FALLEN VALKYRIE DUET

By

J.E. Taylor

Fallen Valkyrie Duet © 2023 J.E. Taylor

Cover Art by Luminescence Covers

FALLEN VALKYRIE DUET

Book 1

ANCIENT GODDESS

A soldier. A war. An ungodly order.

My name, Kara Mist, means wild, stormy one. I once was a battle-ready warrior, an elite member of Odin's Valkyrie force. But the centuries of peace have softened the Valkyrie to the point our battle practice consists more of cajoling than sparring to keep our skills sharp.

Although the other Valkyrie are complacent, I am unsettled. My bones ache for adventure. When peace between the realms crumbles, bringing with it a bloody and world-altering war, I am ready.

But Odin's order to reap an innocent soul from Earth is not the adventure I signed up for.

Refusing Odin is not something any Valkyrie has done before, and the consequences of disobeying are deadly.

Do I blindly follow orders, or do I rebel and face my own demise?

CHAPTER ONE

EVERY AFTERNOON FOR THE last millennia, colors of the Bifrost shimmered on the ceiling of our training hall at the precise moment the suns passed in the sky. Light filled the gallery, turning the golden walls into a heavenly rainbow. It was as glorious as the day before, and the day before that, and yet I was abysmally bored.

The peace Asgard had lived in for the last few centuries had made the Valkyrie army complacent. But I won't fall prey to this pretense of peace. It never lasts, and this time, I didn't want to be caught unaware. The last time we had turned complacent, we lost more than half our numbers in a bloody battle.

I sighed and turned back to my sparring partner, redoubling my efforts as internal frustration mounted under my skin.

"Mercy!" Amala cried as my sword struck hers, spitting sparks from the contact. She desperately tried to ward off my attack. Her short-cropped, sweat-soaked flaxen hair clung to her pale skin, evidence of her valiant, but sub-par effort.

"Do you think our enemies will accept a cry of mercy," I roared and struck again. Steel met steel with a burning clang.

"Enough, Kara!" Freya snapped from the other side of the arena.

I turned to the head of the Valkyrie army. Her wings appeared in a challenge to my excessive use of force on the training field. Her silver-gray eyes flashed at me, and the stern set of her lips told me I had gone too far. Again.

I threw down my sword and stomped off toward the showers unable to stay for the reprimand Freya was about to deliver. My aggravation ran through my veins, heating my skin enough that the chilly air wafting down on us didn't cool me down. Something had me on edge, and I didn't have a clue why. It was as if my senses were on high alert the way they used to be during the war for the realms nearly a hundred years ago.

This unsettled restlessness had kept me sharp, and it kept me alive back then. I wasn't about to second-guess it, either.

The metal adornments on my shoulders and chest came off easily, unlike the armor we used to wear in battle. Those magnificent suits of armor used to take at least two of us to remove. This new style was crafted with peace in mind, not war. I tossed them into the storage area and turned to head to the showers to dull this fiery anger burning in my core.

Freya blocked my path. Her muscular arms crossed over her chest as she stared down her nose at me from a slightly taller position. Her silver eyes matched her tightly drawn hair, which never seemed to fall out of the ornate bun at the back of her head. "What are you doing?"

"Sparring. Isn't that the point of these daily exercises? To keep us battle-ready?" I waved toward the colosseum, where the rest of the team was swinging swords as if there wasn't a care in the world. It was ludicrous.

"You are more vicious than ever out there. What is wrong?" Her stern glare took me in and pushed buttons inside me as if she were mentally prying my secrets out.

Unease pounded my muscles, and I sighed. "I don't know. A strange anxiety has overtaken me, as if the realms are on the edge of bloodshed, again." I shook my head, trying to pinpoint why, but the feeling persisted.

She studied me. "There is no sign of war to be battle-ready for, so I don't see the need to spar until blood is spilled. But yes, the daily sparring is meant to make sure our skills are not forgotten in the event Odin calls upon us."

I pressed my lips together against the comment that wanted to escape.

Her eyes narrowed. "Speak," she ordered.

"This is not keeping us sharp. It is merely going through the motions." I didn't mean to, but the words came out in a derisive hiss. I turned away.

"Do not wish for war," Freya warned.

"I do not wish for war. I wish for purpose." I slung the words over my shoulder as I turned the corner, out of her sight. Purpose and this biting edginess to go away. I knew I would be pulled aside once I had calmed down, and the prospect of another lecture had me lingering under the warm waters of the showers.

When the sound of the others coming in from practice echoed off the walls of the showers, I turned the water off and wrapped myself in a plush towel and wrung out my long, blonde hair. But even the hot shower did not penetrate the restless knots in my muscles.

I stepped out of my heated bliss and toweled off before dressing and retrieving my armor. As per the rules, we were required to polish our armor after every sparring session. I didn't see the reason. Armor in battle was far from gleaming—it was usually splattered with blood and gore.

But I still must follow the rules, even if I detested them. I took the first seat in the shining circle and started the tedious process of cleaning my already shining armor.

Amala stepped out to join me, clean and refreshed, but still the palest-skinned warrior of all of us. Instead of taking the seat next to me as custom dictated, she took the seat opposite me with a seasoned glare. "Do you have a problem with me?"

"No. I have a problem with sparring for show. Not one of you is battle-ready." I continued to alternate between the wax and the shine rags.

"And you are?" she asked with an undertone of hostility.

I glanced up at her, raising my eyebrow and Amala dropped her gaze and started to shine her armor. She knew I was more prepared for a true fight than anyone else in the army.

Before she could come out with a rebuttal, the ground buckled bad enough to throw us from our chairs. My heart slammed in my chest and all the saliva in my mouth dried. Amala's wide eyes met mine, and panic filled her irises.

We both stood, but an explosion rocked the building, sending us on our asses again. A plume of smoke belched from the gallery into the armor room. Through it, Freya stumbled, and for the first time that I could recall, her hair was amiss.

"Kara, Amala, get your armor on. We're under attack!" Then Freya disappeared back into the fray.

My heart contracted hard enough to jolt me to my feet. I didn't hesitate and my armor was on in seconds, but Amala just stared as if this were all a bad joke. I stalked to where she stood and delivered a hand-stinging slap to get her to focus.

Amala held her cheek where the outline of my handprint still registered red, and she blinked at me as her jaw dropped in indignation.

"You heard our general. Get suited up." I didn't wait for her. I grabbed a sword and rushed into the smoke.

Blood exploded in the air and the clash of steel-on-steel rang through the space around me. For those who had never seen war, I recognized the shock flickering on their faces. My muscles, though weary from sparring, still remembered what to do without thought, and I struck, parried, and spun to strike again, ignoring the horrors surrounding me.

Hesitation in battle was deadly, and there were more than enough bodies littering the ground to prove my point. We were not ready for anything of this scale.

I didn't immediately recognize the species we were fighting. They drifted like smoke around us, and only materialized into a solid, black faceless form to slash out or hurl an explosive in our direction. My sword clashed with another just in time, and I pushed off as my adrenaline spiked. It took my mind a few minutes to latch on to the reality of what exactly our attackers were.

Wraiths. Deadly and ruthless. And they hadn't been seen since the last time Asgard battled for rule of the realms.

My heart plummeted.

They were just as brutal as I remembered, and I did not go unscathed. My arm burned where their metal cut. Same with the back of my thigh. Despite my injuries, I kept swinging my sword, blocking theirs, because stopping meant death.

The slam of Thor's hammer sent a shock wave that rammed through me. It had the wraiths running, but it wouldn't keep them away for long. Now that Asgard knew the wraiths were back and bidding for war, nothing would stop Odin from hunting them down and squashing them like the bugs they were.

Silence befell the city as the wraiths disappeared, leaving only our wounded and the dead of both species soaking the ground in blood.

CHAPTER TWO

I LOATHED SITTING STILL. Even if it was for the dressing of my wounds. I'd rather be helping others in more dire need than I was, but Freya insisted I take a break and get my wounds dressed. She stood over me like a mother hen, making sure I was attended to. I grumbled under my breath, and her severe expression landed on me.

"How did the wraiths get free from the magic that bound them to their world?" I demanded of her. My gaze was just as hard as hers. I wanted to know how they bypassed the magic that the

Valkyrie, along with Odin had stitched into the fabric between realms.

Her jaw muscle twitched. "I was just going to ask you that question."

Freya's comment sent a rash of chills through my form, bringing bumps to my exposed skin. I blinked at her as the implied claim under the biting words sunk in.

"You think I had something to do with this?" I pointed to my chest, bothered by the implied slight. I may have been unhappy with our lack of diligence in sparring, but I certainly would never set the wraiths free out of spite. That was traitorous.

"Only a Valkyrie soldier could reverse that spell." Her arms crossed and her lips pursed in irritation. "And you were more on edge than normal today."

I stared up at her as her accusation raked fine nails across my back. She thought I was capable of freeing one of our worst enemies in all our history. I slowly shook my head and pushed the medic away. I rose and faced her, stepping so close that the huff of her breath caressed my cheek. As hurt as I was from her denunciation, I needed to rein in my anger. I inhaled and let my breath out slowly. In her shoes, everyone was a suspect, and rightly so.

"I have been on edge, but it wasn't because I intended to set the wraiths free. It's because I sensed a darkness creeping toward us, and I couldn't put a name to it." I tried to express myself in a way Freya would understand.

"And you expect me to believe you." Her knuckles on the hand gripping her bloody sword turned white.

Heavens, Freya was ready to strike me down right here. I took another slow breath and stared into her eyes. "I swear on my mother's soul, I did not let the wraiths free." I prayed she would believe me and kept eye contact, silently conveying my innocence. If she didn't, I was as good as dead.

The thought that someone intentionally let these beasts free had my blood boiling, but I remained in place awaiting Freya's judgment.

Freya searched my gaze, narrowing her eyes. Her lips thinned and her nostrils flared.

I did not move my gaze away, and I stood still. Fidgeting under her scrutiny wouldn't send the right message. A bead of sweat slid down my back, tickling me enough to want to wipe it away.

Finally, she stepped back and nodded. "When you are finished getting patched up, you can help the medics with the rest of the injured."

"And after everyone is patched up?" I wanted to search and destroy right now. Eliminate all the wraiths and find the traitor who opened the flood gates to our world.

Freya understood the feral quality of my question.

"After, we hunt." Her voice carried enough of the fury contained in her being to understand her anger surpassed mine. One of her warriors did this, and it was unforgivable.

I grinned my approval and gave her a curt nod before I turned back to the medic, giving myself over to his patchwork. As soon as he finished, I shadowed him and helped take care of the others. My need for vengeance grew with each injured Valkyrie we repaired and each innocent hurt in the cross fire.

Our force had been cut down to a third of what we had been. A third was not enough to defend against another strike. Those of us who were still on our feet were like me, sporting injuries that weren't life threatening, but they were a hinderance if there was another attack.

I wiped the sweat from my forehead on my sleeve and followed the medic, whose name I'd already forgotten, to the next patient. I gasped as I stared down at Amala's bruised and broken form. Her face was split by a deep laceration that decimated one of her eyes. Her good eye darted around as she moaned indecipherable words.

I took her uninjured hand and squeezed it but refrained from placating words to soften the truth of her injuries. If she lived, most potential suitors would run from her personality and the rest would shy away because of the battle scar. It was enough to send a plume of pity to the surface.

When Amala's gaze found mine, it narrowed.

Her grip on my hand tightened. "You should be dead," she hissed between cracked lips. "They weren't supposed to declare war on all of us."

I searched her gaze as the ugly truth hit. "You let them loose?" Her crazed smile sent chills down my form, and I attempted to pull my hand away, but her grip was too tight to escape. I still could not comprehend such a vile act.

"Your death for their freedom," she cackled.

I glanced at the medic, who had stalled in his care. His jaw clenched and his hard gaze found mine. He slowly shook his head and pulled his medical bag away from the turncoat among us.

"Freya!" I called without losing eye contact with the medic.

Wind blew my hair as Freya slid next to me in an instant. She glanced between the medic and me, and then down at Amala's hand gripping my wrist to the point her nails had broken my skin and blood slid down my hand.

"Amala let the wraiths loose." My voice shook with rage, and I cut my gaze to Freya's.

Freya made a dismissive noise and turned to leave, as if my words meant nothing. It burned enough for me to yank my hand from Amala's grip, tearing more of my skin in the process. I grabbed Freya's shoulder, spinning her back toward us.

"She admitted it to us," I hissed.

Before I could say more, the medic said, "I heard her confess." He packed the rest of his medical supplies into his bag. "I will not waste my services on a traitor."

Freya blinked and looked between the medic and me before looking down at Amala. Amala, one of the weaker Valkyrie who had not been in the battle a hundred years before. She had no battle experience at all. Which was why I had been so hard on her.

"Why?" Freya demanded with a chill in her voice.

"I wanted her dead," Amala snarled and glared at me, as if I had wronged her in an unforgiveable way. "Her beatings must stop."

I blinked and glanced at Freya as the medic wrapped my wrist, covering the damage done by Amala's nails.

Freya's eyes hardened, and she bared her teeth in disgust. "Sparring is supposed to be a challenge. You have gone soft, and worse than soft, you have become a traitor to Asgard. You set the wraiths free and for that, you deserve death." She stepped back, drew her sword, and before anyone could intervene, the blade whistled as she swung it down, neatly removing Amala's head from the rest of her body.

Blood spurted rivers from her severed throat and puddled on the floor below the cot.

Without another word Freya turned and headed out of the makeshift sick bay that the injured occupied. The medic and I stared at the brutal and swift act of justice before turning away to the next patient in need.

CHAPTER THREE

A S SOON AS THE last patient was patched up, I headed toward the exit of the makeshift triage tent. I needed sustenance and a stiff drink. But before I broke free of the tent, Freya intercepted me.

"Odin would like to speak with you." She nodded toward the great hall where Odin's throne sat. The line of people loitering, waiting for their viewing with the king, was longer than normal. They probably wanted answers. Answers Odin likely didn't have yet.

"Does he know that one of the Valkyrie set the wraiths free?"

Freya shook her head. "I did not speak with him. I'm just passing the message on." She tilted her eyebrow up.

I shivered. "Thor?"

She nodded. It was common knowledge that Thor was on a mission to get me into bed. I was the last holdout of all the Valkyrie, and rumor had it that he wanted a clean sweep of us all. And I was not interested. He was too vain for my tastes.

I just wanted food and a bed, and the line stretched out far enough so I wouldn't get either until well into the night. I wasn't in the mood to wait, and I leaned my head back with an exaggerated sigh. I didn't need to ask if I had to stand in line. Freya's insistent gaze moved my feet to the back of the queue, where she left me with a smirk.

This was not going to be pleasant.

My stomach grumbled loud enough for the man in front of me to turn. His irritation smoothed out as he took in my marred Valkyrie armor. He nodded before offering me a piece of sweet jerky he pulled from the recesses of his pocket.

I took it with a smile, even though the rags he had on announced this was probably the last meal he would have for a while. "Thank you." Hopefully, the jerky would keep my stomach from rumbling loud enough to wake the dead while I had an audience with Odin. That would be as embarrassing as letting a smelly fart go. And with how hungry I was, that might actually be a reality if I ate the jerky. Still, it didn't stop me from taking a bite. My taste buds jumped into overdrive as the sweet-salty treat tickled all my points of interest. It was almost as if the jerky knew what I needed to satiate my hunger. I devoured the piece before the line even moved forward a pace.

Grumbling began at the front of the line as people moved back and guards marched forward until they reached me. My mouth dropped open as they grabbed my arms and dragged me forward as if I were a common criminal. Even though I was pissed at the way the guards manhandled me, I gave my best apologetic look to the angry crowd as the guards pushed me in front of the gates.

I turned on them with a growl that had them stepping back. "Do not ever treat a Valkyrie like that. Especially if you value your life."

"We were told time is of the essence," one of the guards said as the other one spun me around and pushed me through the gates of the now-empty hall.

I stepped to deliver a good ass kicking, but the doors slammed shut in my face. Silence gathered around me, but I could feel eyes on my back. I composed myself before turning toward the dais at the far end of the great hall.

Odin sat on his throne like a regal ruler, but I knew he had a ruthless streak. If he felt slighted, he would not hesitate to smite if he thought it was the right thing to do. His long white hair danced on a breeze that only seemed to encompass his throne. His piercing eyes glowed even from this distance.

I had never been in the great hall with only the ruler of the realms present. Usually, the rest of the Valkyrie were gathered here with me, and I found I was intimidated without my sisters surrounding me. My steps faltered as a shadow moved behind the throne. I swallowed hard, and my feet moved faster.

When Thor stepped out of the shadows into the spot next to his father, I slowed down. His smug smile snuffed out the intimidation and replaced it with a burning irritation. That smile always set my rage meter off. I wanted to scrub it from his face. He winked, and my teeth clenched.

The man was incorrigible. I was never interested in being another notch on his very marked-up bedpost. Other Valkyrie had fallen for his wiles over the years, and he always crushed their hearts. And his attempts to woo me had always fallen short because I could see through his god façade. He was just a power-hungry jerk, and I wanted no part of him.

Odin shifted forward in the chair, setting his elbows on his knees as his gaze narrowed. I gathered, from his frown, he'd caught the nuance of change in my demeanor when his son appeared.

As I stepped to the foot of the stairs, I dropped to my knee, showing my respect to the king of the realms. If it had only been Thor on the dais, I would have flipped him off and marched right back out the door.

"Kara Mist." Odin leaned back. His voice carried a chill with my name that tickled my spine. "I have a task chosen just for you."

My attention was now solely on Odin, and my heart thundered. I had to school my features to show no emotion. Odin didn't like seeing Valkyrie gushing over anything; he liked us stoic and in charge of our feelings. Even so, my heart galloped away at the thought of being handpicked by Odin. Perhaps he saw my valiance on the battlefield today and maybe I'd be leading the charge against the wraiths on their home turf. There was nothing I wanted to do more than tear those bastards to pieces.

"Yes, my king." I looked up, catching the smirk on Thor's lips before he suppressed it. Based on his expression, my stomach plummeted. He wouldn't be smirking if this didn't involve him in some way.

"I am sending you to Earth to collect a young doctor. Hippocrates," Odin said.

My gaze jumped from Thor to Odin, and I stared up at him, processing his words. I blinked and cocked my head as confusion layered over me. "Earth?" Earth did not have a stake in the war of the realms. Why was he sending me there?

"Yes." He provided no other explanation.

Thor was openly smirking now.

"But I...I'm Valkyrie?" That was all I could get out. Stunned did not begin to describe this. Why would he send me to Earth when the wraiths were loose?

"Yes." Odin's brows lowered, and he looked at Thor. "I thought you said this one was smart."

"I said she's vicious on the battlefield, and perfect for this kind of mission," he clarified. But his tone wasn't that of a compliment.

"But I want to be here to protect the people." The words were out before I could stop them.

Odin pounded his staff and glared at me with one eye. The other was obscured by a patch, hiding the damage done in the first war of the realms. "You will do as I order." His voice rattled the windows.

I lowered my head and nodded. I had no idea who this Hippocrates was, or how he played in the future of Asgard, but an order was an order, and any further arguments would land me in Hel's underworld for the rest of eternity. "Yes, my king."

I turned, but before I could take a step toward the hall gates, he gave me my timeline.

"Bring him to Valhalla before the next new moon, Kara. Do you understand?"

My stomach dropped. Bringing someone back from Earth was different than killing them. I glanced over my shoulder, startled. He wanted a human dead. Not just delivered. I swallowed, glancing at the end of his staff because I could not bring myself to look at him.

"Understand?" The word came out in a growl as if he were getting ready to strike me down if I didn't comply.

"Yes." I nodded. I didn't wait for more instructions. I had to get my head wrapped around murder, which I didn't comprehend at all. Valkyrie protected the innocent here and abroad. This was in direct contrast to everything I'd ever been taught. I marched out the door with my head down, passing by the restless crowd. Their rumblings were more aggravated than before. But my mind was elsewhere, trying to decipher the order in light of the danger to my home.

A dead human made no sense. A dead healer, no less. Why? I needed to find out the why before I could strike down an innocent. Even if Odin ordered it, I wasn't sure I could follow through.

My mouth tasted bitter, and all I wanted was a stiff drink.

Freya stepped next to me as I stopped before the ruined training building. She stood silent as I pondered my order. Could she know about this? I turned to her, wondering whether she understood the order I had been given. We were supposed to protect the realms, not assassinate the innocent.

"Are we going to war?" Her face remained stoic, but her question gave me enough information to ascertain she didn't know the particulars.

"You may be, but I am heading to Earth." I couldn't help the bitter tone in my voice. And I wasn't sure I could expand on anything more than that. Odin did not tell me to keep this quiet, but he also didn't give me permission to tell others. The room had been cleared for the conversation, which meant it was probably a private affair that I needed to keep secret.

Her eyebrows darted up her forehead, rendering her surprise in detail. Her mouth even popped into a small O. She looked at the devastation around us as if the reality of being left without her best warrior was unheard of, but she didn't question Odin's order. She ran her hand over her hair, smoothing the flyaway hair into place. "What do you need?" she finally asked when she composed herself.

I had no idea what I'd need, and I shrugged.

"Earth's atmosphere is much like here," Freya said. "At least you'll be able to breathe without magic," she added with an uneasy smile.

"I'll probably bring my dagger since I don't know if swords are normal there." Besides, a sword wasn't good for getting in close proximity to this doctor. My stomach clenched at the thought of burying a blade into an innocent.

I looked down at my stained armor. "This probably won't do." I sighed, wondering how to blend into a world that I'd never been to. Instead of continuing to lament my crappy situation, I headed toward my quarters in the section of the building that wasn't demolished.

Perhaps a long hot shower would loosen the tight muscles riddling my body.

When I entered my room, I stalled. An outfit was laid out over my couch in the living area of my apartment. The top looked more like decorative armor, with spikes on the edges of the chest and hips and a neckline of ornate metal that didn't look like it attached to the bodice, but, on closer inspection, it did. The skirting of floor-length black panels fell to the ground, with slits all the way to the top of the skirting. One for each leg. The shoes caught my attention. Open sandals with ribbons to tie around my ankle. This was so far off from my current attire that I nearly laughed.

I picked up the dress. It was lighter than it seemed. When I ran my fingers over the spikes, they gave under the pressure, bending away from me like a soft blade of grass in a heavy storm. These were just decorative and not meant to cut like I initially thought. When I turned it to inspect the back, I was pleased to see the cut was low enough to accommodate my wings if I chose to display them. I wasn't sure what to think about it, except I'd never worn anything quite so sexy, and the thought stuttered my mind.

It looked as though it was made for seduction and not anything indicative of war. I dropped it back on the couch and then stripped on my way to the shower to clean off the blood and grime from the attack and helping at the hospital. If I hadn't been given the jerky in line, I would be raiding my refrigerator, but between the snack and the order, my stomach wasn't the first priority. Being clean before I tried on the outfit was higher on my list at the moment.

The water ran red for long enough to spike my nerves, but I remained under the hot stream until it finally cleared. I soaped my body, and the suds not only cleaned my skin, but stripped the bloody streaks off the fine gray marble lining the shower floor. My hair was a nest of knots, and I hand combed the shampoo through to the tips, smoothing out my blonde mane as I rinsed.

As soon as my fingers pruned from being in the shower so long, I begrudgingly turned off the water and stepped out, wrapping my body in a warm towel. I slid a comb through my hair, getting the last of the snags out before I headed into the living room to put on the dress.

A breeze filtered through my apartment, and I glanced at the shadow on my balcony. I gripped the towel tighter just as Thor stepped through the balcony doorway with his hands behind his back, uninvited. He gave me that leering grin I just wanted to smack off his face. But before I could ream him with some snarky response, his hands came in front of him with two plates loaded with his mother's famous roast beast sandwiches on her homemade muffins that melted in your mouth. Alongside the sandwich sat one of her famous marble brownies.

My mouth watered despite my irritation with him.

"I figured with everything going on, you probably haven't had a chance to eat." He set one of the plates on the table and took a seat at the far end of the couch before digging into the treats on his plate.

It was highly unusual for Thor to think of anyone other than himself, but I wasn't going to shun this miracle away just because suspicion raked its nails over my skin. I shifted and glanced at the towel and then the dress. I didn't know which would be more suitable for eating.

To hell with decorum. I slid into the chair across from the couch, taking the food. I didn't want to drip on the pretty dress, and my towel was long enough to keep my lady bits hidden.

"Thank you. That was thoughtful." I dug into the food without meeting his gaze.

"I'm to escort you over the Bifrost to make sure you end up in the right realm at the proper time," he said around a mouthful of food.

I was perfectly capable of making sure I got to the right place, but right now, all I cared about was the food on the plate. I ate it without reservation, scarfing up the last of the crumbs with my finger.

I licked my lips and then put the plate down, meeting Thor's stare. His lips cocked back into that smirk as he grazed me with his eyes. When I stood, he stood and closed the distance. His fingers trailed down my arm, and I knocked his hand away.

"I brought you food," he said, as if that was enough for me to drop to my knees and suck him off as a thank-you.

"And?" I glared up at him.

His mouth pressed into a thin line and his eyes narrowed. "And you should show me some gratitude."

"You should find someone who is willing to grovel at your feet to feed that over-inflated ego of yours." I sidestepped away from him and gathered the dress off the couch.

When I moved to pass by him, he grabbed my arm. "You will beg me someday."

I laughed at him and headed toward my bedroom to change. Movement caught my eye, and I glanced over my shoulder. Thor was a few steps behind me. "You are not invited into my bedroom." I stepped inside and slammed the door before he could speak. The audacity of some men. They bring you a meal and expect something in return. I never understood them and had yet to find anyone who was deserving of my heart.

Thor certainly wasn't. He was far too cocky and far too pretty for my tastes.

I pulled on the dress and had to contort a little to get the zipper up, but I managed it without help. Then I straightened out the bust as I crossed the room in search of a pair of black underwear that would match the dress. Once I was fully dressed, I glanced in the mirror, raising a critical eyebrow.

It didn't look too bad. I think I could sell it if I had to, but I wasn't going without at least a dagger clasped to my thigh. I put my foot on a chair and rummaged through the nightstand for a suitable holder. I found one that my mother had given me long ago before she passed on. It matched the dress perfectly. The band was adorned with gold and rubies that matched the hilt of the blade. I clasped it on my thigh, where it was accessible and visible. I hoped it was enough to deter any more of Thor's advances.

I stepped back into the living quarters and crossed to the chair I had been sitting in for my meal. I reached for the sandals, making sure the blade was in full view. Thor looked on with a bored expression as I laced the ties around my ankle.

"You about ready?" he asked with his arms crossed over his chest and the breeze ruffling his hair.

I glanced around the apartment as if this would be the last time I saw it. It was a ritual of mine any time I left. I cataloged all I had and gave a moment of appreciation for the blessings in my life just in case the rug was yanked from under me. Then I turned and gave Thor a nod, stepping to his side.

With one last glance over my shoulder, we moved out onto the balcony, and I willed my wings to sprout before I dove off the building and soared into the painted sky.

CHAPTER FOUR

WHEN WE LANDED ON the entrance to the Bifrost, colors gleamed through the magically thin layer between worlds, lighting up the sky with every conceivable color. I had always enjoyed walking this thin slip of rainbow, even as a child. It held mystical wonders just by existing, and every step created a small jingle. When we as a Valkyrie force ran along it, it created a symphony of sound that filled me with both awe and excitement, but right now it only sounded like wind chimes ringing in the distance. And I was not enthralled with the sound or this mission.

Thor studied me as we walked. At least he wasn't leering anymore.

"What?" I finally snapped.

That tilting smile appeared. The one I wanted to wipe from his lips. It held his arrogance in that one expression. "You don't like me very much."

I gave him my best "what makes you think that" side-eye, but I didn't confirm or deny his statement. Truth be told, when I was young, I had a massive crush on him. But as soon as I became a Valkyrie and saw firsthand how he went through the entire force like some sex-crazed asshole, I lost all respect for him. I had never fallen for his lines or his charm, and I certainly wasn't going to now.

He cocked an eyebrow at my silence.

I sighed and kept walking. My attempt at enjoying the sounds of our footsteps on the Bifrost was quickly souring. "Not particularly."

"Why not?"

His entitlement astounded me. He truly believed everyone should drop down on their knees and thank the stars above if he graced them with his attention. "Because you are an arrogant fool," I muttered under my breath, thankful to be approaching our destination.

His lips thinned, and he faced forward as the transport building neared. Hostility radiated from him as if I had woefully bruised his ego.

But I did not give a damn about the God of Thunder or his ego. "You just want me to like you because I am the only Valkyrie you haven't slept with." I threw caution to the realms. I might be as close to immortal as he was, but I was only a beheading away from death.

He grunted in a derisive manner and sent me a withering glare.

I smirked and looked away. I successfully pissed off Thor, and I liked that I'd gotten under his skin. If he ever changed his ways and became less selfish, I might consider him a suitable liaison. But that hadn't happened in millennia, and I didn't see him changing his spots any time soon.

"Why am I going to Earth to kill an innocent, again?" I asked, hoping to catch him off guard, so he'd provide me with some viable reason.

He grabbed my arm and turned toward me, stopping us. "This is a high honor." He waved toward the building that would whisk me away from the war.

"Then you go and do it. I wish to remain here to defend our people!" My snarl sent him back a step.

His eyes narrowed. "Can you do what I did?" He pointed back to the city.

My jaw clenched. I couldn't banish an entire army of wraiths like he had, and it burned that I had to admit that. I slowly shook my head. "But I am battle-ready." I stared into his blue eyes as they darkened with his anger. "Not many others are."

"That is the reason why we picked you." His finger jabbed into my chest. "Earth is in its infancy, and we need a warrior who can defend herself and carry out Odin's orders without fail." He crowded me, attempting to intimidate.

I continued to glare without yielding. His words seeped their way through my stubborn resolve, and I blinked, narrowing my eyes. "I do not understand the significance of this Earthling. Why is he so important?" I tried again in a different manner to understand this task.

"Because Odin says he is."

That wasn't a good enough answer for me, and I huffed at Thor and turned, ripping my arm from his grip before I trudged toward the structure that held the transport station that would ferry me to the world that Odin wanted me in, regardless of the consequences. I couldn't imagine why, so my mind filled with even more questions. Questions that needed to be answered before I followed through with this mission. I wasn't one of Odin's blind followers, despite being a Valkyrie.

Thor's sharp stare and narrowed lips announced his displeasure. I couldn't care less what the pampered prince thought of me. I still believed this mission was bogus, and for the life of me, I couldn't figure out the why of it all. And yet, here I was, still following orders like a good little soldier.

The Bifrost keeper, Henrick, stood stoically as we entered the transport room. His hair and eyes were without color, and the rest of him visible outside of his armor was as dark as night itself. He held the sword that allowed us to travel between realms when it was buried in the center of the large golden circle and turned. It had been ages since my last foray into the realms, and I smiled at the keeper. If he were to be compromised, the realms would fall. The keeper was as old as Asgard and would remain in place until Ragnarök took us down.

"Earth," Thor said before I could even greet Henrick.

I glared at Thor, and then Henrick raised an eyebrow. I nodded, confirming my destination even though everything inside me balked. "Earth."

Henrick dropped the blade into the slot in the center of the circle and twisted it around three times before finally clicking it into place with a scraping ring. The portal to Earth started in a small circular kaleidoscope in front of where I stood, capturing my attention.

Thor shoved me toward the widening portal, and I was sucked into the ether, tumbling as I tried to gain my bearings. At this rate, I'd be spit out and land flat on my face at my destination. My chest tightened in response to my apprehension.

Thor's words surrounded me. "Do not fail your mission, Kara, or you will feel *my* wrath."

CHAPTER FIVE

I LANDED IN A crouch in the middle of a meadow bordered by trees at the foot of a mountain. The Bifrost channel scorched the ground around me, and my chest finally eased, allowing me to draw a healthy inhalation of clean air. I straightened and inspected my environment.

Mountains and meadows surrounded me. When I cupped my hands over my eyes to shade the sun, I caught a glimmer of water beyond the trees on the other side of the field. The natural beauty of this place reminded me of home. I glanced at the sky, surveying for any type of craft, but the heavens were empty of people traveling from place to place.

I closed my eyes. Fresh scents of pine and sea air mingled, and I sighed. Such a beautiful place for such a dastardly job. I didn't have the motivation to get on with my task, even though I wanted to get home as fast as possible. I couldn't return without this job being completed.

I opened my eyes and took my first step forward toward the unknown. The trees blocked the view of any sort of civilization, and I hoped the sandals I had on would last because I wasn't sure just how far I had to walk to find humans. The meadow challenged me with its uneven ground. My toes found more than a couple of rocks, and each time I'd curse these open shoes. If I had my boots on, I wouldn't be sporting a cracked toenail and swollen pinkie toe. At least the dress was nice and light. My armor would have been much too hot.

Once I reached the forest on the opposite side of the meadow, it took me awhile to find a clear path. The dress snagged a few times on bramble bushes, but the thorns didn't tear the fabric the way they scratched up my skin. A part of me thought this was Thor's fault. He had chosen the outfit to make me as uncomfortable as possible on my journey.

Perhaps he thought if I injured myself, getting close to a doctor would be easier, but a stubbed toe and some scratches weren't going to be enough for me to seek out my target. I still needed to figure out the why before I executed this mission.

When I broke from the trees, waving grains blocked my view, but at least there was a path between the shoots and the woods. I followed it until I came to a crossroad in the wheat. The stalks were taller than I was but the path to my right hinted at water in the distance. The one I had been on seemed endless before another crop of trees interrupted the walkway. Toward water was my best chance at finding people.

As I walked, I stretched out my arms, letting my fingers run over the stalks. Their silken skin swayed with my touch. When I finally emerged, a dirt path, twice the width of the one in the middle of the crops, headed down the hill into a noticeable settlement and the blue water beyond the town beckoned me.

Short stone buildings glistened in the bright sunshine, and I headed in that direction. The closer I got to the settlement, the more people I encountered. Every single one stopped dead in their tracks and just stared at me with their mouths dangling open. My outfit had a vibrance that theirs didn't. The colors here were muted, as if there were no dye to treat them in, leaving only the blandness of cotton or hide. Although I did catch glimpses of jewelry of gold and silver with colorful rocks, that was where the color spectrum ended. It was a complement to the surrounding scenery, which bred vibrant florals of varying greens and purples, pinks and yellows.

I stuck out as someone who did not belong. Damn Thor. He had been to this planet before. He had to have known I wouldn't fit in. At least if I was in my armor, I'd be more at ease, but this outfit left me exposed.

A young child took off down the road, calling in a strange language. More people gathered. I didn't stop my stride, and people scattered when I got near, as if touching me would burn them to ashes on the spot. Some dropped to their knees and bowed with their heads on the ground as if I were a goddess, but the rest continued to stare as if they had fallen into shock.

My skin itched under their stares. Unease filled me as the masses occupied the space behind me, blocking any logical escape. I nearly called forth my wings and took to the sky, but their chatter didn't sound hostile. It actually sounded reverent.

I tried to remember my schooling of the different deities associated with each realm but I never quite grasped all of Earth's, considering there were so many variations. I inclined my head as I passed, acknowledging their courtesy, even though it made me shudder inside.

With the path behind me closed off, I could only move forward farther into the crowd as they continued to jabber words I didn't understand.

The far side of the crowd parted as a man taller than I stalked toward me, offering placations to the crowd that silenced them. He seemed to be a man of authority. His bright eyes that reminded me of Thor's landed on me, and he faltered, blinking as if he couldn't quite understand what he was seeing. His dark hair fell in wild curls and his trimmed beard outlined a strong chin. His full lips pressed together as he studied me on his approach.

Something in my chest stirred at the sight of him. An overwhelming sense of rightness encompassed me, and his blue eyes twinkled as if he experienced the same strange connection.

Then he dropped to a knee in front of me, bowing over as if I deserved to be revered. The rest of the crowd followed suit.

I was neither royalty nor a god, and this reaction made me shift under an uncomfortable weight. "No, no, no." I shook my head and motioned for everyone to rise. "I am no goddess." I gestured again for everyone to rise.

I caught the word "Aphrodite" between his jumbled words, and that goddess's name rang a bell from my studies long ago. And I was annoyed Odin didn't send me here with knowledge of this language. Communicating, especially to find my target, was going to be one hell of a challenge.

I shook my head and pointed at my chest. "No Aphrodite."

Murmurs filled the crowd as they slowly stood back up. I nodded as they repeated "No Aphrodite" even though none of them sounded sure.

I met the man's gaze and patted my chest. "Kara."

He stepped closer, his face a mask of wonder.

"Kara," I said again and tapped my chest.

"Kara?" His head cocked, and my stomach clenched at the curiosity bred in his eyes. He was by far the handsomest man in the crowd surrounding me. He'd definitely give Thor a run for his money back home. Thankfully, he was intelligent enough to understand my meager hand signals.

I nodded and smiled.

"Hippocrates." He patted his chest.

My stomach plummeted, but I kept the smile plastered on my lips. This was the man I was supposed to reap? This gorgeous being? He wasn't yet even a quarter of a century old, with his sun-bronzed skin and muscled torso peeking out of his tunic. The why of it all burned. I licked my lips and inhaled. "Hippocrates," I whispered, saying his name aloud for the first time.

That strange sensation tingled across my skin, warming my soul.

A smile graced his face, showing his white teeth along with dimples despite the thin layer of a beard. His eyes sparkled as if he were enamored with his name on my lips.

Dread filled every fiber as he beckoned me to follow him. People around us spoke with a tone of warning that Hippocrates waved off. The crowd dispersed slowly, but their gazes lingered as if I were some sort of omen for the town...as if I would destroy them in an instant if I wasn't their goddess Aphrodite.

Hippocrates motioned me to walk alongside him as he headed toward the distant water. He pointed to things around me as he continued to talk in a language I didn't understand, but his voice soothed me to the point I didn't care what he was saying. I just wanted to listen to him for hours on end.

Deep down, I knew I should act to complete my mission. But I was hesitant, especially with the warm feeling layering over my skin like a blanket on a cold winter night.

I could not fathom why this man was a threat to Asgard, not with his wide smile and eyes glinting with interest and mirth. There must be a reason, and I was unwilling to follow through until I received answers.

We stopped a little more than halfway through the town, and he waved me toward a tree that looked as if it had stood for more than a century in this same spot. The trunk was too big for two people to hold hands around. Hell, it might have been even too big for three people to join hands together. The healthy sprawl of branches above granted a large patch of shade where the ocean breeze seemed to caress me.

Hippocrates took a seat next to a tray of olives, grapes, and bread, and some leather-bound journals made of thin paper. He patted the ground next to him as he continued to speak.

I daintily sat, trying to keep myself modestly covered. He held the tray out and nodded to the food. His voice coaxed me. I stared at the food and then at him. I wasn't hungry since Thor had brought the meal to my place, but I didn't wish to be rude. I picked up a thin piece of bread and nibbled on it, tasting the oats used to make it with every small bite. He put the tray between us and picked up his journal, along with a black stone that left lines on the paper as he finished his drawing.

He jabbered as he drew. I didn't understand a word, just his intensity as he scribbled on the page.

I glanced out at the ocean, closing my eyes as a breeze filtered through my hair. Hippocrates touched my arm to capture my attention, and energy flowed from his fingers through my body, shocking me. My gaze snapped to his.

"See." He showed me his drawing of an elaborate sketch of someone with their shoulder over what looked like a half wall as someone pulled the arm down. "I wanted to capture how we fixed a dislocated shoulder." He pulled the picture back and stared down at it, and then looked at me as if I hadn't understood a word he just said.

But I did, and all it took had been a touch. He was the first person to actually touch me since I arrived. If anyone before him had grazed my skin with theirs, would I understand the language, or was it this connection I felt with Hippocrates that caused it?

I blinked and then studied the picture again.

"Wouldn't it be less painful just to pull the arm directly out while someone else jambs the heel of their palm to the front or the back of the shoulder depending upon how it is dislocated?"

He moved away from me with wide eyes, studying my face before he looked at his picture.

"This is essentially the same. Just a little gentler." He tossed the book onto his notes and turned to me. "How do you know medical procedures?"

I shrugged. "I have triaged wounded." My mind wandered back to the last few hours, helping the wounded back on Asgard. "I am not a medic. I was just there to lend a hand with the injured." I offered my best humble smile. "How do you know medical procedures?" I nodded toward his journal.

"I am a doctor, as my father was before me. I am trying to find better ways for healing our people." He glanced over his shoulder at the building near us. "That's where our practice is."

I glanced at the building he indicated. Perhaps on the street level it was more inviting, but this side just had a door and crude stairs made of stone. I smiled even as my thoughts swarmed.

Why in the world did Odin want a doctor reaped?

CHAPTER SIX

I FOUND HIPPOCRATES FASCINATING as we discussed his medical theories and the processes he wished to fix. It wasn't until a man stepped out of the building he had pointed to earlier and cleared his throat that Hippocrates stiffened and glanced over his shoulder.

"I'm sorry," he said as he collected his things. "I should have been back, helping my father, ages ago." He picked up the now empty tray and paused. "Do you have a place to stay?"

Stay?

My mind stalled. I had not considered that this mission would take more than a day. I slowly shook my head as my mind conflicted with my mission. I should whisk him off to Valhalla right now, but I could not muster the motivation to kill him.

"No," I whispered.

He glanced over his shoulder and then took a deep breath before he focused on me. "Do you have money?"

Money. Ha. Odin didn't send me with anything but the clothing on my back. The only thing that I had of value was my mother's dagger, and I wasn't hawking that for coin. I shook my head. "This is all I have." I waved at myself, wondering what the hell I was doing. I should be reaping this man and going home, and yet I found I couldn't. Not without a valid reason. And I hadn't seen one yet.

But I certainly was going to look and if I found one, I wouldn't hesitate.

He worried his lower lip for a moment. "Wait here. I will return in a few moments." He didn't wait for a response. He turned and rushed over to where the other man—his father I presumed— stood with his foot tapping impatiently. Although I couldn't hear the hushed conversation, both men were animated enough for me to get they were not on the same page with whatever was being said. But the glances my way certainly confirmed I was the topic being discussed.

Hippocrates hung his head and nodded before turning on his heel and heading toward me. I climbed to my feet and faced him as he reached into his pocket, pulling out some coins. "Go to the tavern and tell them I sent you. This should get you a room for the night." He took my hand and dropped the silver into my palm.

"I cannot take this," I said, but he closed my fingers gently around the money.

"I'll help you find a suitable place to stay if you choose to linger here in Kos." He smiled at me. "And I would very much like you to stay." He backed away with that smile that both thrilled and terrified me. And then he turned and climbed the steps, disappearing into the building behind his father.

I turned away with the money tucked into my tight fist. At least my hunger had been tamed with the bread, olives, and grapes. But soon enough my stomach would be growling again, and I would need sustenance. I just hoped it was enough for both food and bedding because it had been more than a millennium since I slept on the ground, and I still remembered how uncomfortable it was. I doubted I would get more than five minutes of rest even with a comfortable bed with all these heavy uncertainties swarming in my head. I also wished I had something more than just this skimpy outfit.

As I walked through town, looking for the tavern Hippocrates spoke of, I noted there weren't any dress shops like back home where one could get almost anything they needed. The town had a few blacksmiths and some pastry shops, but nothing like the mecca that was Asgard.

Damn Thor and his misogynistic attitude. I would freeze in these clothes out in the open.

I spied the tavern, and the scent of fresh baking bread had my mouth watering. Food first, then lodgings. And then some serious reflection because as of this moment, I had disobeyed orders and would have to answer to Odin soon enough.

The moment I entered the tavern, all conversation stopped. Everyone's gaze swiveled to mine. Anyone standing shuffled toward the walls or the farthest points away from me. Fear tinged the air with a bitter taste, and I couldn't help but roll my eyes.

"I am not one of your angry gods," I said, although pretending to be might have its advantages. "I am just passing through, so please do not incense me with your fear." My gaze swept the room, and many people seemed to relax at my words. But what replaced the tension had me second-guessing my announcement.

Their gazes reminded me of Thor's. It was as if I had openly invited them to my bed instead of scolding them for their fear. I might need to put a few of them in their place if they dared to approach me. My back itched, but I ignored it. If I pulled out my wings, I didn't know what these people would do. As it was, my outfit was enough to shake them; wings would likely drop them to their knees again. As I stepped to the bar, I wondered whether that might be the wiser choice rather than fielding advances.

"What can I get you?" The leering bartender reminded me of a few of the crooked and greedy shop owners in the bad section of Asgard that the Valkyrie had to crack down on every now and then to get them to deal honestly with the public. What was left of his hair was mangy, like a street mutt and his teeth when he smiled made me shiver in revulsion at the brown and black marks splashed across what once may have been white.

"Food and drink." I placed the coins on the counter, pushing them toward him.

His eyes widened, and he smiled in a manner that made me suspect he was as greedy a bastard as I initially thought. I just wanted him to not smile because that truly would kill my appetite if I had to stare at his mouth full of rotting teeth.

"That should cover both food and drink, and lodging for the night." I smiled sweetly as his gaze locked with mine. "Or I will introduce you to my good friend death." I did not mention that Hippocrates had sent me. I had been in enough taverns on Asgard to hold my own.

He paled at my words, but his greedy eyes didn't stop their assessment of me as he swiped the coins off the counter. "As you request." He executed a half bow and hurried away behind the corner. Hushed whispers reached my ears, and I turned to stare at the crowd, who had yet begin to converse like they had been when I pushed through the door.

Before I could make a determination of foes in the crowd, the bartender returned with a plate of fresh bread and fruits, sliding it in front of me as he poured a strong-smelling liquid into a glass. He placed the mug next to the platter and gave me a nod. "When you finish, I will bring you to a room."

"Thank you." I dug into the bounty placed before me. This bread was fluffy and warm, as if it had just come from the oven. The fruit was sweet and satiated my thirst. And the drink...the drink was strong. Stronger than anything I drank on Asgard. This one made my limbs heavy, as if I had drunk an entire bottle of Asgardian wine.

I finished the food in the midst of hushed whispers, and then the bartender handed his apron to another behind the bar and came to my side. He gripped my upper arm as if he now owned me. It reminded me of Thor's grip on my arm on the Bifrost.

I yanked from his grip. "Do not touch me," I snarled.

I hadn't anticipated his backhand, and it stung my cheek and rocked my head to the side. Red veiled over my vision as my fury ignited.

When I turned my gaze back to him, his eyes widened with surprise, as if he had expected me to fall with the power of his weak strike or perhaps blubber because the mean man hit me.

Oh, this fool had no idea who he was dealing with.

A growl ripped from my throat and my wings fluttered into existence on my back. I flexed them, spreading them out far enough to make everyone in the tavern drop to their knees.

The little bartender's fear radiated through the room, mingling with the edge of surprise and terror gripping the patrons. But his fear also mingled with the acrid stench of urine. The front of his wrap darkened.

"You dare raise your hand to a Valkyrie?" I thundered, clenching my fists in an attempt to keep my temper from flaring beyond control. If I lost it, I would wipe out this entire bar in a matter of seconds.

The man stumbled back, catching his heel on a chair, and promptly fell on his ass. "I thought you were a whore," he cried, as if that gave him the right to strike a woman.

I reached down and grabbed the front of his wrap, lifting him up off the ground. "You have no right to treat women like that. You have now made me into an angry goddess." The stench of urine nearly made me gag, and I tossed him into a group of men, knocking them all over before turning on my heel. Before I marched out of the tavern, I seized the corked bottle of the drink he poured me, and took a fresh loaf of bread that had been placed on the bar for someone else, and then left with it, my hands full so I didn't take out my aggravation on the nearest person.

I took flight before I let this anger burn into an uncontrollable fire. I wanted to rip that bartender to shreds for his actions. If a bartender on Asgard dared to strike a Valkyrie, he would find himself in Hel before he even blinked.

Why couldn't Hippocrates have been as nasty as that bartender? That type of greedy bastard would have been easy to put down. But no, I had to deliver a saint instead.

CHAPTER SEVEN

I HAD NO IDEA where to go, so I returned to that magnificent tree as the sun dipped below the horizon. But this time, instead of facing the sea and the rest of the town where I could easily be spotted, I took the opposite side of the tree, hiding me from most of the town. The only door I faced was the entry to Hippocrates's office. My wings fluttered, and I considered snapping them away, but they would offer me some level of warmth in the cooling night.

I settled onto the hard earth and uncorked the bottle, hoping to drown out all thoughts of my mission. The long swig burned as it flowed down my throat, but I kept chugging as if it were cool water instead of a potent cocktail. When I pulled it away, only half the bottle was emptied. My stomach flopped and then righted just as warming numbness shot to my extremities. My limbs became heavier as the alcohol seeped into my cells.

I tore a piece of the bread and nibbled on it to try to counter the drink. I pulled the bottle close, staring at the writing, but I couldn't make out what kind of alcohol it was. After another piece of the bread, I took a sip, swishing the sweet crispness around in my mouth before swallowing. That produced a kick that I had experienced in the bar at the end of every sip, and it nearly had me wincing.

The bread didn't seem to dilute the buzz at all like I hoped. Well, I wasn't sure what I hoped to accomplish by drinking, except it seemed to dull the ache in my chest every time I thought of killing Hippocrates. So, I focused on something less stressful. Like all the things I could have done in that bar, and each one heightened my irritation with the entitled attitudes.

"What wankers." My auditory mutter startled me, and then I chuckled at myself.

Drinking made me careless, so I was thankful I hadn't been in this condition when the bartender hit me. I would have wiped the bar with his ass. As it was, I made the man piss himself. I snorted a laugh at that memory, and then brought the bottle back to my lips and emptied it. This time, the warmth was immediate and when I came up for air, a burp broke the silence surrounding me. I tossed the empty in the direction of the building.

If I happened upon anyone, I'd have to be very careful what came out of my mouth. Alcohol had a way of stripping my defenses and inhibitions. I might confess my intentions or worse.

The door to the building cracked open, grabbing my attention from my alcohol-soaked thoughts. Hippocrates stepped out as if he were headed to town with a worried crease in his brow.

I snorted in derision. I should be reaping this man, but my heart just wouldn't allow it. It felt wrong on so many different levels.

Hippocrates turned toward the noise and squinted into the darkness. His gaze landed on the bottle on the lawn between the tree and the building. "Hello?"

My black feathers surrounding me hid my form in the shadows, so I snapped my back, making them disappear before I attempted to stand.

The sound made his gaze jump to where I stood, leaning on the tree for support.

"Kara?" He moved closer cautiously, as if approaching a scared deer. "I thought I told you to go to the tavern," he said as he stopped in front of me.

I lifted my chin. "I did, and those idiots thought they could manhandle me."

He froze in place, and his eyes widened. "You told them I sent you?"

"No. I just asked for a meal and a room for the night. And after I ate, the bartender grabbed my arm and tried to drag me somewhere. When I refused to go, he slapped me." I brushed my hair back from my shoulder and stood tall, despite feeling the earth moving under my feet like a slow rolling sea. "I don't think anyone from this village will attempt to touch me in that manner again."

"What did you do?" His voice held the trepidation reflected in his bright eyes.

"I lifted him in the air and threw him after I told him he just made me a very angry goddess." My wings snapped out again of their own accord, reacting to the aggravation layering over my skin at the memory.

Hippocrates stumbled back as his gaze took in what he could see of my ebony wings. He dropped to his knee again.

This was getting old. "Get up," I demanded.

"But…"

"But what?" I didn't understand the reverence.

He waved at me with his eyes still averted.

I stepped closer, wobbling enough for him to look up. "I am not a goddess. Get up."

"Are you drunk?" he asked before his gaze moved to the bottle and then back to me.

"Maybe," I said and promptly stumbled to the side.

Hippocrates leaped to his feet and snaked his arm around my abdomen, brushing my feathers with his knuckles in the process.

That single brush of my wings unnerved me and set me on fire.

His arm steadied me against him.

On instinct, I pressed my palm to his chest. His warmth coated me, and his heartbeat ricocheted off my hand like a fluttering bird trying to take flight. Being this close to him nearly ignited my already awakened libido and without a clear head, my body ruled my actions.

His eyes widened at our proximity and his grip around me tightened, pulling me flush against him.

I didn't fight being in his hold the way I had the bartender. Being against his chiseled chest sent my blood pounding in my veins with something other than anger. Something deeper and more insistent. I stared into his bright eyes.

His lips tilted into a smile. "I have never held a goddess before," he whispered in a husky manner that I could listen to for a millennium. "Do you think I'll be smited for it?"

I snorted laughter, and my wings wrapped around us in a cocoon against the night. "I'll protect you," I whispered. Although if Thor or Odin were to show up, my protection would mean nothing against their wrath. I'd be lucky to survive it, and this frail human holding me would be dust.

His free hand ran across the top of my wings, caressing in a manner that sent a shiver down my spine. "Nike?" His eyes found mine.

His reference to another goddess of this realm threatened to derail the heat layering over me. "Kara. I was not lying when I said I am not one of your goddesses." My hand remained on his chest as his heart drummed a beat that echoed mine. Stalling on my mission was putting me in peril, but I couldn't tear my gaze away from his, or pull out of the comfort of his arms, even though I knew it would damn me.

"But you are a goddess."

I slowly shook my head, wishing this entire community would stop with the goddess references. "I am a warrior."

It was his turn to laugh. "A warrior with this face?" His hand caressed my cheek. His thumb moved gently over my lips. "I think not."

I snapped my wings out of existence and pushed my hand on his chest with the intent to step away from him, but his arm didn't budge from around me. If anything, he pulled me closer.

"You intrigue me." His lips were a breath away from mine.

I had the urge to close the distance, but I refrained despite my inebriated brain. If I fell into a kiss and all that his eyes promised, I'd never reap him like my duty dictated.

Hippocrates closed the distance before I could escape him. And the moment his soft lips caressed mine, I balked, opening my mouth to protest. That only seemed to ignite him, and his tongue slipped past my teeth, tangling with mine in a slow dance that left me breathless. He tightened his grip on me, running his hand into my hair, deepening the kiss.

I planted both hands on his chest and pushed, breaking the kiss.

He stepped back to keep from falling and stared at me. A buzz of electricity sizzled between us as his chest rose and fell in time with mine.

The damn half smile on his lips brought a familiar wetness between my thighs. It was far sexier than any smile bestowed on me, weakening my knees with that and the intensity in his eyes. Thankfully, the corset I wore hid the fact my nipples were hard enough to cut through glass. Need flushed me, and I took a step back to distance myself. I could not give in to this insanity.

The war of emotion on his face kept me captivated. It was as if Hippocrates argued with his sensibilities as much as I did.

I leaned back, pressing my hands to the trunk behind me as air raced in and out of my nostrils.

Hippocrates raked his hand down his face as his gaze dropped from my eyes and traveled down my body like a lover's caress. "May the gods strike me dead," he whispered and stepped in, pressing me against the tree as his mouth found mine again. This time, his hands didn't wrap around me, they wandered, stroking whatever skin he could reach. When his hand dipped between my thighs, I moaned, helpless to stop this bliss.

It was as if I were a teenager all over again. Hormonal and urgent, I pulled at his clothing, forgetting my purpose. Forgetting everything but the sensations he created with his hands and his mouth.

He stilled and his lips withdrew before he leaned his forehead to mine. "Have you put me under some sort of spell, goddess?" His eyes closed.

"No." My breath heaved. "But I am under the influence of whatever that bottle contained." I pointed to the discarded decanter. I studied his face as he stepped back.

"Then perhaps we should not follow whatever is possessing us." He slid his hands away from me. His flushed cheeks and the tenting of fabric on his toga told me he had much more self-control than I had ever had.

And now was no different. "What if I disagree?" Damn the alcohol, even more than Thor and Odin for sending me on this fool's errand.

He blinked as if he could not process what I had insinuated.

I stepped forward and slid my palm against his hardness. The sound that escaped him made me grin. I reached behind me with my other hand and unclasped the dress, letting it fall to the ground around my feet.

He moved us to the back of the tree, dragging my dress with me. "If anyone sees you..." He inhaled deep as he glanced down at me in the shadows.

I peeled off my undergarment and tossed it on the bodice of my dress, my actions be damned. Who knew what the morning would bring, but at least I'd have this experience before I reaped the man.

"Kara," he whispered reverently. And then the fabric covering him was on the ground, and he pulled me close enough to cement my decision. Our bodies fit together as if they were made for each other. "You are the definition of beauty."

My hands ran up his abdomen and into the nest of soft chest hair. I marveled at the silky feel of it. None of the men on Asgard had chest hair, so this was a novelty.

His lips tickled the side of my throat as he kissed his way from my jaw to my breast. This man was not without expertise, and I found his subtle strokes and alternating pace fascinating as he moved his way down my body. This was a slow kind of burn that engulfed me with its intensity.

I leaned against the tree, reveling in the sensations as he explored me with his hands and his mouth until my legs were trembled with need. I think I whined because Hippocrates worked his way back up my body and hiked my legs around his waist. His gaze met mine, and he plunged into me hard enough to pull a gasp.

The look he gave me shined on the possessive side, and with each thrust of his hips, it flared in his eyes. The minute I started to moan, his mouth captured it. He wasn't tender and thoughtful like some of the lovers I'd had. No, this was demanding as he pounded me forcefully into the tree like a claiming of old. His kiss required just as much attention as the motion of his body. It was as if he had been as starved of physical connection as I'd been.

The intensity of his grip on my hips along with the growling moan against my mouth was enough to catapult me to the next plateau. My eyes rolled back with the force of my release, and I squealed into his mouth as my body tightened and then released, milking him into his own release.

He slowed his pace and leaned back to see my face before he looked up at the sky as if waiting to be struck dead. When his gaze fell back to mine, he smiled. "Next time won't be so rushed."

I cocked my eyebrow at him. "Next time? That's mighty presumptuous of you." I couldn't help the retort. He's assumed I'd be around long enough for a next time.

His smile faded. "You will come live with me now." This was delivered in such a way that it flipped the switch on my irritation.

I opened my mouth to argue when my brain decided to weigh in. I had nowhere to go, and if I went home without his soul, I would face Odin's wrath. I nodded and dressed quietly, wondering where the hell this common sense was a little while ago. My gaze landed on the bottle, and I nearly huffed.

That's where my common sense had run to. It nearly drowned in that damn bottle.

My dress easily slipped on and clasped, and my undergarment slid on in seconds. I waited for Hippocrates to stop fiddling with his tunic, glad for the simplicity of the dress I was wearing. I did not give this outfit the credit it was due when I first saw it.

"Women are not supposed to be unescorted," he finally said after he adjusted his cover and met my gaze. "I do not know where it is you come from, but your lack of an escort concerns the townspeople greatly."

I crossed my arms and jutted my chin. "I come from a place where women are not suppressed." We were the warriors who protected the people.

He rolled his eyes. "I understand. Especially since you carry such a weapon as the one on your thigh. But here, the traditions are thickly embedded, and you must adhere to them. Otherwise, what happened in that tavern is likely to happen again. The only females without escorts are the whores."

My arms fell to my sides, and my mouth dropped open.

"Which is why I told you to tell them that *I* sent you." He sighed and wiped his face. "Come." He called me closer with his fingers.

Temptation to reap him filled me, but my heart squeezed at the thought. I took his offered hand, and he led me out of the shadows and onto the dark streets.

Curiosity tickled my center. "Why would telling them you sent me have mattered?"

"Because I am one of the few healers on the island." He glanced at me. "They would not have attempted anything with you had they known you belong to me."

I stopped and ripped my hand from his. "No one owns me." My voice came out feral, and I found the hilt of my dagger. I didn't unsheathe it, but temptation had my fingers itching to do just that.

"No?" His hands found his waist, and he cocked his head, challenging me.

I stepped close, narrowing my eyes. "No. You do not own me. I am agreeing to your kindness of a roof over my head while I am here. And if I feel the need to strip you down and take you again, it is within my right to act upon it. But if you attempt to bed me without my permission, I will dislocate both your shoulders and then show you the most agonizing way to fix them."

His mouth popped open, and his eyebrows arched before he recovered. Dimples appeared in his cheeks before he started to chuckle. "Noted." He took my hand, and we continued the short journey to his abode.

CHAPTER EIGHT

HIPPOCRATES'S HOME WAS MUCH more rudimentary than anything on Asgard, even those considered below the poverty level. Again, I was smacked with the reality that this realm was so far behind than those I had encountered. It was almost laughable. Odin didn't need a Valkyrie to do this job; he just needed an errand boy. I smiled and showed my appreciation when he brought me to a small room that was probably the size of my closet at home. A single bed sat in the corner, along with a small bureau and a pot on top that he referred to as a chamber pot.

"Thank you." I turned just as he stepped out into the hallway. "And where does one relieve oneself?"

He pointed to the chamber pot on the bureau and gave me a strange look, as if I should have already known that. "It will be emptied in the morning."

I nodded and glanced at the pot, trying to formulate my next question, but my brain had stalled on relieving myself in a pot. "Where is your room?" I blurted as he went to leave again.

He crossed to the window and pointed to the other side of the building. "On the other side of the courtyard, where the rest of my family resides."

His comment took me by surprise. Did he have children? Had he just been unfaithful? My fingers brushed my knife.

"Family?" My shock filled the one-word question. Depending upon his answer, it might be far easier to carry out my orders than I previously thought.

"I live with my parents. My father and mother." He pointed to an open doorway leading out to the courtyard. "That's my room." Besides an arched opening next to his, I barely made out another door closer to the entry of the home. He turned his face toward me with a sly smile. "Was that jealousy I detected?"

I laughed, and the tension seeped out of my muscles. I didn't dignify him with an answer either. There certainly had been a darkness that flared inside me at the thought of a wife and children of his own, which conflicted with what he had done with me at the tree near his office. He kept giving me more reasons not to follow through on my mission just by being such an innocent in thought and deed.

"You can help my mother with the garden tomorrow." That smile still played on his lips.

I glanced at the flower beds and vegetable gardens in the long, wide courtyard, along with the various fruit trees in bloom. The light of day would illuminate the many colors that were muted by the night.

"Okay." I nodded. I hadn't done simple gardening in eons. Perhaps the task would put me back on the right path. These innocent diversions stripped away my will to follow Odin's orders. Although, I should be practicing my forms to keep sharp, because if I waffled on this job for much longer, I'd have to face Thor's wrath, per his own parting words. "Do you have a sword?"

Hippocrates recoiled, as if the question itself were a weapon. "Why?"

"I'd like to practice. To keep in battle form." Deep down, I knew I'd need to be battle-ready because Odin wouldn't wait for me forever. From the waxing crescent in the sky above, the new moon was less than a couple of days away. The sands of time wouldn't wait for me to find the will to follow through on my orders.

"We are healers, Kara," Hippocrates said, bringing me back from my momentary reverie.

As if his vocation mattered. Our medics knew how to wield weapons just as efficiently as scalpels. "Healers don't practice self-defense?" I challenged him, because I couldn't fathom being willingly ill-equipped to defend myself.

"We don't sword fight, if that's what you mean." He stepped away from me as if I might stab him in the heart.

Which wasn't such a far-fetched idea at the moment. However, even with his ridiculously naïve views, I couldn't draw a blade on him. His sureness in society and himself had me completely derailed.

I sighed. I guess I could do my forms with the knife, but it wouldn't be the same as the heavy steel in my hand. "Fine."

"And please stay here until I return." He splayed his fingers at me as if trying to keep me from losing my temper. "Wandering the streets would invite another disaster like at the tavern."

Even though I knew he was trying to protect me, I glanced at the small room and then at him. "You want me to hide in this room all day?"

He smirked and shook his head. "Heavens no. You can be out in the courtyard." He waved at the window. "Helping with the garden. Or in here resting. Just not unescorted out on the streets."

I took a deep breath and let it out slowly, studying my surroundings as my options played out in my head. I was certain Odin would be getting antsy. After all, how long did it really take to reap a soul, especially when deposited right in the town where said target was? So, perhaps hiding out here with his mother wasn't such a bad thing.

I nodded my assent.

He paused at the door again. "I'm not sure who I am keeping safe...the town or you." He glanced back at me. "But I'm compelled to make sure there is no harm done to my village." He closed the door before I could formulate a response.

Good heavens. Why?

Why this man?

He didn't seem to carry any malicious intent in any of his actions. Thoughts swarmed, and I threw myself on my back on the bed, staring at the ceiling. But the moment my muscles relaxed, my thoughts became sluggish and slow. I hadn't rested since before Asgard was attacked, and all the excitement pressed down on me, pulling me to sleep as effectively as a noose around my neck.

Dreams came quick. First, reliving the sweet bliss of Hippocrates taking me against the tree. But a foreboding slunk into the warmth. Henrick's white eyes blotted out Hippocrates's smiling face, wiping out any lingering sweetness. My heart thundered in my ears as he demanded a status, but it wasn't Henrick's voice ordering me to spill my secrets.

It was Odin's.

I struggled to surface, but Henrick had a vise-grip on my mind. One that I couldn't seem to break. But I could shut down my thoughts, safeguard my memories behind walls of subterfuge. Instead of answering his demands, I asked why this man was so important to Asgard.

I received a snarl in response, along with a growling command for a status.

I stalled. I certainly wasn't going to let them have access to my memories. Although I wasn't totally honest, I recounted the episode at the tavern to give credence to my fib about not being able to locate Hippocrates. With the townspeople afraid of me, information wasn't forthcoming. I hoped that would hold Odin off, but Henrick just repeated the timetable Odin had given me, along with a hiss to get the job done.

Henrick released his hold, and the world spun. Awareness filtered in, and I shook off the connection, disturbed by the intrusion of my mind. I trembled, trying to pull in a full breath, but my lungs had tightened so I could only draw half breaths, fanning the flame of panic rushing over my skin.

I hadn't been aware that was a possibility, and yet I should have known. The timer hanging over my head was nearly empty. If I didn't complete the mission, I'd have to live with the consequences.

Unnerved wasn't a good enough description for the quaking in my stomach. The lingering effects of the psychic intrusion pounded in my head, and I didn't think sleep was an option for the remainder of the night. If he intruded on my sleep again, would I be able to keep him from the truth?

Could Henrick break down the barriers in my brain and pillage my memories?

CHAPTER NINE

I STARED AT THE blackness surrounding me. Not even the stars cast light into this dim room. Had I been laying here for minutes or hours? At least I was breathing normally now, but I couldn't tell how much time had passed while I was trapped in a panic attack. All I knew was sleep was not happening, even though my eyes seemed to droop with exhaustion. I glanced out the window and let my eyes adjust as I zeroed in on Hippocrates's closed door.

I craved the safety of his arms, wondering whether he could chase this worry gripping every cell away. Waiting until daybreak seemed unsurmountable enough to yank me from the bed. I felt my way along the wall to the entry to the courtyard on my side of the abode. Once outside, my eyes adjusted, and I was able to easily skirt around the table and chairs between my section and the family's bedrooms. I bit my lip at the two doors. I believed his was the one closer to the archway. If I was wrong, that would at least make for an amusing story in the light of day.

Uncertainty gripped me, and I closed my eyes trying to recall which one had been open when he pointed. I chose the one farthest from the front entry. I stood before the door as doubts regarding my actions swarmed.

I was already shirking my duty, but that cold fact didn't stop me from reaching out and turning the latch. The door creaked as I pushed it open.

Blue eyes peered out from the dark, and I prayed it was Hippocrates.

"I cannot sleep." I wrapped my arms around my midsection and cupped my elbows.

Someone slid out of the bed and crossed the distance. I held my breath until he stopped in front of me. I had not chosen the wrong door, and I let out a sigh of relief.

Hippocrates's hair was in disarray from sleep, but his kind smile warmed me, along with the view of his naked form. "So, you decided to come and have your way with me again?"

The mirth in his voice heated my cheeks. I hadn't come for more sex. I had come to have his strong arms wrapped around me, to keep Henrick out of my head. But now that I was there, that option didn't sound half bad.

He took my hand and studied my face.

"What are you doing?" I whispered as he stepped into the courtyard. I had expected him to draw me into his room and not back outside.

"Bringing you back to your room, where any noise we make will not disturb my parents' sleep." He glanced back at me.

"Oh." I let him lead me the rest of the way. When he dropped my hands and closed the shutters to the courtyard, the darkness wrapped around me. Only the soft swish of his feet on the floor preceded his arms pulling me flush against his naked form.

"I promised you a more leisurely experience, and yet when I am this close to you, my body borders on frantic, as if it knows something we do not." His lips found mine, and the kiss started with a slow tongue swirl that brought a growl into his groan.

My entire form flushed with heat, and for the second time tonight, my dress puddled at my feet. I gave in to the sensation of him because I knew this was temporary. My bubble would burst soon enough, and I vowed to make the most of this while I could.

We explored each other with the tenderness of lifetime lovers. I memorized every swipe of his tongue, every caress of his hands, and every sound he made. I cataloged the way he tasted in my mouth, from his tongue to his cock and every centimeter between. His musky male scent enveloped me, and I couldn't seem to get enough.

After hours of decadence in each other's arms, we laid side by side, breathless and staring at the ceiling. The light in the room had changed enough for me to see his profile as I turned my head.

His lips were as swollen as mine felt from being kissed, sucked, and nibbled with gusto.

He gazed at me with a hint of a smile. "I am going to pay dearly for all this nocturnal activity today." He wiped his face. "But it was worth the exhaustion that is surely to set in later." He pressed a kiss to my forehead and started to sit up on the edge of the bed.

"Where are you going?"

"I need to try to get some sleep before I leave the house." He glanced toward the window. "And my parents will not be welcoming if they knew I stayed in your room tonight."

His smile, along with the red glowing in his cheeks, made me relent, even though I didn't think I'd get any more sleep than I had before Henrick invaded my mind on behalf of Odin.

Still, after Hippocrates slipped away and I threw the shutters open, welcoming the coming of dawn, I lounged on the bed, and my eyes fell closed.

CHAPTER TEN

THE DAWN CREPT IN before I was fully aware. I must have fallen asleep again and slept soundly until sunlight pierced my eyelids. Birds chirped, and the sound of feet shuffling had me sitting back up on my bed and glancing out the window.

The courtyard gardens were indeed vibrant in daylight. Oranges, yellows, reds, and rich greens painted each planter, and the trees clustered in the back of the yard even had shades of bright colors. The entire area pulled a smile to my face and the thought of helping his mother tend to such an array of color and life created both a thrill in me, alongside trepidation.

Plates of newly cut fruits graced the table in the center of the courtyard and four plates sat on the table across from each other. Muffled voices argued in the distance, and I tilted my head to hear more clearly. The deep timbre of Hippocrates's voice filtered through the bird calls.

Guilt bit at me like a thousand fire ants. I should not have let my libido get the best of me, even if Hippocrates was a fine man who set my world on fire. I had a mission. Time was ticking, but I could not take an innocent's life. *Was he going to turn evil in the future? Was that it?* I could not see the goodness in him souring.

I stretched and put the dress back on because that was all I came with. I should have brought a change of clothes, especially with my reservations about this mission, but I only wore the outfit I was given. It was all I had. I didn't think I would still be in Kos at this point, but my mind and my heart were at odds with my mission. I wasn't sure a family conversation this morning was a good idea, but when Hippocrates stepped out of the house across the courtyard with a tray that held a pitcher and four glasses, it looked as though I didn't have a choice.

He looked much more rested than I expected, and I found myself drawn to his magnetism and the energy he radiated. Heck, I could feign sleep, but it wouldn't do any good. Besides, my stomach growled loud enough for him to notice me. His gaze met mine, and his lips stretched into a forced smile that didn't quite reach his eyes. He set down the tray and nodded for me to join him.

I wasn't sure I was welcomed based on the tone of the voices arguing moments ago, but I made my way outside anyway. Hippocrates pointed to a chair, and I sat down. He took the seat on the bench next to me without a word. He shook his head when I opened my mouth to speak, as if he sensed the question on my mind.

"Did you sleep well?" he asked in a hushed tone. A dimple appeared in his cheek.

"Yes. Thank you." I hadn't had much sleep but when it came, it was blissfully soundless.

A smile that announced everything that had happened last night sprouted on his lips before he suppressed it, as if showing that much transparency was not a good thing. Hippocrates poured juice into a cup and handed it to me before he served himself. "Help yourself." He waved to the food gracing the table.

Although I was hungry, my mission made my stomach clench. I didn't know whether I would end up with an aching belly if I ate. But I certainly didn't want to be rude. I took a couple of small pieces of fruit and tore off a tiny piece from the fresh bread loaf, leaving more than enough for three other people. I didn't want to impose on their meal, either.

Hippocrates reached over me and plucked two more pieces of fruit and put them on my plate, and then filled his own with the same amount. "You don't have to be shy. There's more than enough for all of us."

"I did not wish to assume." I peeled the skin from the orange-colored fruit and then bit into it. Citrus danced on my tongue and filled my senses with its sweet tang. "Is this fresh picked?" I asked after I'd swallowed the bite.

He grinned and pointed to the back of the courtyard where orange trees lined the paths. "There's plenty more as you can see."

I practically inhaled the food on my plate before his parents stepped out into the courtyard. They regarded me with open disdain, as if I were some poor pauper in their midst. They remained quiet as they sat opposite us, but their hostile glare said more than words.

"You know how we feel about whores," his father snarled, as if having one of Hippocrates's dates at the table was a normal occurrence.

"Then it is good that I am not one." I spoke before Hippocrates even had a chance to swallow the food he was chewing.

His father's gaze moved to mine. "Know your place."

His snarling words rankled me. I shot to my feet and slammed my fist down on the thick table. The thick wood snapped in half, sending food and liquid flying. I pointed at his father. "Do not *ever* speak to me in that manner."

Perhaps Odin had it wrong and it was Hippocrates's father who should be reaped. I could do that without a second glance. Especially with his demeaning attitude.

They both gasped and scuttled backward. Their eyes were as wide as the mouths of the shattered cups that had held our juice.

Hippocrates had his cup halfway to his mouth and had frozen at the display of my power. He glanced at me before looking at his parents with an "I told you so" expression. He sipped his drink as if ruining a table with just a fist was normal here on the island.

His mother dropped to her knees and bowed her head, mumbling a prayer to Athena to try to appease me. If my memory served me, Athena was more appropriate than Aphrodite to describe me. This time, I did not correct her or make her get to her feet like I had to the masses yesterday.

His father had frozen in his spot, as if my display had shocked him into a non-animated state. It would have been quite amusing if I hadn't been so pissed off.

"She will not harm you." Hippocrates looked up at me. "Right?"

I glared at him. How dare he presume that. "I will send them to Valhalla if they continue to show me such disrespect."

His eyes shaded with worry. "But you won't hurt them, right?"

"Will they show me the respect I deserve?" I turned my venomous stare at his parents. They both nodded emphatically, as if their son's words had finally sunk in and broken their paralysis. I glanced at the destroyed table and sighed. I guess my strength here in this realm was somewhat magnified. I could honestly say that I'd never broken a table back on Asgard. "I apologize for ruining your breakfast." I crouched and started to collect the sprawled fruit and broken pottery.

"Please, let me," his mother whispered, as if my helping was some sort of sin.

I met her gaze. "I made this mess." I couldn't let her clean it up. That wasn't right.

"Yes, but it's only because of our disrespect." She avoided looking directly at me, as if that could smite her on the spot.

She had the right reason for my outburst, but it did not excuse me from taking ownership of my actions. "I will help." I offered a forgiving smile to soften my resolute words.

"What is your name, goddess?" She swept broken pieces into her hand.

"Kara." I didn't correct her goddess reference, especially after the insults, but I continued to help clean up the mess. Unfortunately, the table was a total loss. They didn't have the materials here to mend the wood, and I didn't carry the magic to mend wood. *At least a table being destroyed is better than a son dying*, I told myself.

I glanced up at Hippocrates. He watched with his lips slightly parted, as if he were surprised that I would bend down and help clean up. Neither he nor his father offered to lend a hand, and I sat back on my haunches. This was unacceptable to me. It was another display of this civilization's disregard for women as a whole.

"Where I come from, women are not slaves to men's whims. We are the warriors who defend the crown and the people." I stared him down and then pinned my judgmental gaze on his father. "When a woman drops to her knees to clean up, men help. Especially if it was the man who caused the mess." I tilted my eyebrow up at him.

His gaze dropped to the ground and then back at me as if I had just sprouted another head.

Hippocrates got the message and slid his chair out before he squatted next to me to help gather the fallen fruit. Much to his mother's amusement, his father joined us in cleaning up the mess. His mother suppressed her grin and winked at me, forming a tentative bond.

A bond that pressed down more guilt on my shoulders. I should not be building any sort of relationship with these people, but I couldn't seem to help myself. With the exception of his father, these people seemed so simple and endearing that I couldn't fathom the pain I would eventually cause.

We cleared the mess quickly, and I moved the table to the back corner of the courtyard, next to a gate as his father instructed. He stayed with me to direct me where to deposit it, as if I wouldn't follow through with his instructions without oversight.

"I will have it taken to be fixed," his father said as I set down the last of the broken table pieces.

As we walked back, Hippocrates watched us with a tilted smile. My stomach clenched at my subterfuge. I came to this place to take his life, not insert myself into it. My heart hurt with the brutalness of the truth. I couldn't keep up this farce for much longer.

His mother handed a sack of fruit and bread to his father as he approached. "Remember to eat today. Both of you." Her gaze slashed between them, and his father leaned over to peck her cheek.

"We will try. Enjoy the day with Kara," Hippocrates said just before they slipped inside the house.

A door closed in the distance, and silence fell between his mother and me.

She turned to me, her face lined with worry. "What do you want with my son, Goddess Kara?"

Boy, she was direct. I formulated the words carefully because this was just as daunting as facing Odin. "I want nothing from your son." Which was technically true. But Odin wanted his soul, and for the first time since I met the man, I wondered whether I could hide him from a god.

She pondered my answer. "Goddesses usually do not show up without a reason."

She needled me with her statement.

Even on Asgard, her statement would ring true. Gods and goddesses never did anything without a reason. Whether that reason was valid or even sane was another discussion altogether.

Instead of waiting for an answer from me, she headed to the nearest garden patch and dropped to her knees. She inspected the growth and started plucking things from the earth.

She wasn't harvesting the plants, and I was at a loss. "What are you doing?"

"Weeding the garden so these don't choke the healthy plants." She waved the weeds at me before dropping them in the growing pile next to her.

I moved closer, studying the pile and then the plants she left untouched, trying to discern a difference. They looked so similar, and she noticed my interest. When she held the weed next to the plant, I could make out subtle differences in the leaves.

I knelt in the path on the opposite side of where she was and pointed to what looked like the weeds she was pulling.

She blinked at me and looked horrified. "Oh, Goddess, you do not need to weed the garden."

"Four hands are faster than two." I pulled the weed and started a pile of my own. "And then when we are finished, we will have time for me to teach you some defensive moves so you will know how to defend yourself in the event of trouble.”

“Men protect us,” she said with a cock of her head.

“Where I come from, the women are not relegated to cower when there is danger. Men are at our sides as we charge into the fray.” I wiped my forehead with the back of my wrist before I dropped the handful of weeds I’d plucked into my pile. “We have gardens as well, but it has been years since I’ve tended to anything but being battle-ready.” I met her wide-eyed gaze. “What is your name?”

“Sophia.” She still stared at me as if I had developed some horrid disease.

“Well, Sophia, before I leave this place, I will see to it that you are prepared to defend your homestead instead of delegating that peace of mind to the man of the house, who is not here most of the day. Am I correct in that statement?” I tilted my head down and looked through my lashes at her.

“You are correct,” she said, but there was no conviction in her words.

“Have you ever handled a sword?”

“Oh goodness, no.” She shook her head as if handling a sword were forbidden. “Kos is no Sparta.”

I was flabbergasted with this society. "Well, you will before I leave." I just had to find a couple of swords. Training ones would be better, but I had yet to see a military presence here to procure what I needed. "Are there any military barracks on this island?"

Her gaze narrowed at me. "Why do you ask about military barracks?"

"Because they usually have training swords. If I try to train you with a real one, that could be dangerous." As it was, the thought of procuring swords from the hands of men slithered doubt under my skin. Especially if the men of Kos carried the same attitude as the bartender and Hippocrates's father.

"Oh." She glanced down at the garden. "And if I choose not to train?" She shifted down the path to the next section.

I was even more speechless, and I guess it was broadcasted on my face because she lowered her eyes and her cheeks flamed red.

"I am not comfortable with waging war." She began to pluck weeds out with adept fingers, avoiding my stark gaze.

Her words soured my mood, and I continued to pluck weeds, unable to conceive of not wanting to learn to defend myself. But this was her home, and I must respect her wishes. I nodded. "You can watch and decide if it is something you might like to learn. Do you have anything I could train with here? Something similar to the size of a sword?"

My question stumped her. A deep crease appeared between her eyebrows as her forehead crunched in thought. It was the same look Hippocrates wore while he drew the pictures yesterday. When the creases smoothed, I gave her my full attention.

"Would a broom work?" she asked with a voice as meek as a mouse.

It wasn't ideal, but I could make it work. Although I might have to break the broom piece off, so I didn't smash myself in the face with it. "Do you have an extra broom in case the one I use breaks?"

Her expression fell and her lips pulled down as she shook her head.

Well, there went that thought.

She cocked her head. "How about a walking stick?"

"That would work." I really wished they had swords, but I'd make use of whatever she could lend me to at least keep my forms up. And without a broom at the end of the stick, I had little concern that I would break it.

We finished weeding the garden in quick time, and she retrieved the walking stick. It was a little longer than my sword back home and much lighter, but it had a nice, smooth handle. I stepped through each of my forms, explaining them to Sophia as I practiced, helping her to understand what each one should be used for in battle.

When I completed every move at least twice, her eyes were wide with awe. Awe wasn't something I was used to seeing, and it was daunting. Because she should not be in awe of the woman sent to kill her only child.

CHAPTER ELEVEN

IN THE MID-AFTERNOON, HIPPOCRATES'S father stopped by the house, carrying a large bucket. "Lampus decided today would be a good day to pay us for treatment." He grinned and held up the bucket, filled to the brim. "Prawn. This will please the goddess?" He glanced at me with a glint of hope in his eyes.

The idea that he offered his food to please me twisted my gut just as much as Sophia looking at me with awe had. Even though I had no idea what prawn were, I nodded and tried on a smile that felt as fake as Thor's interest in me.

His grin widened, and he handed over the bucket of unprepared prawn to Sophia. "We will not be much longer. Hippocrates was not at his sharpest today and the rest of our afternoon is light." He caught a kiss before he left.

"Have you ever had prawn?" She tipped the bucket so I could see the little sea creatures.

"No." The briny smell that drifted from the bucket was not enticing at all.

"Come. I will show you how to prepare these." Without words, Sophia headed into the house, waving for me to follow. She wasn't shy about pointing to the spot where she wanted me before she set up the counter with the bucket and a large bowl and put one of the more beat-up bowls on the floor between us.

"Garbage." She indicated the bowl on the floor and raised her eyebrow to make sure I understood.

"Garbage," I repeated and pointed to it.

"Yes. And this one behind the bucket is for after they are prepared." She pointed to the bowl on the counter.

"I understand."

"We peel and remove the vein before adding it to the bowl on the counter." Sophia took a prawn from the bucket and set it in front of me before taking one for herself. "Watch." She tore off the crusty legs and outer shell of the creature and discarded those into the garbage bowl on the floor.

"Now you."

I repeated what she did, de-shelling the miniature beast.

Then she handed me a knife and showed me how to slice into the back of the naked and curved prawn to remove the vein visible through the entire length of the creature.

Once we were both done de-veining, she cut the head off hers and threw the head and vein into the garbage. The naked and deveined body went into the bowl on the counter. I followed suit and dropped mine next to hers in the bowl on the counter.

"Now repeat until we have done the same to the rest of these." She smiled as if this instruction was in her element, and she no longer seemed bothered by my perceived goddess status.

We continued preparing the prawns in relative silence, except for the lovely tune Sophia hummed as she worked. It was almost hypnotizing, and I found I was almost falling into a trance. Enough so that when we finished with the last ones, my lower back twinged enough to tell me we had been standing in one place long enough for an ache to form.

I glanced out the window into the courtyard and noted the shadows lengthening. "We have been in here for quite a spell."

"Yes. And we are not done preparing the prawn yet." Sophia dipped a towel into a bucket of water at the far side of the counter and cleaned off her hands before she handed the cloth to me.

"What are you making?"

She smiled. "We, my dear. *We* are making one of my son's favorite meals. Honey prawn."

"We?" I cocked my eyebrow at her.

Her cheeks flushed pink, and she nodded. "If you are to be with my son, you must know how to prepare his favorite foods."

Guilt bit deep enough for me to step back at her presumption. "I am just passing through." I licked my lips trying to find words to wipe away the frown now pulling on her lips. "But I can learn."

She thawed slowly as she studied me. Her lips formed a slight smile at what she saw in my gaze. Even so, her eyes carried a wariness that I had seen at breakfast, as if I had been sent here to break her son's heart. She handed me the pot and took my elbow, leading me through another hallway to what looked like a prep station, where there were jars and spices along with a clay pot large enough to hold the prepared prawn. She dumped the bowl in the pot and then added olive oil, fish sauce, and honey to the pot, stirring the prawns to coat them in the sweet-smelling mixture.

Once the mixture was to her satisfaction, Sophia moved us farther down the hall to an open kitchen, where the fire brick oven emitted a low light along with enough heat to immediately bring perspiration to my skin. But with the heat came the scrumptious scent of fresh baked bread. It lingered on the air as if a thousand loaves had been made in this room and it would always carry this mouthwatering scent.

This was the first room where I encountered people other than Hippocrates and his father. The help had been soundless all day, as if making a peep would have been a deeply awful transgression. I glanced at Sophia, and she waved her hand at me as if shooing a fly. The workers kneaded dough on the counters and then one of them crossed to the oven and pulled out a fresh loaf, setting it aside to cool.

Sophia slid the pot over the open flame and used a long spoon to stir the contents. My mouth watered, and I forgot how hot this room was. My stomach growled, and I was reminded that we had not stopped to partake in any food during the day. It had been full of activity, just the way I liked my days to pass.

It didn't take long before Sophia pulled the pot off the fire and waved me over to look at the concoction. The gray prawns were now a healthy pink and the scent of honey drifted up from the pot. She stirred it a few more times, coating each of the prawns thoroughly before she gave a nod to the servants. She escorted me back into the courtyard. It was only then that I saw a replacement table where the large thick wooden one had been. This one was a little more modest, more like the size of my coffee table as opposed to the size of a banquet table. The benches almost overtook it, but it would do.

She set four plates out and just as the last dish hit the table, Hippocrates and his father strolled in. Hippocrates yawned through a smile with tired, puffy eyes that took me in as if he'd been starving for my presence.

Time ticked away, and the servants brought the prawns and fresh bread out, along with olive oil and spices to dip the bread in if we chose. I was painfully aware of my mission and my failure to follow through as I tried to swallow the delicious meal. I didn't even taste what passed through my mouth, even though Hippocrates raved to his mother that this was the best batch yet.

Night encompassed us by the time we finished the meal, and only the stars peeked out of the black backdrop of the sky. No moon shined, and I shivered. Tonight, it would be clear to Odin and Thor that I had failed this mission.

Tomorrow might bring my death as well as Hippocrates's, and I could not enjoy this last meal.

Hippocrates took my arm and led me out of the house for a walk. I strolled in silence as he chattered about his day. When quiet fell between us, I glanced at him. His brow furrowed as he studied me.

"What ails you?" he asked, noticing my melancholy.

I chose my words carefully. "I do not believe my mission here is worthy."

"And what is this mission?"

If only I could divulge that to him. I shook my head and stared out at the water as we approached it. Waves licked the shoreline in a calming cadence. "It is not important. But my failure to succeed may come with ramifications when I go home."

He stared out at the calm ocean before he spoke. "Why go home then?"

"It's home. It's where my sisters-in-arms are." Even as I said the words, I knew going back was not a viable option. Freya herself would behead me—that was, if Odin didn't want to make an example out of me. My arms broke out in gooseflesh, and I rubbed the chill out of them.

"You can choose to stay with me," he said softly without looking at me, as if speaking the words any louder would cause the gods to strike him down.

I turned to him and palmed his cheek, making him meet my gaze. "I don't think that is possible. But if I could stay, I would." I glanced at the sky, expecting the Bifrost to open and send the Valkyrie army after me. When nothing happened, I returned my gaze to his.

I didn't know which to fear more. My sisters-in-arms or Thor. Would they send the Valkyrie force for me? Or would Thor show up to dole out his twisted brand of justice?

I stepped closer to Hippocrates with the intention of enjoying our night before his world fell to pieces. I just prayed that when the end came, it was swift and painless.

CHAPTER TWELVE

HIPPOCRATES MADE GOOD ON his promise to take his time. He made slow, sweet love to me tonight, the kind that moved the earth in a much different way than the frantic thrusts of our first christening. And just like the prior night, I memorized his tender touch. When we laid spent and exhausted from passion, I curled into his arms, letting him hold me as he drifted to sleep.

Melancholy hit and my chest hurt enough to squeeze tears from the corner of my eyes. That imaginary clock in my head kept spinning faster toward my demise. I had to figure out a plan to get this man somewhere where I could keep him safe.

I kissed his temple and then smoothed his hair from his brow. "Would you leave Kos?" I whispered.

"No," he whispered back in that sleepy way I wasn't sure whether he was fully awake. When he turned and met my gaze in the dark room, I knew he wasn't asleep. "So, you need to stay."

I wanted to spill my secrets and convince him to run away with me in the night. But the look on this face stopped me. I nuzzled into him without giving him any indication of my plans.

I drifted off, and that tingle started in my brain just before the intrusive voice boomed in my head for an update. I sat up with a gasp, shaking Henrick out of my mind. I mentally slammed the door on Asgard without answering his call.

"Hey. Are you all right?" Hippocrates asked with a groggy voice.

"Yes. Just a nightmare," I muttered and slid back into his grasp. But I was too wired to sleep, unlike Hippocrates, who began to snore almost immediately.

I listened to his breathing, trying to let my body relax and rest without drifting off. I did not want Henrick to invade my mind again, and sleep seemed to be the thing to allow him entry.

But sometime in the wee hours of the morning, I fell into a dreamless slumber, only waking when Hippocrates moved from the bed. I curled onto my side and watched as he slipped out of the room to get ready for another day at work while I puttered around with his mother.

I was tempted just to grab him and fly out of here with him because time was not on my side now that I'd passed the deadline. But I had a feeling he would fight me and that wouldn't do, especially if we were in the air. I didn't know how long I'd have before Odin would send someone to check on me.

But my answer came a little after noon when a boom echoed from the mountains. I straightened, with my heart slamming against the walls of my chest.

Here we go.

Sophia hopped to her feet next to me just as fast, and the weeds we were pulling were forgotten as a winged warrior flew directly toward where I stood, as if she could track me. The armor glinted in the sun, and I stepped back reaching for the walking stick, my mouth as dry as the sun's surface.

The warrior landed between us and the fruit trees, and my chest stuttered. Odin sent Freya after me.

"You have failed."

Freya's voice hit a nerve. It was the same voice she used after the battle when she accused me of calling forth the wraiths.

Hippocrates's mother stared in abject horror as Freya pulled out her sword and pointed it at me.

"I have not failed." I swallowed hard. Without my own sword, I was at Freya's mercy. "I have not been given a credible reason for the mission." My voice wavered.

"Odin ordered it. That is reason enough." Freya's eyes turned to slits.

"We are supposed to protect the innocent." I gripped the walking stick tightly in my right hand, even though I doubted it would hold up against the sword's edge and reached my left hand protectively toward Sophia.

"It was an order, Kara. We do not disobey orders." Her nostrils flared in that familiar way of hers when she was disappointed.

"I will not kill an innocent man." I straightened my back, shifting my feet into a battle stance.

"You were sent to kill someone?" Sophia asked.

"A man named Hippocrates. Do you know him?" Freya snapped.

Sophia paled. Her eyes widened with accusation, but she was cognizant enough to shake her head. Her eyes never left me, but I couldn't look away from Freya without risking death.

"I think she's lying." Freya charged forward with the intent to skewer me.

I pushed Hippocrates's mother away, ignoring her squeak of surprise, and stepped toward Freya, ducking under the swing of her sword and parrying with the walking stick. It snapped cleanly where the sword connected with it, as I thought it might. But the deflection was enough for the blade to miss me.

Close contact with swords, especially when one was within arm's length, was difficult and before Freya recovered, I grabbed her sword wrist and threw a brutal punch to her exposed throat with the hand holding the walking stick.

She gagged from the force of the hit, and I twisted her sword arm hard enough for a crack to echo in the courtyard. The clang of metal on stone resounded.

I kicked the sword out of reach. Burning pain sliced my shoulder. I twisted away from Freya, hissing at the pain. A bloody knife glistened in the sunlight.

"Freya, please." I reached for my own knife. "I cannot kill an innocent. But I can kill you if you insist on this insane mission. Hippocrates is a healer, for goodness' sake!"

Rage filled Freya's features, turning her feral. There was no reasoning with her, and I stood between her and her sword. She pulled a second knife and launched another attack.

Block, parry, slash, hit. Actions on repeat, over and over until I lost my temper. I spun, sending my elbow into her chest. Freya flew into one of the fruit trees, nearly tearing it out of the ground.

I didn't have time to categorize my wounds, not with the guttural cry from Freya. She climbed to her feet. As she stalked toward me, I swiped her sword off the ground. The view behind me startled me. Hippocrates's mother sat on the ground, with sightless open eyes. Blood covered the wall above her. Right about where her head height would have been if she were standing.

Damnit. I had tried to push her to safety but sent her to her death instead.

I turned back to Freya, who held blades in both fists. Either she hung onto them, or these were an extra set just for carving her enemies to pieces.

Instead of trying to block with the sword, I twirled away, hissing as she landed another slice across my back. But my maneuver gave me the advantage, and I swung her sword with all my might before she could even turn in my direction.

Freya's wide eyes met mine just before the blade tore through her spine, sending her head flying and drenching me in the torrent of blood pluming from her neck. Her body stood planted in place for a few moments, and then the lack of brain signals to muscle groups caused her body to fall.

My raspy breath dragged in and out of my lungs as the past few minutes hit me. My dress was no longer clean, it was dripping with Freya's blood. Just as bloody as the mark on the wall where Hippocrates's mother's head smashed into the stone.

I couldn't catch my breath as the truth squeezed my chest. These deaths had horrific ramifications.

CHAPTER THIRTEEN

M Y DREAD AT THE situation only worsened as Hippocrates barreled into the courtyard. His eyes echoed the same franticness that thrummed through my entire body, making it hard to breathe. He stared at Freya's headless body and then her head a few feet away, breathing out slowly. He took a step in my direction as his eyes inspected my wounds before he surveyed the rest of the courtyard. When his gaze caught on his mother's dead form, he froze in place.

Both my arms bled from Freya's strikes. She got at least one strike on my back, maybe more with the sting radiating across it. The clang of metal hitting stone sang in the courtyard, and my head spun as I staggered into a sidestep.

"I pushed her away to keep her safe." I stared at the blood dripping down the wall as my failure compounded. "I must have pushed harder than I realized."

Hippocrates's head snapped in my direction. "You killed my mother?" His voice cracked.

"I did not mean to. I only wanted her safely away from Freya's sword." I waved at the metal at my feet.

His eyes narrowed at me and a hardness I had never seen seeped into his face. "You need to leave."

The growl in his voice caught my breath in my chest. I didn't answer him. Not while my mind was in complete panic mode. It was only a matter of time before Odin found Freya in Valhalla. I needed to hide her body, and I spied the tree nearly yanked out of the ground. The hole was deep enough to hide a body and it would nourish the tree.

"I cannot leave you here unprotected." I leaned down to grasp Freya's ankles. I dragged her toward the hole.

"What?" Hippocrates asked as he hunched over his mother, just to make sure she was truly dead.

I stopped halfway to Freya's final resting place. She'd curse me for not taking her body home to have a proper burial, but if anyone else came through the Bifrost, I would rather not have the evidence so apparent.

"I can't leave you unprotected."

"This was about me?" He straightened and glared at me.

I opened my mouth and glanced down at Freya. "In a way." I resumed dragging her body across the stone, leaving a path of blood as I navigated to the hole. I pitched her in and then crossed to collect her head. I wondered whether I should add the sword to the macabre grave. If I was in possession of Freya's blade, everyone would know I took her life. I picked up the steel and sighed as I trudged back to the hole and dropped it in next to her. Then, with very little effort, I righted the tree, covering Freya with the frayed root system.

When I finished, I wiped my hand on my dress, as if that could wipe away the blood. But my hands remained stained along with the dress. I glanced at Hippocrates.

He approached me with fiery eyes and flaring nostrils. "Explain."

I stared at him and then closed my eyes. "I abandoned my mission." When I opened my eyes, his jaw clenched so tight I could hear his molars grinding.

"What mission?"

"I am supposed to bring you to Valhalla." I chewed on my lower lip.

His eyes narrowed. "You threatened Valhalla earlier."

I nodded.

"What is Valhalla?"

I grappled with how to explain the afterlife to Hippocrates in a manner that he would understand. I pressed my fingers to my temple and stared at the blood seeping into the cracks of the stone, trying to remember this realm's personification of death. "Hades." My gaze lifted back to his.

His eyebrows rose. "You came to kill me?" His cheeks flushed red, and his eyes blazed.

"I am supposed to escort you to Valhalla. But I cannot see the reason in the order." My voice sounded meeker than I wanted. "I disobeyed, and I fear they will send more soldiers to reap you and drag me back to be punished." I took a deep breath. "So let me take you somewhere safe where they cannot find you." I didn't know whether that was possible with how the Bifrost keeper could invade my head, but I had to try.

"I will not leave my home." He crossed his arms.

"If you are worried about leaving your father, we can take him as well." I just wanted to protect him.

He shook his head. "This island needs my services and teachings."

His stubbornness infuriated me. "If you stay, you will die, and I cannot guarantee others won't die alongside you."

"People die every day."

His hard tone set my teeth on edge.

"But you are important to this realm in some way. Otherwise, Odin would not have bothered with this order." I still did not understand my order, but considering Freya, the leader of the Valkyrie force, had been sent, I expected the big guns next. Thor. And he wasn't a man who hesitated. He would strike down Hippocrates and then punish me in ways I couldn't fathom. I shook with fear. "Please."

"No." He pointed at the door. "Please leave."

I hung my head before shaking it slowly. I could not leave him. If Thor came, I had to

protect this weak human. But I knew, deep
down, he was just as doomed as I was.

CHAPTER FOURTEEN

HIPPOCRATES COULD NOT PHYSICALLY kick me out of his home, but he certainly could give me the chilliest of shoulders while I scrubbed the rocks of blood. He gently laid his mother out on a thin sheet, wrapping her as he sniffled.

"Do you need me to build a pyre for her?"

Hippocrates glared up at me. "We bury our dead. We don't burn them." The venom in his voice had me backing up a step.

"Then would you like for me to dig you a hole?"

He stared at me and then his gaze moved to the fruit grove. "Like you did for that warrior you killed?" He jutted his chin in that direction. "I would prefer to give my mother a proper burial."

I shook my head. "No. I was hiding that body." I dropped back to my knees and continued to scrub the rocks and then sat back on my heels as the shock of the day hit. "That was my commanding officer." Shakes gripped me and my teeth chattered. "She was sent here to kill me." The cloth dropped from my hand, and I wrapped my arms around myself, holding my elbows to try to stanch the tremors.

This hadn't been a battle against wraiths or other monsters we had encountered in our lifetime. This was killing someone I had respected. Someone who wasn't a monster. My gaze landed on Hippocrates's mother, and my chest squeezed tighter. Even though it had been a mistake, the responsibility of her death slammed home.

My vision warbled under a sudden mist, and then heated paths slid down my cheeks. "I am so sorry," I whispered, still trembling as if I were a child and had seen a monster for the first time.

Hippocrates hissed and climbed to his feet, crossing to me. He grabbed my wrist and then pressed his to my forehead. "You are going into shock." His words were softer than before as he inspected my wounds.

A high-pitched buzz whirred in my ears as he spoke, drowning out most of what he was saying. He disappeared into the house and returned with his medical bag. Stinging sensations cascaded down my back, and I bowed away from him.

"I'm cleaning your wounds." His gaze pierced mine just before that sting returned.

At least the buzzing stopped with the new level of pain. It cleared my head enough for me to regain my senses. "I am fine." I leaned forward to continue scrubbing the rocks. I'd made it almost to the grass near the tree where I buried Freya.

"Stop moving. That's an order." The snap in his voice made me obey him. "You are not okay. This is deep enough to require sutures, as is the wound in your shoulder."

I turned my head, trying to see the wounds, but they were back far enough that I couldn't even glimpse them. "Once I am able to rest, I will heal."

He didn't stop cleaning my wounds even though his face was pinched in anger. Like he was warring with himself over helping the person responsible for his mother's death. "I do not know what I am going to tell my father." His voice was low, almost a whisper as his eyes flicked toward his mother and then back to my wounds.

His devastation peeked through his stern expression for a moment, and my heart clenched in my chest. I was responsible for that haunted look.

"Tell your father I tried to protect her from harm, but I miscalculated my strength." I met his gaze. "Make sure he understands no one is safe from Odin's wrath since I have abandoned my mission."

He stopped cleaning my back. "You had every chance to kill me yesterday and the day before when you arrived. Why didn't you?"

"It wasn't just." I glanced away. "Killing monsters is just, but killing a healer?" I continued slowly, shaking my head. "I could not find reason in the order."

"Do you often disobey orders?"

His disapproval bled through into his words despite the fact we were discussing an order to kill him. I glanced at him, unable to find the words to explain why I did not follow through. There was more to it than it being unjust. He stirred something deep inside me that had been dormant for too long.

I arched against the sting of the cloth he used to clean my wound. "I do not blindly follow."

"So, yes." He continued swiping and then added balm over my wound, soothing some of the sting. When he finished, he tucked his supplies back into his bag. "Go rest." He pointed to where I slept last evening.

I glanced up at him. "You told me to leave."

"I am a doctor. I cannot throw an injured patient into the street. Especially one who can devastate this village." He pointed to the bedroom and there was no leeway in his tone. "If your back is not healed by nightfall, I will suture it. Understand?"

"Yes." I climbed to my feet with his help and crossed to the room, stripping the ruined dress before I fell face-first on the soft mattress. Darkness claimed me, pulling me into fitful dreams of torture and death.

CHAPTER FIFTEEN

MY SLEEP WAS RUDELY disrupted as I was lifted right out of the bed by my hair. Pain entombed my head as my eyes blinked open to Thor's angry gaze. Darkness surrounded us except for the halo of lightning surrounding Thor. I grabbed his wrists, digging my fingernails into his skin.

"Let me go!"

His gaze lowered to my naked form still streaked in blood. "What have you done, Kara?" He met my gaze again and narrowed his eyes.

"I have done nothing!" I hissed, still struggling in his grip.

He slammed me against the wall, dazing me. "You murdered the general of the Valkyrie."

"It was not murder." Crap. That wasn't supposed to slip. "It was self-defense. She came here to kill me." My toes barely hit the floor beneath me, and my scalp screamed. If Thor did not put me down, I was afraid my hair would be ripped out by the roots.

He pulled a clear ball out of his pocket and fog swirled inside it. "You deserve what punishment comes to you." The magic ball slowly cleared, with a view of Hippocrates and me against the tree the first night. "You defied Odin's orders and slept with the man you were supposed to bring to Valhalla?" He shook the orb and another scene of me striking down Freya came into view. "You are a traitor to Asgard."

I knocked the orb out of his hand, where it crashed on the floor and disintegrated. "Hippocrates is an innocent. Valkyrie stand up for what is right, and reaping him is not right." I could not help the snarl in my voice. "He is a healer, for goodness' sake!"

"You were given an order."

His face was so close that the electricity stung my skin.

"An unjust order," I screamed at him.

He lowered me so I could stand on my own, but his fist still held a handful of my hair. "Just or not...it was an order that you defied."

The statement sent a rash of gooseflesh over my skin. "You have defied your father," I pointed out. Thor had gone against his father's orders and taken matters into his own hands before.

His eyes darkened. "I am the God of Thunder."

"I am a Valkyrie," I volleyed back with the same venom and tried to twist out of his grip.

He slammed me harder against the wall, and the stones behind me shifted. Dust puffed around me, and I coughed.

"You cannot run from me, traitor." His eyes lowered again to my naked form. "You've run long enough. Now it's time to pay for your sins." Then Thor did the unimaginable. He slammed his lips against mine.

I gasped, and this tongue plundered my mouth. This was not the sweet bliss of Hippocrates's kiss. This was an arrogant assault from a god who believed he had the right to do anything he pleased.

I tried to push him away, but he yanked my head back farther and pinned me with his body.

His free hand squeezed my breast hard enough to leave prints on my skin.

The creak of the door followed, and Thor's lips curved into a smile as he continued to kiss me. Then he pulled away and smiled at the man with the lantern gawking at us from the doorway.

Bastard.

I swung at him, but he caught my arm and clasped bindings on my wrist. I struggled against him, but he spun me face-first into the wall and linked my wrists together in the bindings.

I screamed my frustration.

"I have always wanted to hear you scream," he whispered in my ear, just before he hauled me over his shoulder.

"What are you doing?" I continued to struggle as he grabbed Hippocrates with his other arm and then launched through the roof of the house, taking us high enough for the frigid wind to leave me shaking. At least Hippocrates had clothing on, but the thinness of the air rolled his eyes back and he went limp.

I closed my eyes tight as my heart thundered in my chest. "Where are you bringing us?"

"To a place you will never be found." His voice was as icy as the wind. He streaked across the sky as fast as lightning, and when we finally dropped, it was into a bank of clouds that obstructed my vision.

He brought us into a cavern, and my eyes widened at the chains embedded in the walls near the back. I struggled, but I was no match for Thor. He dumped Hippocrates on the ground and then took me to where the chains were.

I jumped and kicked. My foot landed on Thor's chest, but he was only sent back a couple of steps. "I wish I could scratch your fucking eyes out!" I tried another kick, but Thor grabbed my leg and twisted, sending me onto the ground with enough force to knock the wind out of me.

Before I could roll and get to my feet, Thor dragged me by the ankle back to the chains and clasped me in. My legs were wide enough for panic to set in, especially considering I didn't have a stitch of clothing on.

He tugged me up on my knees and pressed against me. I tried to swipe my nails at him, but he grabbed the chain holding my wrist together and yanked upward.

My arms screamed with pain. A cry escaped my mouth, echoing off the walls.

"I should tame you, but that would take more time than I have."

He hauled me to my feet and circled in front of me. I was at his mercy with my legs bound and my arms clasped behind me.

He gripped my jaw hard enough to bruise. "Would you like to know what it's like to fuck a god?"

I glared at him. Even though the look in his eyes was deadly, I couldn't help mouthing off. "Piss off, Thor."

He sneered at me with his teeth visible, and then he backhanded me.

Stars bloomed behind my eyes as my cheek flared with agony and I listed to the side, stunned by the pain. I shook my head and attempted to twist my arm from his grip, but iron clamped down on my wrist hard enough to pinch. But I still had one arm free, and I punched Thor in the throat.

It wasn't nearly as hard as the punch I had hit Freya with, but it did send the mighty Thor back a step. I strained against the chains, but they did not budge.

Thor coughed and then snarled before his fist slammed me in the stomach.

I folded as much as I could with the chains, and my other arm was pulled taut and the binding was as painfully tight as the one on my other wrist.

Thor grabbed my hair, pulling my head back, so I had to look at him. "Magic wards the chains, as it does this cavern. If humans are to happen on it, in their eyes, the cave ends near where your lover lays." He pointed at Hippocrates. "This is your punishment. An eternity chained in isolation."

He grinned in such an evil way that I began to shake.

As Hippocrates stirred, Thor moved to the space behind me. He pressed his body against mine in a way that turned my blood to ice. His hands roamed to unwanted places, and I tried to jerk away. But the chains restricted my motion, and all it did was push me further into Thor. "Perhaps if you had said yes to me on Asgard, I might have overlooked your treasonous behavior."

Hippocrates's head snapped up at Thor's words.

"Do not touch me," I hissed, but I was helpless to stop his brutal exploration.

Hippocrates climbed to his feet, taking in the chains holding me in place and the bastard violating me with his hands. "The lady said not to touch her."

Thor continued to pinch and rub me like I was his toy to play with as he pleased. And he certainly wanted me to squirm. "You fucked the traitor. Was she worth it?"

Hippocrates's face turned red, and his eyes locked on mine. "Take your hands off her," he growled, and his fists clenched.

I shook my head to stop him from challenging Thor. That was a recipe for a slow and painful death.

Thor laughed. "And if I don't?" He forcefully tilted my head to the side and licked the side of my throat.

"I will kill you." Hippocrates's tone fell to a hush as if what Thor was doing to me was a sin worth killing for. The doctor I knew was gone, replaced with a feral being that I did not recognize.

Thor's hands came off my body, and he moved in front of me slowly, like a panther tracking prey.

"Run," I yelled, but Hippocrates stepped closer, bringing his fists up. He was nearly as tall as Thor but did not have the pure muscle mass of the god. And he certainly didn't have the strength of a god.

The fool ignored me.

Thor lifted his hands but didn't fist them, and let Hippocrates play. He bobbed and weaved each punch Hippocrates threw, or easily knocked the punch away as if he swatted a fly.

"Please, Thor...please don't kill him." I fell to my knees. My hands rose high in the air and my wings popped into existence. They quivered with the same boiling fear that ran through my veins.

Thor looked my way, and Hippocrates's fist caught his cheek square. But he didn't budge. His eyes hardened as he glared at me. And then a sadistic smile surfaced just as he shot out a punch of his own.

His fist caught Hippocrates in the shoulder.

Hippocrates flew into the cave wall with a yelp. He stumbled, dazed by the punch, and then shook his head before he stepped back into fighting form. But he held the arm Thor hit closer to his body, as if protecting it. It looked dislocated from this angle.

Thor toyed with Hippocrates, slowly beating him until he was bloody and broken at my feet. Each punch, each snap of bone, wrenched a gasp and a plea from my lips that Thor ignored. When Hippocrates could no longer lift himself from where he landed, Thor grabbed a handful of Hippocrates's hair and pulled him to his knees, dragging him to the spot in front of me.

Hot paths slid down my cheeks, splashing on the ground in front of me. "Please don't," I whispered, even though I knew it was futile.

"Any last words?" Thor asked and pulled a blade from the sheath on his hip, pressing it against Hippocrates's throat.

Hippocrates stared at me through swollen eyelids. His once handsome face was distorted with a crushed cheek, and blood dripped from his mouth. "Kara," he mumbled, sounding in as much pain as he looked.

It broke my heart. "I'll do anything." I turned my gaze to Thor's.

What I saw in his eyes crushed me.

"You will kneel for a human, but not for me?" Thor's eyes grew colder.

Odin appeared behind Thor. His gaze was even harder than Thor's. "Kara Mist. You are sentenced to an eternity chained in this cave." He nodded at Thor.

The blade at Hippocrates's throat sliced deep into his flesh as Thor dragged it from one side of his neck to the other. Hippocrates's blood baptized me with heat as my scream rang against the rocks.

His death could have been swift and humane, but Thor beat him to near death before he ended him. And from the glint in the bastard's eye, he enjoyed the torture and my wailing cries.

Thor held Hippocrates so I had to watch the light fade from his eyes. Once the man I forsook my mission for was dead and gone, Thor scooped up his body and took flight, leaving me shaking and at the mercy of his father.

I sobbed, not caring that Odin studied me as if I were a horrifying bug on his nicely prepared meal. When my tears dried up, Odin crouched to my level.

"Without Hippocrates and others from Earth's history who were pinnacles in their fields and helped to advance society in ways that were lasting through millennia, Asgard will not have to deal with some nasty scientific discoveries that could devastate the planet. And humans have always been willing to destroy their own home rather than be ruled over." He smiled, as if that reasoning made any sense.

He stripped this realm of a good man just for his own personal gain?

I glared at him. "You bastard."

"I am playing a long game of chess, and this was one of many critical pieces. Ragnarök is inevitable, and when it destroys Asgard, we will rule this pitiful realm as the gods we were meant to be."

"You are a sick fuck," I hissed. The chilled blood covering me made me shiver. The chains rattled in response.

Odin gave me a frightening smile. "When we return to this realm, you will be nothing but skin stretched over bones. Your mind will be gone. Your eternal torture will be gratifying." He straightened and regarded me with disgust. "His death seems humane in comparison." He turned and faded away.

"No!" I screamed until my voice went hoarse. I was left with Hippocrates's blood painting me and the memory of the light in his eyes dying.

CHAPTER SIXTEEN

P AIN RAKED OVER MY emaciated form. The times humans and animals found solace in this cave were beyond numerous. And the only beings that sensed me and whined were the wolves. Outside of them, no one acknowledged my rantings and ravings from beyond the magical veil. My existence was such slow torture that my mind had fallen into visions of vengeance.

My stomach stopped growling eons ago as my body feasted on its own fat and muscle structure. I was uncertain I could even walk at this point. My captors left me with little wiggle room—stand or kneel, but there was no motion forward or backward and I had fallen to my knees so many years ago that moving my arms now sent pain through every joint.

The floor was littered with what was left of my feathers, and I could not feel my wing bones any longer. It was as if they'd shriveled like the rest of my body.

I did mathematical problems in my head to keep my mind sharp, because when Odin came to kill me, I did not want him to win. If my mind broke, he won. I sang until my voice failed and then fell into a restless slumber out of sheer exhaustion.

The only indication of the passage of time was the change in weather, but they all blended into a shivering cold that had settled into my bones permanently. The sunrises and sunsets seemed endless. Either endless light or endless dark, blending centuries into one another.

My hair wrapped pools around my body and my fingernails had grown to the point they could scratch the side walls. I'd even tried to dig the chains out of the walls with them, but they snapped every time I'd tried. My toenails constantly broke because of the kneeling position I had been in forever.

I would have died long ago had I been mortal, and I would have been with my Hippocrates now in the afterlife. Damn Odin and immortality. Damn this cave and the slow progression of days.

All this because I couldn't steal Hippocrates's knowledge away from the human world just because Odin demanded it. I hated the fact I wished for death, but this existence was far worse than anything death could bring. I wished for Hela's mercy, but it never came.

Darkness fell again, and my eyes adjusted to the night. I counted my breaths. In. Out. In. Out. In a continuous pattern. A thin glow illuminated the outside of the cavern, and I blinked as it got closer. It was probably another explorer. They'd been coming more frequently, bundled up in heavy gear that I had never seen the likes of. And a part of me envied the bulky clothing. But I had long ago stopped shivering.

Usually, explorers came in a party of two or more, and they'd set up a camp in the cave for a blink of time. Their campfires provided a flash of warmth in an otherwise frigid existence. And although they could not see or hear me, their company provided a reprieve from my crazed thoughts.

A lone explorer stepped into the cavern and scanned the back wall with his lantern. I only saw a silhouette, but he was tall enough and broad enough to give me pause. And the way he approached the magical wall, grew a foreign feeling in my chest.

Hope warmed me, but I doubted it. I could not allow that into my soul because the moment this stranger left, my spirit would be crushed.

He set the lantern on the ground, pointing it to the ceiling and I caught his profile. His eyes were aquamarine, and his cheekbones were severe as if he had been starving just as long as I had. But it was the pointed ear that sent a jolt of shock through me.

Fae. I blinked and tried to remember a fae entering the cavern in all the time I had been chained and came up empty.

He mumbled and reached for the wall of magic separating us. His hand brushed against it and sparks jumped from his fingertips. He smiled and looked down at something foreign that sent its own light on his mesmerizing face. His hair was dark and pulled back from his face.

"I am coming for you, goddess," he whispered.

I shivered as his voice rolled through me in a wave of expectation. *Is he talking to me?* I could not afford hope, and I closed my eyes, even as it bloomed in my being.

He glanced over his shoulder and then back before he waved his hand in an arc, chanting a spell of his own. His magic blasted into my space, tasting like cinnamon and vanilla spice, and it breathed hunger into my bones.

The fae stepped through the barrier, and his eyes widened as they took me in. With a wave of his hands, my binds disintegrated, and I slumped onto the ground, pulling my arms in for the first time in eons. He slowly crossed the space, as if I were a skittish wolf and could bolt at any moment.

I chuckled softly at his approach. I couldn't move, much less run away.

He startled at my laugh, freezing in place. "You are alive?"

"If you call this being alive, then I guess I am. Are you real?" I tilted my head so I could see him clearly. "Either you're real or my mind finally broke."

"Your mind has not broken. I am Reyfyre, and I have been looking for you for decades, Goddess." He crouched down next to me.

"I am no goddess, but I am immortal. Death doesn't touch me, even when I've begged her to." Speaking exhausted me. "I am Valkyrie."

He leaned back and a bitter sneer formed on his lips. "You are one of Odin's killing machines?"

"No. I defied orders. This is my penance." I glanced around the room but couldn't lift my arms.

He sighed and looked at my surroundings and then at me. "You do not look like someone who can help us." He ran his hand through his hair, and locks fell from the elastic holding his hair back.

"I do not know how long I have been locked away, but you are right. I need to be nursed back to health and then get to Asgard to dole out my revenge."

His eyebrows rose. "Asgard is no longer."

That snapped my head in his direction. "What?"

"Most of the realms have been destroyed in Odin's bid to rule all."

I tried to prop myself up, but my muscles had atrophied to the point where they were nonexistent.

"And as for how long you have been locked in this cave...it's been close to three thousand years, if the intel I received is correct." He glanced around again. "It is a miracle that you are not dead."

My mind couldn't wrap around the timeframe he dropped. "I came in the time of Hippocrates," I said, more to myself than to him.

"Who?"

My heart ached, and the vision of his life fading from his eyes accosted me. Instead of focusing on the devastation in my heart, I looked at the stranger, sensing more than fae from him. The hairs on the back of my neck stood on end at his proximity. "What are you?"

His pack slid off his shoulder and he unclasped it, pulling out a clear container. He set it on the ground and reached for me. "Mix breed. Fae and wraith."

I recoiled. Wraiths were enemies of Asgard. But my motion did not deter him. He scooped me up until I sat against him, and then opened the container, pressing it gently to my lips.

"Water," he whispered and tilted the bottle, wetting my lips.

I did not have the strength to pull away. The cool liquid caressed my lips and I could not help but lick the liquid off, savoring the small quench on my tongue. "Wraiths are my enemy," I whispered.

He let out a laugh. "Well, we will see what we become when you get your strength back. It seems I am the last of the wraith bloodline, and you are the last of the Valkyrie."

Somehow, I found the strength to pull away and stared at him.

"The Valkyrie are gone?" My voice cracked.

"Odin slaughtered them after they failed him and lost Asgard." His lips pressed together in a frown. "He slaughtered anyone who had the possibility of standing against him. Wraith, fae, witchlings, Valkyrie." His glance found mine. "He even murdered Loki. His own son. And he rules over what is left with an iron hand with Thor by his side."

I blinked at him, and he brought the water back to my lips. "Take a small sip."

I did as he asked, and the water tasted like the nectar of the gods. I wanted more and whined when he pulled it away.

"What is your name?" He searched my gaze.

I thought twice about telling a wraith of who I was, but he unchained me and even offered me water. "Kara." I nodded toward the water bottle.

"Let that settle for a moment." He dug in his pack, pulling out a blanket and then draped it over my shoulders.

"How did you find me?"

"Thor raved about chaining a fierce immortal traitorous goddess in the mountains. He seemed very proud that you were rotting for an eternity." His lips curled down further. "The arrogant ass."

"Why would he tell you?"

He snorted a laugh. "I overheard him. I was hiding in plain sight as a lowly busboy, collecting intel for the resistance." He huffed. "They decimated the resistance soon after, and I made it my life's mission to find the immortal goddess he spoke of." He glanced at me. "I figure you have just as much, if not more, reasons to squash them like the vermin they are than I do."

"And you think I will work with a wraith?"

He shrugged. "Half-wraith," he corrected. "I could just leave. You'd still be barricaded behind that wall of magic, even without the chains." He started to get up.

I willed my muscles to move, and my hand clasped on his wrist. My nails somehow missed him as they curled in front of us. He broke through Odin's magic, so he must be powerful. "Why don't you take him on yourself?"

"I am not immortal."

I laughed at him. "Valkyrie can be killed. One strategic slice of a blade and we fall."

"Same with the gods. They beheaded Loki. Made a grand spectacle of it, too."

I shivered. Loki always walked the line between what was right and wrong, but he didn't deserve to be publicly beheaded. He chose when he fought, regardless what his father said. I had respected Loki in a way that I never extended to

Thor. I shook the thoughts out of my head and focused on the fae. "Reyfyre, you must have magic that can stop them if you've broken through Odin's magic."

"I do have strong magic, but even my father fell to Odin, and he was stronger than I am. I need someone to have my back and the same motivations as I have to save this realm."

"Why would you want to save this realm?"

"If I had been left in the fae realm, the fae would have killed me—same with the wraiths. So my parents did the only thing they could to keep me safe. They hid me here among humans, taught me to glamour my ears and blend in. And in the dark caves we explored, they taught me to tap into my magic. Then the Asgardians came and destroyed anyone who posed a threat to them. My father and mother included. But they sent me away right before the resistance fell." He stared out the opening of the cavern. "They saved my life. But their deaths were televised, along with the rest of the resistance fighters."

"Televised?"

He grinned at me. "You've been here a very long time. The world has changed as you soon will see." He offered me another sip of water. "Assuming you agree to align with me."

I sighed and glanced at the opening to my cave that had never changed in all these years.

Could this fae-wraith be giving me a line to gain my favor? Wraiths were only interested in destruction—although, if what he was saying was true, a wraith and a fae fell in love. And had a child, no less. What in Valhalla's name would cause such a connection?

Of one thing I was sure; Odin could cause such an alliance.

I nodded. "I will align with you."

With a wave of his hand, my out-of-control nails on my hands and feet clipped to the manicured level they once were, and the weight of my hair eased. I turned my head as Reyfyre opened his bag, and my hair tickled me at mid-back. "I don't know if this will fit you, but it will at least cover you until I can get us down the mountain."

Fabric dumped over my head, and he helped me put on the strange frock, pulling my hands through the sleeves as best he could. It pillowed around my body like a warm blanket and a hood settled on my head. The weight of it nearly crashed me to the floor, but he steadied me as he picked me up off the ground.

Pain gripped my legs as he helped me straighten them, and I gritted my teeth together.

"We have a lot of work to do to get you back to fighting strength."

I wanted to snort laughter at the given, but I had no energy left. I wondered how he was going to get me past the magical wall until he undid his bag to reveal straps and clasps that I'd never seen before. He slid straps around my legs and across my back and over my shoulders, making almost a small seat for me. I was confused when he squatted and pulled the ends of the straps in front of him where clicks echoed in the quiet cave. He reached for the straps that hung over my shoulders and pulled me flush to his back. More clicks sounded and then he stood to his full height.

My legs dangled by his sides, loosely covered by the fabric. I rested my chin on his shoulder.

"I came prepared." His voice echoed as he crouched and picked up the water, tucking it away somewhere I couldn't see.

His magic swirled and a moment later, he shot through the barrier with me on his back. His heartbeat slammed against mine as if he hadn't been so sure it would work. Without another word, he swiped the lantern from the floor and turned it off, sliding it into a holder on his chest.

Then he stepped out into the clear night, and I saw the stars for the first time in three thousand years. I was more than thankful for this freedom, but a small part of me still balked at partnering with a wraith.

And so, let the battle for the realms rage.

THE END

* * * *

Continue with the next installment in the Fallen Valkyrie Duet, MODERN GODDESS on the next page.

FALLEN VALKYRIE DUET

Book 2

MODERN GODDESS

A fallen Valkyrie.

A fae-wraith hybrid.

Enemies become allies to survive a god's wrath.

Odin and Thor relentlessly hunt survivors of the destroyed realms on the only planet that still exists: Earth. Their dark tyranny enslaved this world, and anyone who challenges their rule dies a very public death.

Reyfyre, the fae-wraith hybrid, has been hiding his entire life. When he found me, I was nothing but stretched-out skin over bones. Yet he offered me asylum, as long as I helped him kill Odin.

How could I refuse?

He nursed me back to health and rehabilitated my weakened muscle on the sparring field. Even with his demanding routine, I found peace in our hideaway in the northern territory.

Then Odin discovered my empty cell and put a bounty on my head. And our mountain sanctuary, protected by Reyfyre's magic, was too close to it to be coincidence.

Our only hope now is to make it to New York City. However, that's thousands of miles by foot through a tundra filled with hidden refugees, predators, and thieves.

There's no other option. If we die, no one will be left to stop the callous gods before they destroy the only realm left.

But are we really strong enough to take down a god?

If you like dark twists on Norse Mythology, you will love Modern Goddess.

CHAPTER 1

THREE THOUSAND YEARS CHAINED in a cave does some serious damage to the body, even for an immortal Valkyrie like me. And now my only ally seemed to be my mortal enemy. I glanced at the fae-wraith's handsome profile as he concentrated on the hike down the mountain. His dark hair poked out from under his hat, moving with the brisk breeze assaulting us.

I was nothing more than dead weight on Reyfyre's back for the trip down the mountain from the cave I had been bound in since ancient times. He didn't seem to be impacted by my weight at all as he traversed the mountainside like a sure-footed Dall sheep.

My eyelids drooped now that I had warmth radiating across my front. I didn't know whether it was Reyfyre's magic or his abilities that got us down unscathed, but I stopped counting the times my stomach plunged from some harrowing drops that he navigated with ease. The only indication that Reyfyre might have been stressed by the descent was a sheen of sweat on his neck between his hat and the edge of his parka.

The scent he gave off was gloriously sweet, like something fresh from a bakery on Asgard. My mouth watered, and I closed my eyes, leaning my forehead on his shoulder, allowing the smell of him to envelop me. My mind inappropriately wandered between bouts of unconsciousness.

Magic flared around us, and I startled, snapping my head up. My heart clanged in my chest, and I squinted at the stars, waiting for the gods to strike us down.

"It's okay. I just had to switch out to snowshoes," Reyfyre said in a soothing voice as he set out across the tundra.

Wind whipped over the landscape, bringing with it stinging gales of snow, but I was warmer in this backpack of his than I had been for millenniums. Still, my teeth chattered.

"Where are we going?" I forced the words from between my clacking molars.

"As far away as I can possibly get without leaving a magical trail back to my cottage."

His breath huffed with each word, magnifying the fact I was indeed a burden to him. I couldn't walk two steps, never mind the miles he seemed to cross effortlessly. Magic surrounded us, and the formidable mountain behind us disappeared.

Reyfyre stepped out of the mist into a heavily forested area, and I could no longer see the vast tundra we left behind. I didn't know how far we traveled in that magical sphere, but the sky lightened with the distance. It was no longer pitch dark with only the stars to guide us.

"When we get there, your recovery begins in earnest." His blue eyes glanced back at me, and they promised I would not like what was in store for me.

His magical hops persisted, moving us across the landscape faster than we could on foot. Lightness and dark intertwined as days blended together in one continuous blur of discomfort.

Reyfyre cared for me when he took breaks. Campfires, water, and jerky fed to me by his hand because I couldn't lift my arm for any length of time. I was a damn invalid, and my mind could not wrap around what I needed to do to get back into fighting shape.

A vast wasteland of snow and speckled forests laid out before us. Reyfyre waved his hand and a small sled with enough room for him to stand on a platform appeared, along with a team of sled dogs.

When he stepped on the platform, he yelled, "Mush!"

The dogs leapt forward, racing across the land as if they were the wind itself. I glanced over my shoulder, and I could not make out the towering mountain I had been imprisoned on anymore.

After hours of sledding across the snow, Reyfyre slowed the team to a stop. He stepped off the sled and then waved it away.

"Where did they go?" I asked.

"I sent them back to where I stole them from."

"You stole them?" I raised an eyebrow when he glanced back at me.

"More like borrowed, but yes. I needed to get far enough away from my magical signature to lose anyone searching for you, and walking across Alaska takes too damn long. Besides, I did not like being so vulnerable."

"Oh." I couldn't argue with his logic.

Our long journey ended with his next step. He crossed through a magical barrier that tingled across my skin. It was as strong as

Odin's barrier in the cave and gave me pause. The tundra disappeared, and we passed through a thick forest into a glen right out of a storybook. It looked as if spring had come to this piece of earth and the cottage at the edge of the woods was that of a dream.

But I knew better. This beautiful oasis was the beginning of my true hell.

CHAPTER 2

STEEL MET STEEL AND my muscles protested. I fell on my ass hard enough for my teeth to cut into my tongue, coating my mouth with an iron tang.

"Again," my uncompromising keeper snapped.

"What do you mean, do it again?" I snarled. Reyfyre tortured me daily, pushing me beyond my limits until I was a shaking pile of skin and bone. But at least the bastard was easy on the eyes. He was a mountain of a man, with the refined, sensual features of the fae and the viciousness of the wraiths all wrapped into this luscious package. Too bad there was very little true trust between us.

"Lift your sword and try again." His voice was calm, but his eyes blazed.

I should be grateful, but I was in pain most days, so sparring in the woods with Reyfyre wasn't my idea of fun. I would rather sit in front of what he called television and watch what was happening in other people's lives.

Reyfyre called them soap operas, but they were addicting, and the people on the screen appeared so real. Their stories were so tragically intertwined that watching days on end wasn't enough to satisfy my cravings. He told me they were actors like those who used to act in plays in the old days.

Logically, I got his argument, but I'd been transplanted from ancient Greece to this modern world that surpassed Asgard in most of its conveniences and innovations. My mind could not wrap around all that surrounded me, but I was very thankful for the wonders of working plumbing.

The thing that burned the most: even without Hippocrates, the medical field he had once been a pinnacle of thrived. So, killing him had been all for naught as far as I could see.

I lifted my sword again and charged Reyfyre, but he was faster, parrying my strike, stepping aside, and letting me fall on my face. Again. This was so different than sparring on Asgard had been. In those days so long ago, I had been the ferocious one, but now I was the weaker soldier. The one cursing my sparring partner.

I was sure this torture was delighting the wraith side of the man, but right now, all I wanted to do was curl up and nurse my wounds. I used to be the fiercest Valkyrie. Now, I was just a shadow of my former self, and it stung.

Reyfyre glanced at his watch. "You need food." He sent our swords back to the cloakroom in his house with a wave of his hand, and then helped me to my feet. His scan of me made me shift under his scrutiny. "You are gaining muscle, but not fast enough."

"At least I can walk and hold a sword now." I steadied myself next to him on legs that felt like rubber.

We followed the well-beaten path through the woods; our feet crunched over sticks and leaves from the prior fall. Perpetual spring brought forth a bounty of flowers and berries, along with raging streams cutting through Reyfyre's property. Although the time I had spent healing and training here had nurtured my fury to the point of a finely honed knife.

Every time I saw Odin or Thor on television while I was healing and gaining strength, I wanted to tear through the screen and deliver justice. In that respect, Reyfyre and I were alike.

The only thing that had not revived with sustenance were my wings. I think they just deteriorated over the centuries from lack of use. I had seen my feathers fall out in that cave, and watched as the wind swept them away. But I couldn't even bring the bones to the surface. It was as if the rot of time ate them.

It was just another reason for my hatred of Odin and Thor to fester.

As we entered the rustic-looking log cabin in the remote Canadian landscape, Reyfyre dropped to the overstuffed couch and flipped on the television with a wave of his hand. His magic fueled this place as much as the solar panels. I had no idea how the satellite dish on the roof worked, but Reyfyre said it brought us television reception, which was important, because we needed to know the moment they discovered the cave where they had chained me was empty.

I would have thought they'd know the minute Reyfyre broke through Odin's magic, but no mention of it had come across the broadcasting channels. Reyfyre had also altered my hair with both magic and dye. I felt like a walking rainbow and it reminded me of the Bifrost. After the first few days of shock and indignation, I had grown used to it. I'd even dare to say the look was sexy on me, but I'd never admit that to Reyfyre.

Not only was Reyfyre training me to get back into shape, but he was also teaching me basic magic spells. I had already learned to light the fireplace with a spell. So, I had the basics of fire casting down, which was handy when matches were soggy from being dropped in the stream. I learned how to illuminate a dark space, too, but that was the extent of my magical showcase. I wished I could retrieve things like he could. Or stow them away like he had with our swords, but he said that wasn't spell work. That was an inherent magic that the fae held. And like all things fae or wraith, he did not delve into it further. Even when I battered him with questions.

The screen caught my attention, and I blinked as the press gathered around what used to be the United States presidential address podium, according to Reyfyre. The White House gleamed in the background as an empty podium sat in the center of the screen. The United States emblem had been replaced by Odin's knot overlaying Vegvisir. It was an abomination.

Reyfyre straightened and emitted a low growl, baring his teeth at the television. That was his usual reaction to anything Odin-related.

He wasn't alone in his reaction. Seeing Odin made me seethe. His sentence for my imprisonment had been born of cruelty and not justice. He was not a sovereign. He was a monster in disguise.

But Thor was another story. Every time he appeared on television, I froze, with my heart fluttering with fear. It overrode my common sense, and I couldn't shake it. Whenever I saw Thor, my mind snapped back to that gleeful gleam in his eyes while he raked his blade across a nearly dead Hippocrates's throat. Hippocrates's death hit me all over again, as if it were fresh and not thousands of years gone by. I hated Thor with a vengeance that left me trembling.

Reyfyre's hand grasped my knee, grounding me in the here and now instead of the past. He knew what seeing them did to me. He had seen it countless times since he rescued me. His grip was unrelenting and bordered on pain as his own fury coursed through his body. I covered his hand and squeezed my thanks for his support.

Thor's jaw was tight enough to see the muscles in his neck stand out. His lips were nonexistent and the hushed whispers beyond the camera silenced. His hammer was clenched in his hand, as if he might just send everyone in the near vicinity to Valhalla in one swing. This display of anger was new. It was as if someone had stolen his puppy and they were going to pay dearly for their transgression.

Odin wasn't any more settling as he stepped into camera view. His eyes were infernos of fury.

His nostrils flared as he stepped close to the microphone and when he spoke, chills gripped me.

"A very dangerous adversary has been unleashed from her dungeon." He glanced directly at the camera. "A dungeon that was never meant to be opened."

Odin's growl made me sink deeper into the back of the couch. Unless they had someone else hidden away here on Earth, he was referring to me. Now I understood Thor's feral demeanor. When I had begged for Hippocrates and fallen on my knees for him, Thor had been livid enough to beat Hippocrates to within a hair's breadth of death. Then he had done what I failed to do. He killed Hippocrates, bathing me in his blood. That sadistic bastard wanted to ensure I suffered, and it had nothing to do with disobeying an order.

Reyfyre glanced at me and then back at the television. "Thor looks a little put out by all this."

I snorted at Reyfyre. "I was the only Valkyrie who didn't sleep with him. It was his mission to punish me for my lack of interest."

A twisted smile surfaced on Reyfyre's lips. "I knew I liked you for a reason." His grip on my leg tightened a fraction as he glanced back at the television. "But they're a little slow on the uptake." He sneered at the television. "I've been nursing you back to health for over nine months and they've only discovered this now?"

"The bastard finally decided to kill me," I whispered and then gnashed my teeth. "He waited long enough."

A painting of me from our early days on Asgard when battles frequently raged appeared on screen. One with my black wings on full display and my armor and sword dripping in blood. I glanced toward a mirror on the side wall. I looked nothing like the Valkyrie warrior displayed on television, and I smiled at my reflection.

"A traitorous Valkyrie is on the loose here on Earth. Do not approach her. If you see her, please contact the number on the screen with the location and we will take care of it." Odin's glare was enough to let the audience know exactly what "taking care of it" meant. Hell, from what Reyfyre had said, they had already publicly executed anyone who could wage a fight.

"We also are looking for a witch strong enough to break through the ancient barrier that was set around this traitor. Someone strong enough to climb down a mountain carrying another."

Reyfyre snorted a laugh. "They think a witch could get through that barrier?" He chuckled, shaking his head. "No witch alive could compromise Odin's magic." He glanced at me. "They aren't the brightest bulbs, are they?"

"Do not underestimate them." I stared at the television as some of the information Reyfyre had given me over the last nine months settled into my bones. "We are the last of our kinds."

His sharp laugh subsided. "Yes, Kara. We are the last of the resistance. We are the only ones strong enough to wage war." He returned his glare to the television. "But only if we work together."

I turned my attention fully to him. "Neither of us can survive Thor's hammer."

"Want to bet?"

His venom and audacity shocked me. "No enemy of Asgard can survive Thor's hammer. It is even written in verse on the side of the damn weapon. It's why we as Valkyrie weren't wiped out whenever Thor used it. We weren't an adversary of Asgard. We protected Asgard. But now...now I want to do harm to both Odin and Thor. The hammer would see me as a foe, and a wraith certainly qualifies as an enemy of Asgard." I waved at him, glaring at him as if he had lost his mind.

"Ah. But this is not Asgard."

The sly smile on Reyfyre's face chilled me even more than Odin's glare.

"According to the podium, this is the new Asgard." I pointed to Odin's seal.

Reyfyre's smile faded. "But you as a Valkyrie protect the people of Asgard, correct?" He cocked his head as he spoke, reminding me of a confused puppy.

"Yes. That is true." I still didn't get what he was trying to insinuate.

"Then the hammer will not harm you."

Ah. The bulb blinked on in my mind. I saw what he was getting at. It targeted enemies of the people. And our goal was not to enslave humanity, like Odin and Thor. We were champions trying to free the masses from tyranny.

"But Thor and Odin can hurt us." I stared at the two monsters who needed to be put down.

CHAPTER 3

AS SOON AS THE breaking news ended, Reyfyre stood and started to gather his things, piling them on the kitchen table as if he were planning to leave.

"What are you doing?" I turned to him with every muscle aching from our sparring in the woods.

"We're too close to that cave." He pointed out the window.

I had no idea how far we were from the cave that had kept me in chains for millenniums. But from the way Reyfyre moved, it was not far enough away to keep trouble at bay.

I glanced out the window at the wilderness surrounding us. There wasn't even a town within a hundred miles of where we were. At least, that was what he kept telling me since we arrived. "You're being overly dramatic."

He stopped and sent me one of his searing glares. Anyone else receiving that sharp stare would wither away, but I just rolled my eyes. The low growl of disdain that came from him wasn't unusual when dealing with me. We tolerated each other for our common goal, despite his hand on my leg to calm me during the press conference. That was his sanity check for me. It was part of his nurturing me back to life.

"When my gut tells me to move, we move." His hard gaze bore into me as if willing me to get moving, too. "Gather your things."

"And what if I do not want to?" I crossed my arms, aware that I was being obstinate, but I had grown comfortable here in our hideaway in the wilderness. And going out into the unknown world had me digging my heels in.

"Then I will leave you and when they come to collect you, I probably will see your execution on the television."

His tone already condemned me.

My stomach dropped. He'd leave me to die?

Of course he would.

Reyfyre wouldn't put his life on the line for a Valkyrie.

"Even if Thor and Odin find me here, they will not recognize this form. I have no wings. You've changed my hair. I am wearing sweatpants and T-shirts now, not armor. They would never suspect."

He stopped packing and marched to stand in front of me. His chest heaved with aggravation. "Do not underestimate your enemy." He repeated my own words back at me and then waved at the surrounding house. "We live off the grid. That's enough to make them suspicious. Never mind the magical signature here to make that thing work." He pointed at the television and backed away, returning to his packing regimen.

I knew I was being irrationally stubborn because I was leery of this world. "Where will we go?"

He glanced over his shoulder at me but this time his gaze didn't carry the sureness he had a moment ago. "The most populated area in this hemisphere. New York City. Far enough away from the capital where they now reside, but close enough to get there within a day when we figure out a viable plan to take them down.”

“And with that many people around, where will we train?” My hands slammed into my hips with attitude as I dug in harder.

“We will find a place. Maybe not for sword fighting, but there are several self-defense studios that we can join. It’s the city where I learned of you, and it is big enough to get lost in.” He continued building the pile on the table, silently moving his lips.

He was either cataloging what we would need or cursing me.

“Do we have a place to stay?”

The way he sucked in his lower lip and scanned this place told me enough, but he shook his head to confirm my suspicions. “We’ll have to figure that out when we get there.” He took a breath. “And in order to stay together, we have to pretend to be a couple. Otherwise, we won’t be able to stay in the same shelter.”

I raised my eyebrow at him. In this rustic cabin, we each had our own room, so the idea of sharing space bristled the hair on my neck. My lips pressed together to keep my mouth from running off at the idea.

“I’d sleep on the floor,” he said. “Assuming we are given a private room. If not, well then, we’ll just have to spoon on a cot for a night or two until I can find us an inconspicuous place."

"Spoon on a cot?" My voice cracked.

"Yes. So, make sure you bring pajamas. They don't take kindly to vagrants sleeping in the nude."

"And how do you know that?" I challenged with the narrowing of my eyes.

"Because I've lived in Manhattan. When you're a poor outcast, you have to learn to accept handouts. You have to learn to survive, even if it means letting go of your ego and accepting help." He eyed me. "You learn to be humble."

I smirked. Reyfyre humble? Ha. In some ways, he was more self-righteous than Thor. But at least Reyfyre had walked in poverty and done something to warrant his pompous behavior.

Reyfyre glared at me and then crossed to the closet and grabbed two heavy-duty backpacks— the kind you would see on those survivalist shows where the people were out in the wilderness for days. He tossed one to me and I caught it, but nearly fell over from the weight. "Make sure to wear your good hiking boots. We have a long walk to civilization."

I had no frame of reference of this realm, with the exception of the distance in days from the cave. I had been awake for some of the trek, and it had taken Reyfyre a little over two weeks to get here from there. And we were in an area that actually had sunrises and sunsets, which was welcomed after extended periods without one or the other. I could at least experience the passage of time again in a more normal sense.

"Will there be sunrises and sunsets?" I asked, hesitant to give up that unique experience.

Reyfyre stopped what he was doing and cocked his head. The creases on his forehead deepened as he studied me. When his gaze softened and he took a breath, I knew he read my hesitation for what it truly was. I was purposely stalling because everything outside our little cabin and training grounds was the great unknown. "On most of this planet, you have sunrise and sunset every day. Did you not have that on Asgard?"

"We did, and it was glorious when the suns passed each other in the sky. But in the cave, there wasn't lighting changes as there had been in Greece or here."

He kind of smirked, as if this conversation finally made sense to him. "The regions in the extreme north and south have extended days and nights that last for half the year. The cave where you were imprisoned was in the extreme north."

"I do not wish to go to those areas."

"Neither do I. They are frigid. Much colder than this remote Canadian landscape." He nodded toward the window and the spring in full bloom outside our windows. "But where we are going has none of this quiet. It's noisy and smells like garbage and body odor."

My eyebrows rose at the disgusting sensory imagery. "Then why are we going there?"

"Because we need to blend in. We need to hide in plain sight. Here, we are exposed now that they know you've been freed." He began to pack again. "We will be leaving before nightfall, so you need to get moving."

"Isn't this your home?" I knew I was stalling, but I couldn't help it. His description had me uneasy at the very least—as did leaving this place, and my obvious sense of comfort here.

"No. This isn't my home. This is the place I built after my parents were murdered. It's just a building, which will be destroyed as soon as we leave." He jammed more clothing than I thought possible in the bag. "I've never had a home." His gaze flicked to mine and then back to his task.

A bloom of pity worked its way into my stomach. "I'm sorry."

"Do not be sorry. Just get your damn things packed before our luck fails."

I stared at him for a moment and then nodded, heading to my room to sort through the small number of things that I called mine. Although I didn't want to leave this place, I was also not ready to face either Odin or Thor. I could easily be overtaken and locked back up in that hellish cave for another three thousand years. A cold sweat that nearly seized my muscles swept through me at the thought, but I shook it off.

I focused on rummaging through my drawers, pulling out all the clean clothing that I wanted to take with me. I also grabbed two pairs of comfortable shoes and brought them to Reyfyre to put in the backpack. I headed back into my room because the pile of dirty laundry needed my attention. Tomorrow was our normal laundry day, so my basket was almost full and there were things in there that I didn't want to go without. I sorted out the clothes I could leave behind and folded those I wanted with me. I grabbed my knives that Reyfyre had given me over the last few months and then scanned the barren room. My comb and brush and hair ties on the bureau caught my eye, and I swiped them onto the pile. My comfortable boots and jacket were the only things left.

When we finished stuffing all my things into my backpack, I headed into my room and pulled on my boots before I grabbed my coat off the bed. I gave the room a once-over, pulling open drawers and such before I glanced back at the bed. I grabbed the soft blanket folded at the foot of the bed and brought that out as well. It was something Reyfyre had conjured for me, and I slept snuggled in it every night. I could go without the pillow, but this gave me a sense of peace, as if he had charmed it in some fashion.

I folded it as I crossed to my bag and shoved it inside. There was still plenty of room in the pack. It was almost as if these things were enchanted to hold everything needed but not feel like they were a hundred pounds.

Reyfyre gave me a nod as he stuffed canned and preserved goods into the bags along with the dried jerky he'd made over the last few months. It was enough for me to dread trying on the pack. I was sure I'd just keel over backward from the weight.

When he waved me over, I put on my coat and prepared myself for the weight. He slipped it over my arms and when he appeared in front of me to secure the pack, my eyebrows rose. It felt no heavier than a blanket thrown over my shoulders.

"They're charmed, aren't they?" I asked.

He smirked and put his on his back, clasping it without so much as a word. The last thing he attached to the packs were our swords and sabers. He grabbed his hunting rifle by the door as he headed outside.

"You have the bullets, right?" I pointed at the gun as we crossed the threshold.

"Yes. I have everything we will need on our trek across country, along with papers to cross into what used to be the United States." He strapped on snowshoes, despite the fact there was little snow in our glen. He handed me a pair as well.

I didn't second-guess him because that usually was when he schooled me on something. Instead, I slid my shoes into the webbed feet and tightened the bindings.

We clomped across the forest floor, and he took my hand when we reached the magical barrier surrounding the land the cottage resided on. Once he pulled me through the magic that had been protecting us for the last nine months, I understood the need for snowshoes. Although our haven seemed to be in full spring bloom, the rest of the world outside was layered in winter snow deep enough that if I was just in my boots, I would probably be buried waist high and unable to move.

When we stepped out of the woods into the open air, it was as if we had crossed into a different world from where he'd kept me for the last nine months. Mountains towered around us, and although I had seen ghosts of them at the cabin, here they were in stark relief to the bright sky.

"Canadian Rockies," he said in a soft voice, as if he almost revered these hills of rock and snow. Then he turned back toward the cottage and magic spilled out of his hands, racing toward the barrier like a mass of bullets.

A thundering bang echoed, and I spun around on ground that shook underneath me. A bright plume of light burst through the woods and rolled up at the point where Reyfyre's magical wall stood. The trees trembled from the blast, and then dust rose above the woods in a billow that was swept away from us by the wind.

"There's no going back now." Reyfyre smiled at me and continued to trek toward the towering mountains as if this were just a small hike and not one that would test our alliance.

I zipped up my jacket and pulled the hat and mittens from my pockets, donning them as we moved forward. The fact Reyfyre destroyed our home settled in my bones, along with a dread as to what was to become of us.

CHAPTER 4

BY THE TIME DARKNESS descended, the cold had settled in, chilling me to the point I was almost numb. Reyfyre seemed to be oblivious of the frigid air. The only indication that he was impacted by the temperature was the brightness of his nose and cheeks, as if the wind had whipped them raw. I hadn't realized just how protected our little camp had been from the weather. But then again, these were the Canadian Rockies, where the weather could turn on a dime.

"How far are we from Kos?" I thought of the few warm days and nights I spent with Hippocrates.

"Kos?"

I hadn't spoken much of my time before I was locked up. Reyfyre just knew I had been sent to kill Hippocrates and didn't. He knew of Hippocrates's death and what happened in the cave, but the rest of my short stay had been off-limits to our general chatter. Because Hippocrates was no longer in the history books, Reyfyre hadn't known exactly where all that had taken place. "Where they honor the goddess Aphrodite."

"Greece?" He glanced at me and huffed a laugh. "That's half a world away from where we are. Separated from this continent by vast oceans." He scanned the snow-covered mountains surrounding us. "Is that where you were before?"

"Yes. My only experiences in this realm are Kos and the cave before you brought me to our camp." I took a few more steps on my aching legs. I needed rest, but I wasn't about to admit that to Reyfyre. "And your camp was much more advanced than the homes on Kos. They had no switches that could turn on lights or electronics like the television. Or even indoor plumbing." I recalled the chamber pot in my room and Hippocrates's meager explanation for what it was used for.

"This planet was in its infancy back then." He paused and surveyed the barren landscape and pointed to a small copse of trees to our right. "We can make camp there tonight."

"Outside?"

Reyfyre nodded. "It will be far more comfortable than being in that cave."

He reminded me of my existence before he came any time I started whining. And he was usually right, but this time I wasn't worried about comfort. "But out in the open, there's no protection against predators."

He waved toward the trees, as if that was supposed to ease my mind.

"Aren't there grizzly bears and wolves in the wild here?" The last thing I wanted to do was hurt an animal. Humans I could fight, but a being only acting on instinct and not with malicious intent, I could not harm.

"They will steer clear of us."

"Are you creating a magical barrier?" I pushed as we closed the distance to our intended resting spot.

"No. Fire usually is a deterrent." The clip in his voice told me he had had enough of my questions. He sent me a hostile side-eye.

"Magical signatures can be traced, so no magic until we are hidden in the city."

I let it go but my nerves jumped at every motion in my peripheral vision. I had been protected from scavengers and threats in the cave, and I had seen enough to understand they didn't care that we were intelligent living beings. To them, we were a food source.

Reyfyre guided us to the trees and found a naturally protected area under a large hemlock with a branch hanging down to the ground and earth beneath it instead of snow. It was high enough for us to almost be able to stand upright in and had a large enough circumference for us to lay on our sleeping bags on the hard earth without encroaching on each other's space.

The outside of the branches was dusted with snow, so any heat from below wouldn't cause an avalanche down on us either, which was a bonus. The entrance was also high enough so that fire wouldn't burn the hemlock. Plus, the flames would create a nice barrier from wildlife and at the same time we wouldn't be inundated with smoke.

It was perfect enough for me to question it. "Are you sure this isn't a trap of some sort?"

The glare Reyfyre gave me was meant to wither, but I had developed an overly sensitive sense of self-preservation since he released me from captivity. But he took another look at the accommodation and glanced around at the surrounding trees. None of which had any branches bowed over and their limbs had a good six-inch coating of ice and snow.

He chewed his lip and shook his head. "I don't sense magic, but I can't be sure without casting a spell." He wiped his face. "Fuck." His glare was telling. He wasn't happy with me or the situation.

I raised my eyebrows.

"Magical signature?" he said, as if I were daft.

I leaned down and formed some snow into a ball and tossed it at the opening. It sailed inside, but the moment it hit the ground, the earth started to move. The scuttling of the terrain had us both backing away. A spider nearly the size of the opening surfaced, with pinchers big enough to amputate an arm.

My throat convulsed as my swallow reflex stalled. I hated spiders. I had enough of them race across my skin in the cave to leave me shivering at the ghostly feel of their eight-legged trek.

We continued to back away slowly. Reyfyre pulled the swords from the back of his pack and handed me mine.

At least this time I could defend myself. I gripped the hilt of the sword tight through the mittens, hoping it wouldn't slip.

The thing's black eyes locked on us, and I shuddered. It made an awful clacking sound and the woods around us came alive. Reyfyre planted his backpack against mine, pressing into me. I equalized my weight and focused in the opposite direction, holding my sword at the ready. Dozens of hideous spiders surrounded us, none of which were quite the size of the one in the alcove, but they were big enough to draw my breath in a gasp.

"Just don't slay me, okay?" Reyfyre said without any hint of fear.

"Ditto." My voice shook with trepidation.

"Stab between their eyes and watch out for the barbs on their legs," he added just before the pressure released.

I almost fell backward but didn't dare look behind me. Instead, I held the sword at the ready, wishing I wasn't so tired from walking most of the day into the evening. But I had no choice. It was fight or die. And I'd come too far to just give up now.

I closed my eyes and centered myself for a second. When my lids opened, the spiders had closed enough of the distance to send an adrenaline spike through me. My training from the days on end with Reyfyre, along with the years in the guard, came back to me, and I started to move as muscle memory took over. I spun away from a claw meant to rip my face open and slashed, cutting the appendage off before I stabbed forward, planting my blade between the beast's eyes.

The closest spider fell, and the rest of them scrambled closer.

Reyfyre's grunts came from behind me, along with the whistle of his blade. My mind kept track of where he was as I rolled into my forms, hitting and stabbing my way through the mass of black surrounding me.

When the last spider attacking me fell, I turned toward the covered sanctuary and launched my blade at the largest spider with a roar. My blade sailed true and buried in its face, splitting the thousands of beady eyes in two.

It teetered and then fell hard. I turned, witnessing the results of killing the queen spider. The rest of them fell in silent blobs, as if they were all of one mind. Still, Reyfyre stepped next to each one and slayed the fallen, making sure each one was indeed dead.

Reyfyre turned toward me. His coat over his arm was sliced clean through and the edges of the down inside registered red, as if he had been cut by one of the barbs. He didn't even assess himself at all. His gaze moved to the mammoth dead beast blocking what looked like the only safe harbor for miles. Then he actually grinned at me. "Think you can move that thing out of there while I find some firewood?"

I pointed at my chest and shook my head. "I'm not touching that thing. I'll go for firewood."

His smile faded and his gaze narrowed. "Afraid of a little spider?"

I snorted a laugh. I had no idea why the gods created these eight-legged things, but they creeped me out to no end. "I'd rather find another place to sleep."

"Oh, for heaven's sake." He stowed away his sword and marched toward the entrance where the head still held my blade. "Go find firewood," he snarled at me as he gripped my blade and swung the beast sideways, dragging it out of the entrance enough to allow us to get in.

"Um. I think we will need another place to sleep." The ground was a hole, and it was covered in pulsing black sacs. I pointed.

Reyfyre glanced beyond the beast and stopped moving it. "Shit."

"Is that what I think it is?"

He nodded and yanked my blade free from the spider. "We can't stay here." He sheathed my blade and stalked off, backtracking out of the wooded glen and back into the snowy landscape.

The wind howled, pulling at our clothing as we walked.

"Do you need me to look at your arm?" I asked after a while. The copse of woods was now just a dot on the horizon. Before us lay a barren tundra that offered no place to rest.

"When we stop." He scanned the nothingness as if he expected something to pop up from the snowy wasteland.

"We should make camp here." We weren't going to make the distant mountain range. Not tonight. And probably not tomorrow night. And now that my adrenaline had faded, the full force of exhaustion was making itself known in my sluggish step.

Reyfyre glanced at me. His eyes were rounded by puffy dark circles, making them nearly neon in the dark. All he did was nod, unclip his snowshoes, and drop to his knees. He used one of his shoes to dig in the snow. After a few strokes, he eyed me. "Care to help?"

I unclasped my shoes and knelt next to him. "What am I helping with?"

"Shelter." He snorted. "As meager as it is, a hole is better than being exposed on the surface." He sighed. "It also means we will need to share a sleeping bag to stay warm enough not to freeze. And even then, if a storm rolls in and covers us, it might not be enough."

"I won't freeze."

He stared at me, and his lips thinned. "But I might."

My chest stuttered at the thought. Without his magic, I'd have no hope of defeating Odin. "What about using your magic like you obviously did back at the cottage?" I waved around us. The weather there had not been this brutal, even in the depths of winter.

"I had the perimeter warded to hide the magic. It took months to set that up properly. And until we are ready to launch our attack, I cannot chance using it and exposing us. They are looking for magical signatures. They think a witch took you from that cave."

He spoke to me as if I were addlebrained and it riled up my defenses, but I took a breath to calm the budding anger and focused my aggravation on digging a big enough space for both of us to fit in and be beyond the grueling wind.

"That's enough, Kara." His sharp tone burst through my focus.

I blinked down at the hole we had dug. It was at least seven feet in length and half as wide as it was long, and nearly three feet deep end to end. Deep enough so we could get out easily, and if the sides collapsed on us, it wasn't deep enough to trap us. I was so irritated with Reyfyre that I had nearly dug the entire thing myself. He clipped off his backpack, pulled out his sleeping bag and positioned it in the middle of the cavity and then dropped his pack against the side of the hole. He lined the front with his snowshoes and the foot with mine and then put his hand out for my backpack.

I unclipped and handed my pack to him.

He put it on the side nearest us. "Keep your shoes on." He hopped into the hole fully dressed in winter clothes and put his hand out to help me down.

I jumped down next to him, and he waved me to the side as he unzipped the sleeping bag. He slid in and situated himself on the outside and patted the spot next to him. I raised my eyebrow.

"You want to switch that around?" I pointed at where he stretched out.

He looked at the sleeping bag and then up at me with his forehead creased.

"I'll take the outside. That way, you have me buffering your back and you can curl up to focus heat."

For once, Reyfyre did not argue with me. He scooched over and flipped the covers back wider, leaving room for me to step in at the base.

I stretched out beside him while he worked the zipper up, leaving us with a small opening that only our eyes peered out of. We were sandwiched in with my front to his back, and I glanced over the hood of his parka at my bag lining the front wall of the hole. My blanket was tucked into the pack. I sighed. Reyfyre would just have to suffice in its absence. Still, that unnerved feeling gripped me, like without my safety blanket, Odin wouldn't have an issue pinning down my whereabouts. I folded my arm under my head and slung my other arm over Reyfyre because there was nowhere else to put it.

He grunted at me and curled further into a ball. With my arm over him, I could feel his shivers.

I curled my knees under his, plastering myself against him. I wasn't cold. Not in the way he was. "Rey, are you all right?"

"I'm just cold," he muttered, curling tighter.

I curled with him and ran my hand up his arm. He hissed, and I remembered the cut. I rubbed his side and his thigh fast, trying to produce some heat for him. Even through the winter clothes, his defined muscles trembled.

His chest rumbled as I kept going, and finally his tremors subsided.

His breathing evened out and soon his soft snore filled the sleeping bag. I turned my head to glance up at the bright stars dotting the dark canvas above us. The cold air caressed my eyes, and I closed them, curling into the back of Reyfyre's jacket, praying nothing else would attack us in the dead of night.

CHAPTER 5

T HE SUNRISE CAME QUICKER than I would have liked, and I tried to straighten my body out, but my muscles cramped. Reyfyre groaned next to me, as well. His legs stretched next to mine and the heat radiating from him was almost unbearable in the cramped sack.

He unzipped the bag and stretched his arms, and his face scrunched in a wince.

"We need to look at your wound." I stretched alongside him now that we weren't fully restricted by the sleeping bag. We should have tended to his arm last night.

He rolled his eyes, but he did unzip his coat. I helped him remove it from his injured arm, leaving the coat draped over his back. The sleeve of his right arm was saturated with blood, and my gaze bounced to his.

"Jesus, Rey, what the hell were you thinking?" I grabbed the tear in the sleeve and ripped the tacky fabric away. My heart thundered at the amount of blood still seeping from the wound, but it was the sharp shard still lodged that had me taking air through my teeth. "Get me the first-aid kit. Use your magic if you have to but I need it now!" I barked the command.

He reached over to my bag and unzipped a pocket, pulling the kit out before he set it on his lap. He didn't argue with me or get sassy like usual, and the color from his cheeks had leaked out to a sickly pallor.

I paused and shot him a narrowed eye. "You knew it was this bad."

He nudged his good shoulder and avoided my gaze, confirming my statement. "Can you just get the barb out?"

"You are an ass." I gripped the piece of the spider's barb sticking from his skin. "You should have had me look at this last night."

His cutting glare focused on me. "We had no light and neither of us were in the condition to deal..."

I didn't wait for the rest of his reprimand. I yanked the barb from his skin.

Reyfyre hissed at me. Fresh blood slid from the wound. "With this," he finished through clenched teeth.

On closer inspection, the wound appeared red and puffy, like it was infected. My gaze shot to him. "Yeah, well, this does not look good." I refocused on the emergency kit, hoping like hell we had what we needed to combat whatever had made his skin flare like burning embers. Flipping open the top, I dug out the antiseptic cleaner and a clean cloth. Then I began the painstaking job of cleaning the puncture along with the cut above it where the creature had scratched before they pierced his flesh.

Reyfyre's molars grinded together through the entire cleaning process, but he didn't wince or hiss or display any sort of pain beyond the tightening of his jaw muscles.

"I think it's deep enough to require sutures." I sighed and shuffled through the kit. There wasn't anything to stitch him up.

Reyfyre plucked a tube out of the box and handed it to me. "Try this."

It took me a moment to sound out the words on the package. "Liquid bandage?"

"Yes. It's like skin glue. Just put a small strip on one side and then use these to pull the sides together." He handed me a half dozen little bandages that were attached with a thin strip between them. "Butterfly bandages," he said, as if that would explain things.

I looked at the things in my grasp and then back at him for direction.

"The thick tabs go on either side of the cut."

"Instead of stitches." My brain slowly painted the picture of how to utilize the items he handed me. I thought I understood but the materials were as foreign to me as this realm.

"Yes, and now, since the barb is out, and you've cleaned it, and will be closing my wound with those things, I should heal faster." He pointed to the tube and bandages in my hands. "I couldn't heal with the barb still lodged in me."

I refrained from saying something snide or rolling my eyes. I handed him the butterfly bandages, unscrewed the cap on the tube, and wiped his arm once more to remove as much blood as possible before I squeezed the liquid onto one side of the cut. Then, starting from the top, I planted the bandages one after the other, using them to close up the cut so the liquid sealed on both sides.

It wasn't a half bad job, and the flow of blood stopped as soon as I connected the lower part of the broken skin together. I went to wipe it again, but Reyfyre stopped me. He handed me a large bandage instead.

"You don't want to wipe the glue away. Just cover it."

I ducked my chin in agreement and then peeled the adhesive off the edges of the large bandage. I lined it up so it covered the entire area and then pressed the sides to his skin. I ran my finger around the outside to be sure the seal was tight and then gathered up all the mess into a pile as he pushed his arm back into his jacket.

He scowled as he zipped up. "I'll need to find a new jacket when we get to civilization. In the meantime, we have to keep an eye out for predators. I'm sure my clothing reeks of easy prey."

The idea of the predators that I had seen in the cave hunting us sent a wild shudder through my bones. Neither of us were in any condition to put up a fight if more than one attacked us in this harsh landscape.

He dug a small hole in the snow and took all the garbage from cleaning him and shoved it inside and then covered it before helping me out of the pit. He handed me my snowshoes and then my backpack before rolling up the sleeping bag and tucking it back in his bag.

I watched him in fascination at his efficiency, even while injured. Although, after he clipped his backpack on, he seemed to pause to take a deep breath. Reyfyre tossed his snowshoes out of the hole and then reached out his hand for help.

The man had to be a solid two hundred pounds, but he seemed weightless as I yanked him up the three feet to the solid snowbank I stood on.

Without a word, he strapped his snowshoes on and then started to walk toward the distant mountains due east, where the morning sun framed the mountains in a halo of light. Once it crested the mountaintops, it would be blinding against the unbroken white landscape.

"Aren't we going to eat something?" My stomach growled, punctuating my words.

Reyfyre pivoted toward me and folded his lips shut before he marched back and rummaged in my pack. He slapped a package of jerky in my hand and then slid a bottle of water into my water holder without a word before stalking off.

I caught up to him. "Aren't you eating?"

"No. Not yet." He still held dark circles around his eyes, but both his forehead and cheeks were flushed with fever. "I'll replenish my energy later." He kept traveling forward. "We need to reach the forest at the base of the mountains today."

My eyebrows rose as I scanned the distance. Daunting, but not impossible. I agreed with his aversion to being out here in the open. Our snow gear and coats were not white. We did not blend in, so if anyone was traveling overhead, we stood out like a speck of shit on a pristine blanket of white.

I unwrapped the jerky and took a piece, carefully closing the package and stuffing it into my pocket. I chewed on the end of it, savoring the salty meat flavor. I couldn't tell whether it was dried venison or what, but I didn't care; it satiated the growling of my stomach and energized my poor aching body. "This is good," I muttered around a bite.

The edge of his lip twitched up into a smile.

"How much farther beyond the mountains?"

"We have about thirteen hundred miles between here and where I have a boat waiting in Hudson Bay. Then we can sail down to New York City from there." He focused on the mountain ridges ahead of us.

"How far was it from where you found me to the cabin?"

"About the same distance, but I used magic to get back to my cabin. It took a fraction of the time."

"So how many days do you think this trek will take us?"

He blew out air through rounded lips. It plumed in front of him. "Probably a month or so, unless we run across someone with a vehicle who is going that way. But hitching a ride could be risky, too." He glanced at me. "But I'd be inclined to take the risk if we're lucky enough to run across vehicles out here."

A month?

My brain stalled as it tried to calculate what a month meant. I knew a week was seven days, but a month was harder to define. I glanced at the sky and then the timeframe sunk in. "Is a month a full rotation of the phases of the moon?"

"Yes. More or less. It's about thirty days, give or take. Four weeks and then a couple of days added on."

Reyfyre had been so patient explaining things to me over the time we had been at the cabin. The only time he seemed to get irritable was when I took over the television, or he was hungry or tired. Well, I guess, in retrospect, the only time he wasn't irritable was when he was explaining things of this world to me. Except soap operas. The man hated those things with a passion near to how he felt about Odin and Thor.

Thirty days. His words sunk in. He wanted us to walk for thirty days? My gaze scanned the snowy terrain. "Thirty days out here?" My voice cracked, and I nearly swallowed the piece of jerky wrong, but caught it before I had a coughing fit.

"Consider this your training for the next thirty days." He gave me a side-eye and a smirk. "We're going for endurance instead of skill. And if predators attack, then we can rely on our skills with the swords."

Again, I did not want to dwell on what type of predators were out here. So I focused on another tidbit he had mentioned. "What kind of vehicles would be traveling here?" I waved at the land surrounding us.

"Snowmobiles. And once we get over the mountains, we'll eventually run into roads. Then we might be able to hitch a ride, but that's more of a wildcard than the predators in the tundra."

Oh great. I wished I still had my wings. I'd just fly us to our destination instead of making my entire body hurt for days on end. I stared down the hulking hills in the distance. "Over those?"

"Yes. I know a path through that isn't as harrowing as it looks from here." He glanced at me. "Stop whining and eat your jerky." He nodded toward the partial piece still clasped in my hand.

Although we had spent time together in the cottage, it was usually filled by the television or books or music. The silence of the surroundings made me feel closed in, as if I were still locked in that cavern. Even with the wide-open space, claustrophobia of only the whoosh of our snowshoes had me on edge.

"Tell me about this realm." I only knew what I saw on television at his cabin, and he said that wasn't real. We never really talked much about this realm beyond the fact that Odin ruled it with an iron fist. We never spoke about our pasts, either. Reyfyre had been ultra focused on training and getting me back to fighting shape, so there wasn't time for much else.

Reyfyre laughed. "I don't have any references of anything other than this realm. Tell me about Asgard."

"Deflection much?"

That earned me a tilt of his lips. "I'll tell you about Earth after you tell me about Asgard." His eyes scanned the landscape.

"This isn't a quid pro quo."

"Isn't it though?"

"Rey, stop being an ass and tell me what you know about this realm." I aggressively took another bite of the jerky while leveling my best *stop bullshitting me* glare.

His sigh could have caused an avalanche had we been on a snowy mountain. "I am trying to conserve my energy while I heal. Talking drains me."

"Oh." I chewed up the rest of the bite and swallowed, feeling like a supreme ass for giving him a hard time. "In that case, Asgard was nothing like this." I waved around me. "We did have mountains capped in ice, but the valleys were lush and green and dotted with farms. And the city rose around the Bifrost. It gleamed a glorious gold with the light of our suns. When they passed in the sky, the Valkyrie training room gleamed with the colors of the Bifrost. It was magnificent, and the Bifrost was stained with all the metallic colors of the rainbow. Kind of like what you've done with my hair." I tilted my lips at the memory of my home. "The air was always crisp and clean." I sighed, and then scanned our surroundings. "This realm doesn't seem to have the grand architecture or farmlands like my home did."

"You haven't seen much of this realm, Kara."

"I know. And what I've seen, beyond the cabin, isn't nearly as advanced as Asgard was." I glanced at him. "We had almost everything you had. Except television. That is a new novelty that I don't see myself tiring of."

He chuckled softly and kept the pace moderate. Only the shuffle of the snowshoes and the howling of the wind accompanied us for a while. The sun glare in our eyes faded as the sun rose almost overhead. It was only then that Reyfyre spoke again.

"My parents used to tell me Earth was much less advanced than Faery, as well. When we came, it was only humans. When we arrived, the realms still existed, so Earth wasn't overrun by other species. Even so, I still had to hide my heritage here. Earth had no clue there were other provinces with intelligent societies out there, so my parents taught me the spell that still to this day hides the one easily identifiable trait of my fae heritage." He waved to his ear.

"What were your parents like?"

Reyfyre's eyes went unfocused as he strode forward. "They were militant about keeping our magic a secret. My father had the foresight to keep us under the radar for a very long time. He kept his heritage a secret and hoarded our riches, hiding most of it from being discovered. We lived just barely over the poverty level, but they took me everywhere. They got away with it by saying they were homeschooling me, so no government came after us for missing school. And they taught me fae, wraith, and human history. They made me humble with their knowledge and how freely they shared with me, and even though we lived like nomads, I knew I was cherished. It's funny." He chuckled under his breath. "When I was little, the only time my father used his magic was when my mother lost her temper." He grinned. "She was a holy terror when she was angry, and his magic could only hide so much of her black smoke, so whenever she went ballistic, we moved to another area of this realm. I saw almost every country there is on this planet." He waved his hand at the land around us.

"So, you're more like your father?" I asked, because I had never seen Reyfyre lose his temper.

He snorted a laugh. "My dad said I was more like my mother, and my mother said I was more like my father. I guess I'm a good mix of both of them. When refugees of the other realms started to flock here, that was when they started secretly teaching me complicated magic and trained me with weapons. They didn't want me to be vulnerable. As I said, they had much more foresight than I've ever had."

Reyfyre sucked in his lower lip. "Once they heard what Odin was doing to the realms, they stepped up and started to pull in the higher ranked species on the magical spectrum to form the resistance. And hiding became a matter of survival. Then, more and more refugees from the other lands came to hide from Asgardian wrath as those assholes systematically destroyed the realms." He side-eyed me, as if I were part of the group that shattered so many dominions.

"If I had been there, I wouldn't have let that happen. My superior wouldn't have either." My eyes misted at the memory of Freya.

"Well, she did." His razored tongue lashed his words, as if all Valkyrie were evil beings.

"No. Freya didn't."

Reyfyre shot me a dirty look.

"She died in Greece. I killed her when she came to punish me for disobeying." I plodded along next to Reyfyre. "If I had died instead, she may have questioned Odin's greed." I could not see Freya buying into the destruction of the realms. It was against her nature, just as much as it was against mine.

"Then she would have died publicly."

I snorted in agreement. "She could have led the Valkyrie against Odin." I thought about how angry Freya had been at me for disobeying a direct order, and doubt crept in. She had tried to cut me down as if it didn't matter that Hippocrates was an innocent.

Maybe my recollection had been tainted with my time in chains, and it was only my wish that she would have stood up against this type of tyranny. My stomach tightened, still pushing the belief in Freya's view of what was just and what wasn't.

"They followed him like blind sheep."

Reyfyre's growling response made my stomach twist.

"I'm still not sure Freya would have." I stuck to my gut feeling on that and kept thinking perhaps if she hadn't come in with swords swinging, I might have been able to convince her of how wrong the assignment was. "So, society hadn't advanced the way Odin thought it would had Hippocrates and others not been killed?"

Reyfyre glanced at me. "What do you mean?"

"He sent me to reap a healer who apparently had been historically significant. He said there had been others as well, so this race couldn't build things that would destroy this realm. But I venture to guess it was so they wouldn't be able to fight back when Odin and Thor came to rule here." I scanned the tundra slowly, searching for predators.

He walked in silence with that deep crease between his eyes. "He planned the destruction of the realms as far back as three thousand years ago." He blew a stream of air from his lips that immediately fogged in front of him.

I stopped. I knew Asgard was no longer, but he had never mentioned the remainder of the realms until today. And his words finally sunk in, sending a shiver of dread through my entire form. "Nothing is left?"

He took a couple of steps and then stopped. He didn't meet my gaze right away and when he finally looked at me, he slowly shook his head. "It's why things like those spiders are here. Their realm was destroyed. But they aren't organized enough to be a threat to Odin. There are other things hiding here, too." He glanced over his shoulder. "But Odin and Thor stomped out most alien species that could put up any sort of fight. The resistance consisted of an array of beings along with a handful of humans who did not like this new world order. If we had been able to stop the squabbling between us all, we might have been able to stop them, but there was no trust across species. There was always tension between us and eventually, the humans gave up on any hope. They'd rather live under Odin's thumb than take up arms and fight for freedom."

I started to move again and reached into my pocket, peeling another piece of jerky from the group. I offered it to Reyfyre, and this time he took it. I pulled another strip off and then pocketed the rest. "So why are you trying to save them if they don't want to be saved?"

He sighed. "I've asked myself that same question every day," he admitted. "But then those assholes do something unimaginable to remind me they are not fit to lead this world. Or I pass another starving child who is nearly freezing to death, and it reminds me that we are this world's last hope. Someone needs to stand up for those who don't have a prayer."

Reyfyre was an idealist. Who would have guessed.

"I just want to pound them into oblivion. It's not for the same altruistic reasons as you. For me, it's personal."

He laughed. "Even without his hammer, Thor is a beast."

I nodded. "But he's never gone up against me when I wasn't chained."

"You can barely beat me." A dimple appeared in his cheek as he side-eyed me. "Besides, my reasons aren't as noble as you think. I do carry the same need for vengeance as you."

I grunted around my jerky. We ate while walking. I didn't want to stop if we didn't have to because if we sat to rest, I wasn't sure I'd be getting up.

As it was, when the need arose, squatting to relieve myself was a major pain, but there was no other way around it. There were no chamber pots or facilities in this frozen wasteland.

"I certainly hope where we are going is as well-equipped as your cottage," I muttered as I buttoned up my pants and stepped away from the yellow snow.

"My boat has a well-equipped head." He continued to walk, picking up the pace a little now that he seemed to have all his color back.

I guessed the jerky was the boost he needed. In the distance, I could just about make out another grove of trees, but these seemed to climb the hillside that rose before us. I hadn't realized we had crossed the tundra itself, but I guess the long stretches of silence between us with only the shuffle of the snowshoes were longer than I had thought.

But the idea of another spider-infested forest had my pace slowing and my heart galloping in my chest. Another attack from those monsters might very well kill us.

CHAPTER 6

MY FEARS REGARDING SPIDERS were unfounded. But the forest blocked most of the light, making it difficult to navigate. We found a downed tree and hunkered behind it, using some of the dead brush for a perimeter wide enough that our fire wouldn't catch.

Reyfyre unpacked our sleeping bags and leaned our packs on the tree near where he laid out my bag. He unzipped his sleeping bag and went to sit on it, but yanked his hand back. "Damn it."

"What's wrong?"

He showed me his red palm before wiping it with snow. "It's still tacky with blood." He opened it all the way and laid it with the inside facing the night sky on the patch of snow opposite where mine was. Blocking the exit of our little camp.

"That sucks for you." I dug in my bag and pulled out more jerky, offering him a piece.

He shook his head and busied himself with building a fire. We had enough wood from the branches we peeled away from the dead tree to keep us roasting far into the night. And when he had the fire blazing, his back twitched and Reyfyre looked up at the stars peeking through the trees.

Then he spun on his heels and met my gaze. "We're going to have to share again." His chin jutted to the sleeping bag under me.

I couldn't blame him for not wanting to sleep in tacky blood. Even so, I stared him down, searching for an ulterior motive. When I found none, I offered a piece of the jerky again.

"Is this how you intend to get me into bed?" I chomped another bite and let a smile toy on my lips.

Reyfyre snorted a laugh and took the offered jerky. He settled on the bag with me. "I know it's not ideal." He took a bite and leaned back against the tree, completely ignoring my comment. "But we'll have to take turns feeding the fire tonight, so it's not like we'll be stuffed in the bag together." He bumped my shoulder with his in an attempt at humor.

We stared at the fire in silence.

"I need to get out of these clothes, too." He sighed and unzipped his jacket. He easily removed his uninjured arm, but the other one stuck in the sleeve. "Can you help?" His irritated gaze slashed to me.

I finished the piece of jerky. "What do you need me to do?"

He handed me the portion of the jacket he already took off. "Pull."

I did and nearly toppled over when it finally gave. The inside of the sleeve was a deep red, almost black now, which was different than the crimson from this morning. "You might want to see if you can scrub some of that out with snow and then let it dry over there with your sleeping bag."

"Not a bad idea." He stood, crossed to the perimeter, and crouched, taking a handful of snow to the sleeve. He got most of the offending blood off, but his hands and the snow surrounding him looked a bit like a mini massacre occurred. Enough so that after he laid out his coat, he stripped his shirt and used it to clean his hands and the dried blood caked on his arm.

Reyfyre's bare chest shimmering in the firelight made my eyelids take a beat. Sure, I had seen him sparring with only a tank top before, but I was too worried about where his sword was to actually study the cut of his abs. And my, were they a set of firm, sculpted muscles that I wanted to run my fingers over just to see whether they were made of flesh instead of stone.

His soiled shirt landed in the flames, and Reyfyre shivered as he dug into his backpack for another one. The blue flannel he pulled out complemented his eyes. He slid it on and buttoned it up all the way to the collar. He didn't bother tucking it in as he took the seat next to me again.

"Did you want something more than just jerky tonight?"

I chewed on my lip, debating. His jerky was sweet and salty and so very satisfying, and I'd already had a few pieces, enough to make my belly full. "I'm good if you are," I finally said.

"I could use a couple more pieces." He put his hand out, and I peeled him off a few before stowing the rest away in my backpack.

I studied his profile as I settled back down. The rings under his eyes were dark with exhaustion. Although I was tired, he had been healing himself all day as we trekked across the frozen wasteland.

"I can take the first watch if you'd like."

He chewed on his jerky and nodded. "Thanks." He didn't say much more, just gulped down the jerky and some water before waving me off the sleeping bag.

I moved to the edge of the bag, half on the bottom layer and half in the snow. He stuffed himself in and then looked over at me sitting on the edge of the sleeping bag as if it was a huge inconvenience to lose a half an ass's worth of the material. And my ass was pretty small.

He huffed and settled into the bag. "Wake me in a couple of hours."

I guess when the man put his mind to it, he could fall asleep on a whim. His light snore filled the clearing and I stared at the fire, adding logs when the flames fell to flickers.

SNARLING SNAPPED MY HEAD up, and I blinked at the pit of hot coals. Beyond the firepit, two mangy beasts fought over Reyfyre's coat. His sleeping bag was shredded to pieces. Thankfully the beasts hadn't decided to take a bite out of either of us. Yet.

They weren't big, but what they had done to Reyfyre's sleeping bag sent a shudder down my spine.

I had dozed off staring at the fire.

What if something bigger had come into our space?

I slowly reached out for a log and threw it on the hot coals, where it promptly burst into flame on impact.

The beasts stopped their vicious tug-of-war and their beady eyes snapped in my direction. They bared their teeth, and their low growl sent a rash of bumps over my arms. The fire didn't scare them off like I thought it would. My gaze jumped to where our swords sat.

They were too far for me to reach without leaving Reyfyre exposed.

My mouth dried. If fire didn't deter these beasts, I wasn't sure what would. And from the mess they made of the sleeping bag, their claws were mighty sharp. I did not want to hurt them, but if they got a taste of Reyfyre's blood on the fabric, that would make him a target. He might need to magic them away at this pace. I frantically tapped Reyfyre on the shoulder, and the beasts snarled at my movement.

Reyfyre blinked his eyes open, and started a yawning stretch, but stopped as his eyes focused on the destruction on the other side of the fire. He growled my name and sent a withering glare that had me shivering more from him than the advancing beasts.

"Fuck." He sat up and faced his palms toward the beasts. He muttered under his breath and their growls increased. The fur on their necks stood on edge. "Just go!" he yelled, climbed to his feet, and brought his hands up in the air above his head, making himself appear more like an old crook giving himself up than a wraith. Reyfyre looked ridiculous.

Even the beasts were vexed enough at his antics to stop growling. They seemed to second-guess going on the attack.

They turned to leave, kicking out their back paws as they grabbed both the coat and what was left of his sleeping bag, and fled into the darkness.

Reyfyre slumped down on the bag next to me and reached for another log without so much as a word. But his silence held a reprimand that made me stare at my hands.

"I'm sorry. I didn't even know my eyes closed and then..." I waved toward where they had cannibalized his sleeping bag. Little bits of fabric still littered the snow.

He rifled through his backpack, pulling out a thick sweatshirt. His grumbles were more unsettling than the beasts' growls.

"What were those things, anyway?"

"Wolverines. Nasty little fuckers. If they actually go into attack mode, either you have to kill them, or you die. And it's extremely hard to kill them once their attack instinct is triggered."

"What?" My voice rose a complete octave.

"They can take down bears and moose. And they don't leave any evidence behind. They eat bones as well as flesh." His piercing eyes drilled into mine before they slashed to the firepit. He picked up a thinner stick to tend the fire and remained silent.

Right now, I think I'd rather deal with a wolverine than an angry Reyfyre. His glare was enough to set my teeth on edge. I stared at the remnants of his lost bag. It looked like the sleeping arrangements we had tonight were more permanent than I liked, but I couldn't make him sleep in the snow. Not with all he had done for me.

But I also wasn't all that pleased about snuggling with a wraith.

He pointed at the empty bag. "Sleep."

"Did you get enough?"

He slowly turned toward me, and I shivered as a cold breeze reached inside my jacket and gripped my stomach. "Did I stutter?"

I blinked and scrambled into the bag, leaving him enough room to sit on the edge if he so desired. But he remained crouched by the fire, poking at it with the stick as he scanned the forest for more threats.

CHAPTER 7

MY GUILT FOR SLIPPING asleep while on watch certainly didn't impact my ability to fall into the blackness. I dreamed of wolverines doing Thor's bidding. Nightmares plagued me, and my edginess kept me from getting any true rest. Not the kind I needed for another day out on the tundra.

When my eyes opened, Reyfyre was huddled next to me with his knees nearly tucked under his chin and the fire still roaring. Light brushed the sky in a predawn rainbow.

"Morning," I muttered through a yawning stretch.

He just grunted. "At least you didn't say good morning." He side-eyed me and flicked his eyes back to the flame. "I might have to use magic to conjure a coat."

I took a slow breath. "Are we far enough away?"

He looked to the west and shrugged before his eyes dropped to mine. "It's either that or I freeze, because even all the layers of clothing isn't warm enough in this wind."

"You can take my coat." I started to unzip it.

He laughed. "Thank you, but it won't fit, and you'd freeze."

"I've been naked and chained in this cold for three thousand years. I won't freeze." I peeled off the jacket and handed it to him.

He sighed and tried to put it on; he couldn't get both arms into the jacket because he was too damn broad-shouldered. "See." He handed the jacket back to me.

"How about wrapping the sleeping bag around you?"

He chewed on his lip. "If the inside gets wet, we won't have any alternative to sleep in since mine is gone." He waved toward where the wolverines had stolen his things.

I opened my mouth, and Reyfyre put his hand up.

"I know you're trying to help. But either I need to use magic, or we need to find and kill a caribou. The skin of the caribou would keep me warm, and the meat would last us at least a few days, possibly more if we can freeze it safely, or smoke it."

I shifted in the sleeping bag. Although we had killed for food before at the cottage, we hadn't seen any animals beyond the spiders and wolverines since we set off.

"Do we have enough food to get to our destination?"

He stared at the fire and then glanced at me with a small shake of his head. "Which is why I brought the hunting rifle." He pulled a thick hoodie from his pack and slipped it over the flannel shirt. Then he pulled on his gloves and attached his pack to his back.

I remained in the sleeping bag, just watching him, until he delivered a scalding look that made me get moving. I packed away the sleeping bag and put on my snowshoes while he kicked snow onto the fire, dousing it.

"If I get to the point where I can't hold the gun steady, I will conjure a coat."

I just nodded and snapped the backpack clips together. Hopefully the wind would be at our backs. That would save Reyfyre from the brunt of the cold air and we would have more hope of successfully taking down something that would sustain us and keep him warm in the process.

The trees kept us protected, but the way the tops were swaying, I knew luck was not with us. The steepness of the land didn't help either: it sucked what little energy we had and the moment we got out of the protection of the trees, my eyes watered at the blistering wind and my stomach dropped at the frigidness attacking us. Even I could feel it through my coat.

I could not imagine Reyfyre's discomfort. His teeth started to chatter before we even hit a quarter mile from the wood line. And the terrain left us shuffling along at a snail's pace. I saw no wildlife in this mountainous terrain, and we had climbed high enough to be above the trees or any sort of wind barrier.

The path he took was a wind tunnel, and we fought for every step as we climbed higher into the mountain pass.

"You might need that coat," I said, trying not to let my own teeth clack together.

"It might lead them right to us," he stuttered through a torrent of shivers.

"I would prefer not to have you be a fae-popsicle."

He snorted and glanced at me. "Fae-wraith."

My eye roll actually pulled a smile to his blueish lips.

If he died on me, I'd be lost in this frozen wasteland. My skin warmed with panic. "Reyfyre, conjure a coat, please."

He grabbed my arm and led me to the side of the pass. The ground shifted under our feet, and he yanked me back as the snow we had disturbed slid into a crevasse. A deep fracture. One that, if we had slipped into it, Reyfyre might not have survived.

I stared at the drop and took another step back in case the snow we were on loosened under our weight.

Reyfyre closed his eyes and opened his palms to the sky. Magic swirled around us, engulfing both of us in the storm. When it ceased, he had a black coat that looked too thin to be warm enough, but I had a matching one wrapped around me and could attest to the lack of cold seeping through. When he stepped back into the wind path, he just shifted his hood over his head and leaned into the gale.

I did the same and found it easier to move than with the bulky coat that had been on me before. With this coat, the wind didn't penetrate through the down layers. It just seemed to bounce off us.

"Thank you," I said.

He glanced back. "Don't thank me. I did not create these from thin air. I stole them from one of the shops near Denali. They were too expensive for me to spend my hard-earned money on, even though they touted being one of the warmest coats on the planet."

I stopped walking. "You stole them?" My voice squeaked.

"Are you cold like you were before?" The snap in his voice was back.

"No. But that's beside the point."

"Fine. I'll send them the funds once I get access to my bank accounts. Which won't be until after we have neutralized Odin." He pointed a gloved finger in my direction.

"Stealing is wrong."

"And you wonder why I didn't want to conjure up a coat in the first place." His words dripped with sarcasm. "You should have never fallen asleep last night." He stomped away, leaving me staring after him.

I sighed. "It's still wrong," I muttered under my breath and trudged forward. Who knew what was in store for us around the next bend. It could be a hidden predator, or Odin himself.

Dread wrapped around my chest, squeezing as tight as a snake.

CHAPTER 8

I FOLLOWED REYFYRE AND my judgment of him softened as the brutal wind tore through the mountain pass. The coat he fitted me in made the trek much less daunting. Neither one of us had chattering teeth or shakes that made it difficult to take each step, and I couldn't fault him for outfitting us to better endure this journey.

We rounded a bend, and Reyfyre stopped short. I nearly walked into his backpack. The wind that had been in our face shifted for a moment, and Reyfyre slid the rifle off his pack. I glanced over his shoulder at what had spooked him.

A bear and her cubs stood still, peering our way with wide eyes. They looked just as shocked as I felt. I had seen these creatures enough in the cave to know that they were predators.

The wind shifted again, blowing strands of loose hair out of my face, taking our scent away with it. But the damage had been done. The bears knew we were here, invading their territory.

"Back away slowly," Reyfyre whispered as he shifted the gun.

"You are not going to shoot her." I bristled at the idea. Instead of backing away like he expected, I moved in front of Reyfyre, blocking any chance of him shooting the mother bear in front of her cubs.

"Are you insane?" he hissed from behind me.

The mother roared at me and stood on her hind legs, towering over our heads. The claws on her front legs were long enough to do serious damage.

My chest squeezed, and I gulped down the burn. Fear would do me no good. I had to make the mother feel as if she and her cubs were not in danger and Reyfyre waving the rifle around certainly wasn't conveying the feeling of warm fuzzies.

"Move."

I ignored Reyfyre's order and splayed my fingers out at my sides. "We don't want to hurt you. We just want to pass." I nodded at the other side of the small opening where her cubs had been playing, hoping my calm voice would take the fight right out of her.

"Why are you reasoning with an animal?"

"Because I want her to know we do not intend to harm her children. That's why she's so upset." I waved my fingers toward the bear without moving my arms an inch. Movement would set the bear off, and I quite liked my head attached to my shoulders.

"Idiot," he muttered under his breath, loud enough for me to catch.

Reyfyre's hissed words must have irritated the bear even further, and it lifted its paw, flexing until the claws were out for maximum damage. If that thing hit me, I'd be shredded, if not decapitated. And her paw was coming down fast.

I stepped into her personal space and shot my hand out, catching her at the joint just before her paw and the deadly shards sticking out of it. My arm shuddered with the impact, but I ignored my screaming muscles.

She thundered at me, close enough to actually bite my face off.

Before my brain could freak out, my free hand slid up beneath her chin and I scratched lightly. "I don't wish to harm you or your cubs." My voice rang calm and clear, and I inhaled, letting my shock and fear go. It would not help me in this precarious position.

Her growl faded, and she glanced down at me, meeting my open gaze.

"We just wish to pass." I continued to scratch under her chin like I would a cat or dog. They liked this on Asgard. Even the most vicious of animals became docile with a sincere chin or ear scratch.

This bear was no different. She lowered herself, and I let go of her paw but continued to scratch under her chin until she tilted her head, moving my scratching to the side of her face. I moved my fingers up to the spot behind her ears, and her eyes closed as she leaned into my hand.

Her cubs came closer, curious as to what was happening, and I waved for Reyfyre to go by while I had the mother's full attention.

Reyfyre moved by me nearly soundlessly with the gun still clasped in his hands. But at least the barrel was pointing toward the sky and not at the bear, who I seemed to be thoroughly charming. We locked gazes for a moment, and I swore I saw some awe there, but the irritation was very clear. He was going to have some unpleasant words for me if we got out of this unharmed.

I moved my free hand to the bear's other ear and scratched with the same soothing motions and the mama bear's eyes opened. I smiled down at her. "You like this?"

She moved closer, nudging me as I continued with my scratching. I kept Reyfyre in my peripheral vision and when he stepped out of the opening and behind the safety of a mountain of snow, I pulled my hands away, skirting to the side.

"I need to go."

But she wasn't having it. She wanted more pampering. I ran my fingers between her ears and then behind the ear closest to the wall that Reyfyre had slid against. I pulled my hand away and nodded toward the cubs.

"You need to take care of them." I raised an eyebrow as I spoke.

She glanced in the direction of her cubs and then at me, as if torn by my scratches and her children.

I scratched once more. "Be safe," I whispered, and this time she didn't stop me when I stepped away. I continued to walk in the direction of the opening where Reyfyre stood just outside of the bear's view. The barrel of the gun was still pointed at the bear behind me as I crossed the distance.

The minute I stepped out of the opening and into his direct line of sight, I rolled my eyes at him.

"You could have been killed," he hissed.

"The bear is smaller than most of our Asgardian wolves. I could calm them within seconds, too." I pointed at the gun. "Put that away. Bears aren't food."

The snap in my voice made Reyfyre growl, and he sounded even more feral than the bear had. His glare persisted, nevertheless, he stowed the rifle back into the holder on the side of his backpack.

He marched on in front of me, his stomping footfalls leaving thicker indentations in the snow.

I suppressed a smile at his utter annoyance. "Killing isn't always the answer."

He slowed to a stop as he surveyed the mountainous landscape surrounding us. "Putting yourself in unnecessary risk isn't an answer, either." His gaze slashed to mine. "If you die from doing something idiotic, the world will continue to suffer, so things like that"—he pointed back the way we had come—"are not tolerated."

I blinked at the burn his words caused and opened my mouth in rebuttal.

His hand came up. "I do not want to hear your excuses. You put our mission in danger. You put my world in danger." He huffed and started to walk again, but this time, his footsteps were normal and not like that of an angry child. His head still swung from side to side as if he were still reprimanding me in his head.

I followed him as the words seeped deep inside me. I glanced back the way we had come and sighed. Maybe Reyfyre was right. I did not think before I acted and that could have ended me. It was a risk, but I couldn't let him kill the mother bear in front of her children.

My heart wouldn't allow it.

And I knew deep down that my heart would be the death of me.

CHAPTER 9

NAVIGATION THROUGH THE REST of the mountain pass was uneventful and we started across another vast tundra. As soon as the sun dipped behind the mountain range, Reyfyre stopped and scanned the flat landscape.

Nothing that would count as shelter stood out for miles, and he dropped his backpack before he glared at me. "Looks like it's another shallow hole and sharing the sleeping bag again."

I narrowed my eyes at him. At least on the mountain there had been areas with shelter.

"Don't you give me the stink eye." He pointed a finger at me and then slipped his snowshoes off and used one to start digging.

I sighed and followed suit.

We finished before the last of the light left the sky. Reyfyre rolled out the sleeping bag and scanned the landscape again. "We might have to do this a couple more times before we get to anything worthy of shelter." He jumped in the hole and lined up his backpack and snowshoes against the walls before taking mine and doing the same.

He held his hand out to help me down before he took a seat on the fabric and rummaged around in my bag, pulling a fresh package of jerky out. He peeled off a quarter of the sticks and handed me the rest before digging into the measly dinner.

Soon I'd be pooping jerky. It was good, but I was starting to have a hankering for some fresh meat. Although, as I glanced around at the vast emptiness surrounding us, I realized this was about as good as it was going to get for a couple of days.

The sky above us lit with purples and greens, and my gaze shot to Reyfyre.

"Northern lights," he muttered around a mouthful of food.

I finished my jerky and tucked the rest of the bag into my backpack. "It's stunning." I tilted my head back to take in the streaked sky dotted with stars behind the colored lights.

"Mhm." Reyfyre stared up at the sky as he munched on the last of his jerky, and then he unzipped the bag and waved me in. He slid inside after me and laid on his back next to me so he could get a better view of the light show.

I shifted next to him, my eyes still on the sky. "At least sharing the bag will get us used to sleeping in the same bed and won't make being in a shelter in New York City that much more awkward."

His gaze turned to mine, and he made a noise of agreement.

"You're still mad about the bear."

His nostrils flared, and he looked back at the sky. "That was one of the stupidest things you've ever done."

So, yes. Reyfyre was still aggravated with me.

Good lord, what else could go wrong?

As if the gods had heard me, low growls reached our ears.

"Fuck," muttered Reyfyre, and he swiped his hand across the hole we dug. His magic sparkled just as two wolves launched toward us.

My heart thundered at their bared teeth and the vicious growls. It was fiercer than the wolverines had been, and I braced myself for impact.

They landed, skidding across Reyfyre's magical barrier as if it were ice.

I gasped in a breath as more wolves congregated, scratching at the magic as if they could break it. They could clearly see us. I met at least three of their gazes, which seemed to send them into a frenzy.

"Go!" I yelled and pointed. As if just my tone had any power of persuasion over these animals.

They bared their teeth and snapped at me before digging at the wall Reyfyre held between us.

I huddled closer to Reyfyre, and he glanced at me as though I had committed a cardinal sin.

"Can't you just magic them away?" I mean, one wolf would have been something we could intimidate, but an entire pack, and from the looks of them, a pack of ravenous wolves, we didn't stand a chance against them without the magic Reyfyre wielded.

"No. I can't. It's bad enough that I had to use it to protect us from these beasts. If I sent them to another part of the tundra, that is much more traceable than this. They'll tire and go away eventually."

There were at least eight wolves that I could see. And despite being just skin and bones, they seemed strong enough to pull a sled. I raised my eyebrow at my internal dialog. "What about conjuring a harness and sled and controlling them? That could get us across this frozen wasteland faster."

"Yeah. Let's just lead Thor and Odin to my boat while we're at it."

"No need to get sarcastic. It was just a thought."

"Well, wipe that shit right out of your head."

His snarl made me stiffen, and I rolled so my back faced him. Reyfyre rolled the opposite way, and our backsides did not touch, which was quite a feat in the tight space. But the cold be damned. Neither of us were in the mood to share our warmth beyond what the sleeping bag already allowed.

I closed my eyes, trying to ignore the hostility radiating in the small space along with the snarls and howls from above. But I was too damn tense. My body needed sleep, but I didn't think it would come tonight. Which would make us more sluggish and careless tomorrow.

That was, if we got out of this hole and freed ourselves from the wolf pack.

CHAPTER 10

SUNLIGHT PIERCED THROUGH THE shadows covering us, and I blinked my eyes open to wolves sleeping above us, and Reyfyre's arm draped across my stomach. A flash of irritation swept through me, and I turned to tell him to get away, but Reyfyre in sleep was a sight to behold.

Especially this close.

I held my breath as I studied him.

Dark lashes fanned across his high cheekbones. None of the usual lines of aggravation framed his eyes or his mouth. And his brow was as smooth as a new blanket of snow. His lips carried a rose hue that made them seem petal soft in sleep. He embodied perfection.

I wanted to reach out and run my fingers over his supple lips and through his dark hair. This was the first time since he rescued me that I had the chance to truly study the man. I flushed with unwanted heat.

He is part wraith, my mind screamed, and my gaze darted back to the wolves above us.

I jabbed my elbow into Reyfyre, and his eyes snapped open.

That vibrant blue of his irises flashed at me and then he pulled his arm away. "Sorry," he mumbled as he rolled onto his back. His gaze stopped on the wolf pack above and those irritation lines formed at the edges of his lips.

He was still handsome, but that moment of perfection was marred by his frown.

"Go," he hissed and waved his hand at the wolves with some intricate pattern that shot waves of magic from his fingertips.

The wolves woke with a start and then bolted as if they caught whiff of another prey to hunt.

Reyfyre curled his fingers into a fist and sighed. "Since I've already damned us…" He waved his hand again and I found myself on my feet, and our packs were nowhere to be seen. Our feet were only clad in boots, and I stared at him as if he were insane until he nodded over my shoulder. I spun and stared at the strange machine that sat on the snow with our snowshoes and backpacks attached to a rack on the back. Two helmets rested on the seat.

"You stole this too?"

"Yes. And I'm not sending it back. The owner of the shop was an asshole. And we're going to run this thing until it dies from lack of fuel." He climbed up to the machine and handed me a helmet when I stepped next to him. He started the machine and muttered under his breath. "Which won't be quite as far as I had hoped."

He put his helmet on before I could tell him that karma was a bitch. I climbed on the machine behind him.

"Hang on tight." He flipped his visor closed, and I had barely enough time to wrap my arms around his waist before we took off like a bullet. I caught sight of the wolves turning our way at the sound of the engine. I squeezed tighter, and Reyfyre opened up the throttle, speeding us away and out of range for a possible attack.

The flat snow-covered land sped by, and I clung to Reyfyre as he navigated the landscape.

We crossed what would have taken days on foot in a matter of hours. The whiteness before us transitioned as the sun crawled across the sky and a sparsely populated forest came into view. As we neared it, the engine began to sputter.

The snow machine slowed to a crawl, and Reyfyre turned it away from the direction we were heading. As soon as he completed the turn, the machine stopped and coughed its last breath.

I eased up my hold on Reyfyre, and he sucked in a full breath, as if my grasp had kept him from drawing any significant amount of air.

I peeled off my helmet and muttered an apology for holding on so tight.

His smirk was enough. He hung his helmet on the handlebars, slid off the machine, and untangled our packs and snowshoes from the rack behind me.

I added my helmet to the other handlebar and then swung my aching leg over the seat just as Reyfyre threw my snowshoes on the ground near the side of the machine.

"How much time did that save us?" I asked as I clipped on the shoes.

Reyfyre glanced behind us as he snapped his backpack straps in place. "I think that may have saved us something like ten to fifteen days and more importantly, this means the food we have stored will get us to the marina." He turned the key and read the readings flashing on the screen. "We went a hundred and fifty miles before we ran out of gas, and we've been averaging ten to fifteen miles on foot each day."

"So, we just cut the trip by half?"

He laughed as he held out my backpack. "Not quite that much, but it still was a chunk of time."

I studied the machine. "And it cannot be used further?"

"Not without gas, and I'm not inclined to use magic again. Plus, if it has any sort of tracker, I'd rather leave it out here on the tundra. If we're lucky, our tracks will be covered by the wind within a matter of minutes and maybe some fresh snow will fall to further muddle where we headed by the time they find this." He stared at the tracks cutting through the snow behind us. The wind had already wiped some of the evidence out.

"Did you want to take the helmets?" I busied my hands with clasping my backpack in place. The weight settled on me like an old friend.

"No. I don't want anything of theirs to be tracked to us." Reyfyre turned toward the wood line and started in that direction.

I followed, hoping we did run across another snow machine. I liked the idea of being able to cut the time down like we had. And I'd never admit it to Reyfyre, but I really liked having my arms around him like that. Even though I was holding on for dear life at first, I did like being flush against him and feeling the thunder of our hearts beating together.

I shook the thought out of my head as the woods swallowed us and my nerves jumped on edge, waiting for the next challenge to our journey to present itself.

CHAPTER 11

WE DIDN'T GET FAR before a noise to our right pulled our attention. A large bull moose stood taller than Reyfyre, with antlers that looked like the ends could spear us through. Its nose flared just before it lowered its head and charged.

Reyfyre grabbed my hand and yanked me forward as he sprinted away. I kept up with him as we awkwardly lumbered away from the angry moose. A quick glance over my shoulder sent shock waves through my form, and I pushed faster, this time pulling Reyfyre with me.

The moose was closing in fast. Plumes of smoke came out its nose, frosting the air with its exertion, and its eyes were as wild as any enemy I've ever faced.

We zigzagged this way and that and couldn't seem to lose the damn thing. If we stopped to unsheathe our weapons, it would trample us before we got a shot off.

My chest constricted with my own panting breaths. Reyfyre seemed just as frazzled as I felt and running in snowshoes was not an easy task.

All of a sudden, Reyfyre wrapped his arm around my waist and swerved off the path, diving behind a group of trees at the last second. We skidded to a stop, using the trees as a buffer. The moose collided with the thick pines, shaking the snow off the branches and onto us. But the tree trunks held.

The moose huffed and banged the trees again a few times before realizing it was a futile effort. It walked away, shaking its head as if arguing with itself. The visual was funny, but my heart was still lodged in my throat, cutting off my ability to laugh.

"I think we'll just camp here, if you don't mind." Reyfyre leaned his back against the thick trunks and closed his eyes. His breath still plumed white with each heavy exhale.

I glanced at the space in the little alcove he had thrown us in. It wasn't bad: the ground was now covered with the dislodged snow, but it wasn't deep like the surrounding areas. And best of all, the trees seemed to shelter us from the wind.

"We've slept in worse places," I said, and his eyes opened. The blue pierced through me like buckshot.

"Besides, I am starving," he added as he unclipped his backpack.

My stomach echoed his sentiment. We hadn't bothered to stop and eat at all while we were on the snow machine.

"Gather some wood, and I'll get us situated here and we'll have some real food today instead of jerky."

With our backpacks against the trees and a perimeter of bushes on the back side of us, the space for a fire was limited, but that didn't seem to discourage Reyfyre. When I returned, he had a small ring of rocks that he had filled with small branches. He had a few broken logs and thicker branches blocking us into this small space. I added the wood I was able to gather to his makeshift barrier.

He had a couple of pots out, along with a few canned goods ready to be cooked on open flame once he got our fire started. He glanced at the kindling and then at me.

"Do you want to try to spell the wood to burn?" He raised an eyebrow.

"You want me to use magic?" The few spells he had taught me at the cabin had been hard to master, but I could light a fire. That was the first spell he had taught me and one of the few I was fairly good at. I mean, the evenings got chilly and sometimes Reyfyre was out hunting and with no matches around, it had become a necessity for me.

"Your signature is different, and it could throw them off our trail. Besides, it is a spell and not inherent magic." He glanced at the sticks and waved for me to continue.

I knelt right outside the ring of rocks, faced my palms toward the wood, and closed my eyes before I spoke the incantation Reyfyre had taught me. I visualized a spark and the tinder smoking before it caught fire.

My nose tickled, and I opened my eyes to smoldering wood. I repeated the incantation and the sticks caught fire. Heat drifted to my hands, and I pulled them away.

"Good job." Reyfyre took the space next to me. He held the pots over the flickering fire. "Add some more of the kindling." He nodded toward the pile next to me.

I grabbed some of the thicker pieces of wood, along with a variety of twigs, and added them to the growing flames. He held the pans over the heat and the scent of beef stew rolled from each pot. He swirled each as if stirring and when they started the low roll of a boil, he set them down near our rolled-out sleeping bag and settled himself on one side. When I moved to the other side, he handed me a spoon and then dug into his hearty stew without hesitation.

We didn't talk while we both basically inhaled the contents of the pots.

Reyfyre exhaled and set his dish down on the ground before leaning back against the tree. "I could eat a dozen more of those," he muttered under his breath.

I ran my finger along the inside of the pot, getting the last of the remnants out. Then I licked every last drop off. I agreed with Reyfyre— I could eat so much more than just one can of this delicious stew. But then we'd have no food left and he'd probably starve if the lack of wildlife in the area was any indication. We hadn't even seen a rabbit or squirrel run across our path.

And sneaking up on a moose was next to impossible if you didn't know where to find them to begin with.

I plunked my pot next to his and dumped some snow into each to try to scrub them out.

Just like back at the cottage, if he cooked, I cleaned. However, it was more difficult to clean with only snow at my disposal. Still, I got most of the leftover gunk off the pots and grabbed a couple of leaves off the bushes surrounding us to wipe them down.

"What are you doing?" Reyfyre asked.

"Cleaning the pots." I turned and handed him the relatively spotless pots with a smile.

He grunted and inspected the cleaning job I did. "Great job," he said after a few minutes. "But you don't need to do that. Our bags are charmed, and have similar wards that the cottage had. Which is why we were able to pack so much in them and have them not weigh more than both of us combined." Dimples appeared in his cheeks.

"Things still need cleaning," I said.

"It's self-cleaning."

I blinked at him. "Oh. So, the leftover food wouldn't get on everything?"

"Nope." He stowed the pots and spoons away before he built the fire up as high as he dared. "Get some rest. We still have many days of walking ahead of us." He slid into the bag, leaving room for me behind him, and closed his piercing eyes.

"What other tricks do you have in the bags?"

One eye opened and studied me for a brief moment. "No tricks, just magic protected by wards."

Like that explained everything. I crawled into the bag behind him and laid back with a huff. He could be so frustrating, with his simple answers. I knew there had to be more than just the notion of magic at play and was irritated to not be kept in the loop. I wiped my face, and my mind wandered back to the cottage and Reyfyre stuffing the bags impossibly full. I should have known they were magical. I guess walking for days on end kind of dulled the senses.

But after all the crazy encounters we'd had, I guess my brain blocked out that particular fact. I wondered what else I'd conveniently forget if we ran across some real dangers.

That thought produced a rash of chills; dread at what we might still yet confront gripped my chest in a tight vise. Who knew what would be around the next bend.

CHAPTER 12

ANOTHER DAY, ANOTHER LONG walk and they all blended into one big blanket of green-dotted, snow-filled landscape. Until something shimmered in the distance.

"What's that?" I pointed.

Reyfyre glanced at his compass. "If I am not mistaken, that's our destination. Hudson Bay."

He smiled one of his rare genuine smiles, and I thought my heart stopped for a second. Thoughts about having that sexy grin aimed at me swarmed. I shook my head and diverted my gaze to the distant body of water.

"How long until we reach where your boat is?"

"Just a few more days."

I could not wait until my legs were propped up on a bench somewhere and we were cruising away from this vast winter wasteland. I was ready for civilization, even though I was as equally apprehensive of meeting the inhabitants of this planet. I had encountered enough people back in ancient Greece to wonder about how the human race had evolved.

"Don't look like a few days is daunting," he said, side-eyeing me.

"The walk isn't what is bothering me. Civilization is."

His gaze softened. "You'll do fine with people, just as long as you don't demand anything from them. Being Valkyrie means nothing here except a death sentence. You'll do well to remember that and keep your origins, as well as any of your demands, quiet."

My gaze slashed to his. "What?"

"You are nothing here. Just like I am. Don't expect much and you won't be disappointed. And be thankful for anything we get."

He stared me down as if I were going to be a problem. I had seen that expression from plenty of mothers back on Asgard when their children were on the cusp of misbehaving.

It ruffled me, but I kept my tongue silent.

"Our cover here is we've been hired to take a rich man's boat into New York City." He pulled out a paper, along with a couple of card-like items that had our pictures on them. "Driver's licenses." He waved them at me before tucking everything back into his backpack pocket. "And I have passports, too."

I had no idea what a passport was, but I went along with him. "Okay."

"So, be a good girl and don't question me while I'm bartering for what we need for this trip. I have access to very little with my current identity, especially without magic, so don't blow it for us." He kept plowing forward and from the tight set of his jaw, he expected me to explode.

"Sure. If you need any help bartering, let me know and I can bat my eyes for you." I couldn't help the snark that crept into my tone.

"If I need you to charm someone, I'll let you know." His response came out with a chuckle, as if the thought of me displaying anything but superiority was outlandish.

"I am capable of schmoozing people."

"I am sure you are, but the type of charm these people will likely expect happens with you on your knees, and not using your mouth to talk."

My mind jumped to the tavern owner and my muscles clenched. "You mean pigs."

He nodded. "Yes. And expect some rude comments, but please don't react." He met my gaze. "I will not allow anyone to touch you. Understand?"

I nodded, feeling every inch of his piercing stare. It created a heat in the center of my chest, as if he had just proclaimed me as his. And for some reason, that did not bring ire to the surface. Oddly, it vibrated through me with a pleasant rush that made me shift my feet.

It skewered my view of him just for a moment, the same way seeing his sleeping profile had warmed me to my very soul.

I gulped and kept walking, studying the patterns my snowshoes cut into the white drifts we traversed. *He's a mortal enemy of Asgard. I could not be attracted to him no matter how beautiful he might seem; he still was a brutal killer at heart. Wasn't he?*

With each step closer to civilization, my blood hummed with apprehension. I could not ease the dread pressing down on me, just as surely as I couldn't suppress the growing attraction to

Reyfyre. If I wasn't careful, I'd end up leading both of us right to the gallows.

CHAPTER 13

THE FIRST SIGN OF civilization reminded me a little of Reyfyre's cottage in the woods. Sturdy structures started to dot the landscape around us, giving way to denser packed homes as we got closer to the water. These structures were more in line with the villages on Asgard versus the clay and stone structures I had seen in Greece eons ago.

People were bundled up much like Reyfyre and me, and they rode snow machines or big vehicles with large wheels draped in chains.

We followed the road into the fishing village where old fishing boats sat beside sleek yachts. The attire of this age was more practical than the draped fabric of ancient Greece. It was in line with what Reyfyre wore and what he had outfitted me in. Denim and fleece reigned in this town, along with woolen hats, mittens, and scarves.

We received a few glances, but that changed as soon as we stopped in front of the marina store, unclipped our snowshoes, and walked into the building. A crew of weathered men leaned against the desk at the back, and they straightened the moment the door closed behind us.

Reyfyre removed his gloves and unzipped his jacket, reaching inside to pull out a piece of paper. He scanned the men and then zeroed in on one closest to the edge of the counter. "I'm here to bring my client's boat to New York," he said with almost a questioning lilt, as if he wasn't sure which man was in charge.

The man closest to the edge of the counter put his hand out and Reyfyre extended the paper to him. He perused the instructions and pursed his lips as he raised his eyes from the paper before rolling around to the computer on the other side of the counter, typing like a madman possessed.

His gaze came up, locking on Reyfyre. "Passcode?"

Reyfyre pulled out a folded paper and looked at the typed word inside it. "Gold nugget." He slid the paper back into his coat pocket.

"You sailed a rig like this before?"

"Yes, sir." Reyfyre pulled out another slip of paper. "My boating license."

The man snagged it from Reyfyre's fingers and narrowed his gaze. "Ray Davis." His eyes moved over the information and gave a curt nod before handing it back.

The other two men continued to leer at me and didn't give Reyfyre as much as a glance until their boss snapped, "Get bay 235 ready for boarding." Then they left through the side door, leaving us alone with the boss.

"I'll need gas and rations to get to New York City," Reyfyre said.

"Gas, I can do. But for rations, there's a grocery store around the bend that can help you out." He typed on his computer and then looked up at us. "That will be five hundred even."

Reyfyre blinked and then reached into his pocket, pulling out a piece of plastic as if this were standard, but his strained smile announced to me that this wasn't what he expected. His gaze slashed to mine in warning.

I hadn't even opened my mouth, but his *shut the hell up* attitude got my britches all in a bother. Instead of flapping off at the mouth, I chose to walk outside and see what the others were doing before I said anything that would jeopardize our situation. I had yet to encounter the type of men Reyfyre had mentioned on our way in, though. So, I could only surmise things had changed since his last visit to this quaint coastline.

I crossed the small, paved lot to the railing that surrounded the water access and glanced down at the docks below. The crafts were actually in the water and not hovering over it like they did on Asgard.

"What have we here?" a voice drawled from behind me.

I turned and paused at the five men fanned out around me. They wore ratty pants and thick shirts broken by straps that rolled over their shoulders. I pulled my hands out of my pockets and stared them down. Their interested leers told me these were the men Reyfyre had warned me about. I wondered whether it was because I was unaccompanied like in ancient Greece.

"I am with someone." I scanned each man, but that statement didn't seem to penetrate their feral gazes. "He's just inside the building." I pointed at the structure behind them.

"Yeah, but he's not here now." They stepped forward, grinning. "And you are." One of the men reached in and snatched my hat.

"Hey!" I tried to grab it back, but that just got me within their reach. Hands seized my arms and spun me around, pushing me against the barrier between me and the water below. My brain stalled for a moment as hands grasped at me in ways that made my teeth clench. Fury burned in my core, and I swung my elbow back, connecting with the soft flesh of someone's stomach.

The *oof* of pain was satisfying, but then instead of grabbing my hands, a fist hit my lower back and my knees buckled from the instant pain. I hung onto the railing to keep from falling.

"Get away from my girlfriend."

Reyfyre's voice carried over us, colder than the wind on the tundra, followed by the cock of a gun.

The men around me froze and put their hands up, backing up a few steps. One of the idiots had the nerve to say, "We didn't know she was with someone."

I turned slowly, facing their backs. "I told you assholes I was with someone."

Reyfyre's eyes darkened from the stunning aquamarine blue to almost a deep navy, announcing his displeasure. "Come here, love."

I swiped my hat off the ground and slammed my shoulder into one of the men as I passed. It was an aggressive move that pushed him off-balance, and he had to sidestep to catch himself. I crossed to Reyfyre's side and then glared at the five men who had decided I was their private toy to play with. I reached for one of the swords on his backpack to dole out some much-needed justice.

Reyfyre shook his head. "They don't deserve a death sentence for being morons," he said softly to me and then sent a deadly glare at the men. "Unless they are stupid enough to try to attack us both. Then we'll gladly remove their heads from their necks."

The men paled at the threat.

"Right, love?"

The use of that nickname did things for me that I couldn't have anticipated. Heat scraped my cheeks; my heart fluttered and wetness coated my panties. I licked my lips. "Right." My breathy voice betrayed the fact I was turned on by his protective possessiveness.

His lips tilted up in a ghost of a smile at my response. He held his elbow out and I looped my arm in it. "Come on. The boat is almost ready."

He took a few steps backward toward the boat launch area behind us, never letting the barrel of the gun waver.

It wasn't until we were parallel to the launch ramp that he turned enough away from the men that he no longer presented himself as a possible danger. Luckily, the men took off in the opposite direction once the gun wasn't pointing at them.

"Why did you leave my side?" Reyfyre's sensual voice had disappeared into the one of annoyance that I was used to.

"Because I was tempted to say you had been wrong about the men in this town." I glanced down as more heat filled my face. "At least not inside the store."

"We need to work on your observation skills before we get to New York City." He led me down to a large yacht that was moored by the gas pumps.

"Weren't we going to get supplies at the store?" I asked as we approached the boat.

He huffed a laugh. "Not with what just happened. We'll use the fishing poles for our food when our rations run out, and we have a full tank of water. We can stop at a port on the coast of Maine on the way for supplies if we need to. People there aren't as feral as here."

I grunted. "Daisy Mae?" I asked as I scanned the name scribed on the back of the ship.

"She's beautiful. Isn't she?"

He didn't really answer my question, but the way his eyes caressed the boat, I could tell this was one of his first loves.

"Yes, she is."

He stepped onto the plank and offered me his hand to help guide me aboard. I took it and when his soft palm met mine, I swore I felt sparks between us. But as soon as we were up a small set of stairs and out of sight inside the vessel, his hard look returned.

"You need to stick with me when I tell you to and not make any waves going forward. I know how to hide in plain sight. Situations like that never should have happened. Now stay put while I unlatch our moorings."

"I did not instigate that mess." I slammed my fists into my hips and stared him down. "And I don't like your tone."

"Fuck my tone, Kara. If you were to fight and kill those men, it would bring Odin right to us. Do you want that?" He hissed low enough for me to hear but not loud enough for anyone outside the room to pick up. And then he stormed out on deck.

Shock rattled through my bones, and I shook my head. I did not want Odin's fury aimed at us. I might survive, but Reyfyre wouldn't. And then I'd be imprisoned back in that godforsaken cave again. If they didn't kill me first.

My mind would fracture if that happened.

The thought sent a chilling shudder through me.

CHAPTER 14

THE CAPTAIN'S CHAIRS IN the bridge were very comfortable. Reyfyre sat behind the command center, steering the yacht and monitoring the systems. The moment we pulled out into the open waters of Hudson Bay, he seemed to relax. But he kept an eye out on the radar for other boats just in case some of those lunatics decided to sneak up on us.

"Once we get into the Labrador Sea, we can find a place to anchor, unpack our backpacks, and see what we have left. Then we can get a little shut-eye before we continue on. I won't pull into port until we reach Newfoundland or Nova Scotia." He pointed out the route on the map. "Or Bar Harbor in the United States. Those places are much more civilized than where we were."

I stared at the map. "How long until we get to New York?"

Reyfyre chewed on his lip for a few minutes. "Probably about ten to fourteen days with stops for refueling and sleeping. Maybe a little less, but I'm only factoring in an average speed of fifteen knots. While this baby can go more, the seas are likely to be rough, especially with it being winter." His gaze met mine. "If we're there sooner, it just means these comfortable accommodations are gone for a while."

"Comfortable?" I glanced behind me at the deck we were on and although there were a couple of couches behind us, it didn't look all that comfortable.

"No, honey. There's an entire living level below this one." He smirked. "This was one of my only impulse buys after my parents died and their monies transferred to one of my phantom identities. I had always wanted one and said screw it. If I was going to be on the run from that megalomaniac, I wanted to be on the run in style."

"Show me?" I waved toward the back, itching to see the rest of this boat.

"Not until I know no one has followed us. Besides, this doesn't have any sort of auto navigation system. So, I want to wait until we anchor for the night, then I'll show you around."

"I could explore on my own."

His head tilted to the side as he considered my statement. "I'd rather be the one to show you. I would have shown you much more than just the bridge had we not had to bug out so quick."

"What do you mean?"

"Those guys were asking for trouble. If we hadn't gone out so fast, I'm sure they would have let their stewing anger build enough to attack us on the boat. As it is, their glares promised retribution. And I, for one, would not like to have a murder charge over my head in addition to stealing a snowmobile." He gave me a pointed look. "I don't want our faces plastered all over the continent."

"Oh." I nodded my understanding and promptly yawned. The bridge was heated, so we both had stripped down to our jeans and sweatshirts, laying out our winter clothing across the couch and our backpacks and snowshoes on the floor near the closed-off stairwell he had pointed to.

"But if you wanted to take stock of what we have in the backpacks, you can do that." He hooked his thumb over his shoulder to where the packs leaned against the couches.

It would certainly keep my mind occupied. I stood and stretched before I went over to the packs. I took mine first and set out things in piles. Food and liquids went on the table and clothing went on the couch in a neat pile. My clothing pile seemed so small in comparison to the food, blankets, and utensils in the pack.

"Where do you want these once I have things unpacked?" I held up the empty backpack.

"Closet over there." He pointed to a slim door on the far side of the room.

I stowed my pack inside, noting there most likely would be enough room for his pack once I had emptied it. I went to work on his, and there was a lot more food than I had thought, along with a few pots and pans that we had used out on the tundra. On closer inspection, they didn't need to be cleaned before we used them again. They already gleamed due to the charms on Reyfyre's backpacks.

Reyfyre's pile of clothing was on par with mine. Less than a week's worth of garments were in our stacks.

"We might need some more clothes."

Reyfyre glanced over his shoulder at his pile. "I have more clothing stored here. You can borrow whatever you need until we get to the city and get a job that will give us the funds to get clothing and find an apartment." He turned back to the sea.

"Your shirts are too big for me," I muttered as I continued to pull things out of his bag as if it had no end. And then I unhooked the sword sheaths from the sides and set them next to the shotgun Reyfyre had placed next to the command center. Having our weapons handy would benefit us if we were actually attacked.

I stowed the backpack away and then swallowed a small burp of bile. My stomach had become decidedly sour since we boarded, and I put my fist to my lips, racking my brain as to why.

"Um. I'm not feeling so great." I sat on the couch.

Reyfyre glanced back at me, and his eyebrows shot into arches. He opened the panel next to him and rummaged around inside. Then he threw me a small round canister. "Motion sickness pills. Just take one of the pills with a little water and come sit up here where you can see the horizon."

I stared at the container, reading the text imprinted on the top as to how to open the tube. It took me a few tries and by the time I got it open, I highly doubted I would be able to keep one of these little tabs down. But I did what he said and climbed into the chair next to him, still gripping the container.

"Just keep your eye on the horizon for a while." His lips tilted into an amused smirk.

His expression crawled under my skin. "What?"

"I just never suspected that a mighty Valkyrie would succumb to seasickness."

"Well, our crafts hover. They aren't at the mercy of the waves beneath them." I took a breath and concentrated on the distant line on the horizon like Reyfyre had suggested and prayed the medicine he gave me started to work fast, because otherwise, I'd be making a mad dash to the back of the boat to hurl in the ocean.

CHAPTER 15

I DOZED IN THE seat after the medicine took hold, magically settling my stomach. An odd sound had me blinking. Reyfyre had shut off the engine and the rattle of chains nearly stopped my heart. I snapped my gaze to Reyfyre.

"It's just the anchor." He took hold of my upper arm and helped me from the chair. "Let me show you the living quarters and then we can crawl into the bed and get some sleep," he said through a yawn. His eyes carried the dark circles of the sleep-deprived.

My brain balked at his words, but I was too tired to argue. Besides, we had shared sleeping bags on the tundra. But it still left me unbalanced. Especially after the flare of heat his words had caused in me earlier in the day.

He grabbed the gun and swords, tucking them under his arms, and then swept up all the food contents I had organized on the table. "Those pots are probably good," he said. "Grab them for me. I have dish soap downstairs and I'll make sure they are sanitized after I get some sleep."

I followed him down the stairs. When we entered the living quarters, as he called it, I paused on the stairs, scanning the rich wood and granite that sparkled under the lights. It was almost as big as the cottage living area and had two seating areas, one in the middle with a table and one aft. The bedroom took up most of the forward space beyond the sitting area.

"Pots go in the sink." He nodded with his chin and then set the food on the table before he propped the gun and swords on the inside wall of the bedroom. He turned to me, pointing at a door to the left of the bedroom. "Bathroom." And then he pointed to the opposite side of the boat at another door. "Shower." Then his finger slashed to me, along with a warning tilt of his eyebrow. "But you cannot take your normally excessively long shower, otherwise you will deplete our water supply. Understand?"

I stared at the shower door and nodded, stepping toward the room.

"I get the shower first." The snap in his voice was punctuated by him peeling his boots off and setting them on the floor in the bedroom. He opened one of the closet doors and pulled out a pair of boxers. "When I'm done, you can clean up and if you want a night shirt, have at it." He waved at his closet, which had neat piles of various clothes on each shelf, and then disappeared into the shower.

I turned and stumbled upstairs to grab my pile of clothes and bring them down to the living area and peeled off my boots, setting them aside near the stairs. Then I commandeered an empty drawer I found in the bedroom for my clothing.

I rummaged through Reyfyre's closet and found a soft blue tank top that would probably reach my knees. I took that and a pair of my underwear and crossed to the couch, waiting for my turn to wash off the grime from the last month of travel.

Reyfyre's dirty clothes hung on the hook next to the shower door and I sighed. The only view I'd ever had of his bare chest was the night of the wolverine incident. And that was too brief. I could definitely get used to seeing more skin from Reyfyre.

I let out a soft chuckle. I must be tired if my brain went to objectifying the man. That's exactly what Thor did to me on Asgard, and I hated it. I couldn't start doing that to Reyfyre. Not when it had sent uncomfortable chills through me anytime that asshole leered at me.

The shower went off.

I tilted my head back and closed my eyes, giving Reyfyre some privacy as he stepped out of the bathroom.

"There's a hamper in the bathroom. You can put your dirty clothing there and we'll find a laundromat to wash them once we get to the city. You'll find a clean towel on the hook of the door. That's also where you should hang your clean clothing, so they don't get wet."

"Thanks." I stood, collecting my things. By the time I turned toward the shower, he had already crawled under the covers on the right side of the bed.

"Good night," he murmured just before his eyes closed.

I stepped into the shower and immediately understood why he hung his clothing up outside. The stall was the entire room, with a towel hooked on the door. Soap and shampoo sat on a small shelf and the rest of the walls were smooth, without breaks. The floor had a grate in it where the water drained.

I hung the shirt and underwear up on the hook under the towel and then stripped. I tossed the dirty clothing onto the floor outside of the shower and then turned on the water. Two months of grime sloughed off my body, and I scrubbed my skin and washed my hair twice before I shut the water off. I could have stood there for another hour, but his warning stuck with me, especially considering I had been the one to catalog what we had left, and we were low on water bottles.

I dried my body with the towel and slid on the underwear and shirt before I wrapped the towel around my hair. When I left the shower, I picked up the dirty laundry and headed into the bathroom to put it in the hamper and see whether Reyfyre had a brush or comb to untangle the knots in my hair.

Thankfully, he had both in the bathroom cabinet, and I towel dried my hair, hanging the wet towel on the bathroom hook before I brushed out my tangled locks. I searched and found a couple of unopened toothbrushes and cleaned my teeth with the half-used toothpaste in the cabinet.

Fully refreshed, I turned off the lights behind me and settled into the bed next to a snoring Reyfyre. I curled up facing him, studying his profile like I had under the northern lights. In the darkness, he looked almost cherub-like, and he smelled clean, along with a cinnamon undertone that made my mouth salivate.

The urge to caress the fae-wraith's cheek crawled under my skin, and I turned away before I did something stupid. The shock wave of that sudden need made me shiver under the covers. *I cannot fall for him. I cannot have that kind of weakness again!*

Hippocrates had made me vulnerable. I would never be vulnerable again so long as Thor and Odin were alive.

CHAPTER 16

MORNING CAME AND WITH it, my stomach rolled. Reyfyre was already up in the kitchen, cooking something that would normally smell good, but it only served to make me clench my jaw against the bile lining my throat. I slid from the bed and stumbled to the bathroom, spitting the offending taste from my mouth.

I relieved myself and brushed my teeth to wipe out the horrid flavor.

When I emerged from the bathroom, Reyfyre handed me a pair of sweatpants without a word and then nodded to the table where two plates were set with a pile of eggs and bacon. Fresh orange juice sat in glasses next to the plates.

Despite my sour stomach, my mouth watered. It had been eons since we had eggs and bacon, never mind fresh orange juice. "Did you magic us supplies?"

He shrugged. "There's already a magic signature aboard this ship. I figured out here, it would be harder to track than on land. We are stocked for the full trip, including gas and extra water." He sat down and shoveled the food into his mouth. "We can still fish if you'd like," he added around a mouthful of food.

I took the seat and tentatively took my first bite. My stomach groaned, demanding more, and I shoveled the rest in as if I hadn't eaten in months.

The minute I drained my cup and sat back, my stomach decided that was not truly what it wanted. It cramped, and I scrambled to my feet, temporarily uncertain which way to go. The boat pitched me toward the stairs and that cinched the decision. I ran up the stairs into the frigid air whipping across the North Atlantic and grabbed onto the railing. I leaned far enough over not to splatter the boat, and my breakfast shot out in a disgusting geyser of food and stomach acid.

Reyfyre's chuckle reached me just before his hands collected my hair so it wouldn't get dirty food chunks in it. "You need to take that medicine when you wake up so you're not vomiting nonstop."

"Thank you, Captain Obvious," I said between gags.

When I was sure I had nothing left, I slid to the ground and leaned against the railing, looking up at Reyfyre. "How come you don't get seasick?" I wiped my mouth with the back of my hand.

He crouched down, offering me a pill and a can of soda. "Some people just don't."

I wanted to wipe off his smirk and the humor dancing in his eyes. Instead, I took the pill and washed it down with a minute sip of the soda.

"Do you need help back to bed?"

"I can't go down there with the scent of eggs and bacon on the air," I balked as my teeth started to clatter together with the shivers running through me.

"Then let's get you up to the couch on the bridge." He picked me up in his arms and carried me to the couch like I was an invalid.

Although his actions irritated me, I doubted I could make the walk without hurling the medicine. Reyfyre deposited me on the couch and then disappeared below deck. Running water followed, along with the clank of dishes as he cleaned up. Guilt wormed its way through me. I should have cleaned up because he cooked.

When he finally appeared, he was dressed in a clean pair of jeans and a gray sweatshirt that made his eyes glow brighter. He handed me a zip-up sweatshirt of his and went to the command center. The engine roared to life, followed by the anchor being pulled back up. And then Reyfyre charted out the next couple of days before he steered the boat in the right direction, and we set off.

Most days of this cursed cruise played out the same. It was all one big blur of sour stomachs and Reyfyre's snickers as he fed me the seasickness pills I had left on the nightstand. By the time we had reached Maine, I had been remembering to take the pill before I got out of bed. Thankfully, after that, I didn't hurl after breakfast. The pills just skimmed the sourness enough so I didn't vomit, but I was not comfortable at all.

He finally moored the boat at a marina in Massachusetts and told me to wait on the boat. I was trying to keep breakfast down, so I did not argue with him at all, but I did study the marina and the people moving about the area. I got no dangerous vibe from them—quite the opposite— and it made me relax to the point my stomach settled a little more.

Reyfyre came back and opened the container in his hand. He pulled out a terrycloth wristband and put it onto my wrist. A bump pressed into my arm right at the juncture of my veins. I let him slide the second one on, but cocked my head at him.

"Seasick bands." He met my gaze. "Between these and the pills, hopefully you won't have such a tough time for the rest of our trip." He smiled. "Then maybe we can get some training done on the deck."

I narrowed my eyes. "You got these so you can kick my ass?"

"Precisely." He bopped my nose and left me staring after him as he undid the ropes and then guided us out of port.

Dread wrapped around me as we pulled back into the open waters again. However, the motion of the seas didn't seem to affect me as much. Oh, I still felt the pitches, but it didn't make my stomach go in a terrifying loop-de-loop aimed at making me throw up. And once the pill started to work, I wasn't nauseous at all.

I slid into the captain's chair next to Reyfyre. "These are minor miracles." I held up my wrists. "Thank you."

He glanced at me. "For the first time since we left Canada, you're not greenish."

A burst of laughter escaped. "I didn't realize seasickness came with a color."

"It's not a color that looks good on you." His lips twitched into a smirk.

I didn't have a comeback for Reyfyre. But now that my stomach wasn't in the forefront of my mind, our task at hand raised its head. "What if we fail?" My hands clasped before me, and I refrained from letting them wrestle with my unease.

"Then we die knowing we tried."

His words sent a cold chill right to my bones. I did not want to lose Reyfyre. Something had settled between us on this trip and my wariness of the wraith part of him didn't seem to matter anymore. Somehow, I had come to care about Reyfyre more than just as a trainer. I had no doubt once we settled in and started training, I would almost hate him again. But those negative feelings would be tainted by this softening of my heart.

I took a deep breath and nodded. "Tell me what will happen when we get to the city."

"We pack up our clothing and find a shelter that will let us stay together. Then I'll see if I can get both of us a job at the bar I used to work for. They know me under my alias and are usually hard up for help, so that should work in our favor as long as they are still open." He wiped his face. "After a couple paychecks are under our belt, we'll be able to have enough for a down payment for a small apartment."

"So, another month or so before we start hunting?"

He laughed. "More like another six months for us both to get in shape before we take the fight to them."

"Six months?"

"Unless they find us first. But yes, it will take at least that long before you are at full strength. You still need work, and I need to be in top shape as well." His gaze slashed to mine. "And when we are training, you'll have to pull your punches with anyone else but me."

"Who said I was training with anyone else?"

Reyfyre grinned, and his eyes twinkled in a dark manner. "The gym I used to belong to is the best place to learn to fight again. It's mixed martial arts along with boxing and strength training. So, you'll be pitted against some talented humans. If you go full out on them, you'll broadcast your otherness to them and then we'll be fucked."

"You trust these people?" I couldn't believe Reyfyre would trust humans, especially given the fact they weren't standing up to Odin's rule.

"I don't trust anybody." He sucked in his lower lip. "They think I'm human. You're the only one left on this planet who knows what I am."

"So, you trust me?" I placed my hand on my chest.

The guffaw he let out sent a wave of irritation through me. "As I said, I trust no one."

"Fuck you, Reyfyre." I climbed out of the chair and headed out of the bridge and onto the open deck. A cyclone of feelings swirled inside me, making me dizzy with the intensity.

The engine shifted into neutral and then Reyfyre appeared in the doorway. "I trust you to have my back in a fight. But you've proved you don't listen to me in any other situation, so no, I don't trust you at all beyond having my back in battle." His aquamarine gaze bore into me.

"You would have killed that bear." I crossed my arms, defending the one time I truly did not listen to him.

His eyebrow cocked. "You fell asleep when it was your turn to keep watch. And you did not stay with me at the marina." His arms crossed, radiating the same hostile manner that I adopted.

I opened my mouth to argue and closed it immediately. Both of those things were on me. I turned my back on him and stared at the water, frustrated that I couldn't identify the burn in my blood. Reyfyre did not trust me, and that rubbed my skin like a thousand beetles attacking my flesh. I needed the man to trust me because deep down, I trusted him implicitly. He had never steered me wrong.

"I'm sorry," I said over my shoulder. When he didn't respond, I turned to an empty doorway. He was back at the controls and the stress was visible in the tightness of his shoulders, even at this distance. I let the winter winds slap at my skin for a moment longer before I retreated inside into tension as thick as clumps of rotten seaweed.

CHAPTER 17

THE FRICTION BETWEEN REYFYRE and me seemed to grow as all our unspoken shit festered between us. Thankfully, it was only a few days after his lack of trust announcement that New York City came into view.

I stared at the city looming before us with my jaw dropped open. The tall buildings reflected the sunlight like mirrors, intimidating me into silence. I had never seen a city like this. Sure, Asgard had Odin's castle, but that was one building looming over everything else.

This was something different and almost too big for my brain to comprehend.

Reyfyre leaned toward me. "Your mouth is hanging open."

I snapped my jaw shut and glared at him. "You did not prepare me for this." I waved at the view getting closer and more overwhelming every minute.

"Welcome to New York City, Kara." He grinned. "This is one of hundreds of cities across America, but it is the biggest."

I gawked at the city. It was stunning in the morning light. And it was a far cry from the mud and brick huts I saw in Greece. The human race had evolved beyond measure. And yet, Odin and Thor still reigned over them with an iron fist.

"If they could build this, why did they just lie down and surrender to Odin?" I asked softly as we approached the marina.

"Because they have nothing that can kill a god. None of their best weapons, human or otherwise, was a match to Thor and Odin's power." His lips curved into a frown. "We need to establish ourselves here as Karen Johnson and Ray Davis." He pulled out the licenses and handed me mine. "Do not lose this."

I tucked it into my back pocket as Reyfyre docked the boat. He turned off the engine and glanced at me. "We need to pack our clothes."

Without waiting for me, he headed downstairs.

I followed in time to see Reyfyre pull a suitcase from under the bed. It had wheels on one side and after he slammed the bed back down, he unzipped the bag and started to pack our remaining clean clothing neatly. Once he had our things tucked into the suitcase, he retrieved the laundry bag from the bathroom and spread it over the top of the clean clothing before zipping up the bag.

I stepped aside as he deposited the suitcase in front of me. He went to one of the thin floor-to-ceiling doors and pressed his thumb to the pad under the latch. It unlocked and swung open. Inside his locked cabinet were more weapons: guns tucked into the doorframe, along with some interesting knives. There were a couple of rifles like the one he carried from the bedroom along with our swords. Stowing them quickly, he closed the door and repeated pressing his thumb to the pad. The click of a lock engaging filled the silence.

"It would have been nice to know we were armed to the helm." I crossed my arms.

"Now you know. But only a blade can be used to kill a god." His gaze met mine before he focused on the kitchen, opening cabinets and taking stock of the food. He did the same with the refrigerator.

He handed me what was left of the eggs and a milk carton. "The rest of the things in here will keep." And then he slid his stockinged feet into his thick snow boots, slipped on his jacket and waited expectantly for me to do the same.

After being in heated accommodations, the slap of cold wind as we disembarked from the boat hit like an ice storm. "How long will this cold continue?"

He chewed his lip and started up the dock. "I think we have another six weeks until spring kicks in down here. I'm hoping we can find a furnished apartment by then." He spoke over his shoulder as he led the way into the marina. He headed straight for the counter and unfolded a piece of paper, handing it to the clerk. "Did Mr. Allaire leave anything for me here?"

The clerk glanced at the paper he was handed before looking up at Reyfyre. "Let me have a look, Mr. Davis." He stepped away into the back room, rummaging around for a few minutes. When he came back, he handed a slim envelope to Reyfyre with a smile. "Does Mr. Allaire's boat need any repairs?"

"Not to my knowledge, but I believe he said to make sure you do a service check before you dry-dock it?" The statement came out in more of a question as Reyfyre pocketed the envelope.

"Yes, sir. We do a thorough inspection before we store it. Do you happen to know when Mr. Allaire is coming into town? His contract doesn't specify when we should have it ready for him."

"He mentioned he wanted me to do a return run in the fall, so I'd assume he'll want it during the summer, but you never know what his timing is." Reyfyre smiled. "I'll catch you in the fall."

"See you then, Ray."

He turned and escorted me out of the building, keeping his smile on his face until we were off the property. Then it dropped completely. "I didn't expect to be gone quite this long, so my accounts here are probably near depleted. And I don't have access to Allaire's accounts yet."

"Who the hell is Allaire?" I asked, still carrying the eggs and milk while he rolled the suitcase behind us.

"That is my real surname." His side-eye told me to keep it under wraps. "Just like yours is Mist." A dimple appeared in his cheek before he squashed the smile. "Karen," he added as we crossed the road.

I crinkled my nose at him.

"Karen Johnson," he said with a smirk. "I figured Karen would be easy for you to remember, especially under stress."

"Just like Ray?"

He nodded. "It's close enough for me to stop before I get to the fire part of my name. And I don't think Odin or Thor knows my surname. Otherwise, my accounts would have been drained dry. It was my mother's name, but she took my father's surname when they married, so there's no trail back to it."

"So Allaire is rich?" I waved back toward the marina.

"By what standard?" He glanced up at the towering buildings surrounding us. "If you're comparing my wealth to a king?" He nodded.

"In comparison to Odin?" I only had the opulence of his castle as a comparison.

Reyfyre's eyes squinted as he pressed his lips together. "Before he stole the riches from the wealthy here on Earth, my family surpassed him. But they were only able to hide away a fraction of their wealth. But I'm still in the top one percent on Earth. I just don't have access to it until I take down that bastard. I've done my best to keep it hidden. There are some things like the boat that has a steady stream of money tagged for its upkeep and storage, and there was no provision for the person who moved it from place to place to live on it. That would have raised too many flags." He glanced at me. "So, for now, we are poor and have to live that way. It keeps us under their radar." His blue eyes flicked to mine, punctuating his statement.

As soon as we crossed over from the marina into the city proper, Reyfyre grabbed the milk and then took my hand in his as he propped the milk against the suitcase handle and dragged it along behind him as we were swallowed by the New York City crowds.

CHAPTER 18

WE STOOD ON THE road, staring up at the sign for the bar Reyfyre used to work in: the Stumble In Bar and Grille. I smirked and glanced at him with a tilt of my eyebrow.

Getting here from the marina had taken us through a maze of underground paths and the actual subway. Which, as a first timer, was quite the experience. I can't say I liked being crammed into the space with umpteen other people, but at least Reyfyre had given our eggs and milk to a homeless person on the street before we headed into the subway tunnels. Reyfyre still had the suitcase rolling behind him like a bizarre extension of himself.

"Trust me. They pay well." Reyfyre held the door open for me and stepped into the dark, bustling bar behind me with the suitcase in tow.

Before we even got to the bar, a screeching voice yelled, "Ray!"

I pivoted to see a rotund redhead nearly leaping into his arms.

Reyfyre caught her and grinned as he twirled in a circle with her in his arms, leaving me to man our suitcase.

My gut twisted in an unfamiliar way, and I scowled at the spectacle.

"Man, Charity, you've certainly grown up." Reyfyre set her on her feet as he gave her the once-over. Then he turned to me. "Charity, this is my girlfriend, Karen. Karen, this is Charity, the owner's daughter."

I was still caught on him introducing me as his girlfriend when Charity stuck out her hand. I clasped it and let her pump it more than once and provided a cordial smile in return to her beaming one.

"Actually, I'm the owner now." She pulled her hand away. Her shine faded with the words, like the fact she owned the bar was a burden.

"What happened to your parents?" Reyfyre asked with wide eyes.

Shock radiated from him enough to bring goose pimples to my flesh.

"They didn't serve the gods quick enough," she said almost too quietly as her gaze darted around the bar.

The combination of melancholy and fear in her eyes caught a swallow in my throat. I didn't need any further explanation, and I stiffened as rage snaked through my veins.

Reyfyre's face hardened, and he met my gaze with a small nod. He was just as infuriated by the news as I was, and I didn't even know Charity.

"I'm sorry to hear that, Charity," he said with a voice that held enough sadness for me to get these people had been important in his life. His hand shook as he took mine in his.

I squeezed to show him I was there for him, and the quick shift of his gaze he sent me seemed like an unspoken thank-you.

"It has been long enough that I don't burst into tears anymore when I tell people." She gave me a sheepish smile. "And they haven't been in here in about a year. So, there's that." She seemed to regain her composure. "Can I get you a table?" Her gaze landed back on Reyfyre.

Reyfyre glanced at me before he spoke. "Actually, we're both looking for jobs."

Her eyebrows rose. "You're not still schlepping boats around the world anymore?"

Reyfyre laughed. "No. Karen doesn't take too well to water, so I'm landbound for a while until she finds her sea legs." He wrapped his arm around me and pulled me against him in a possessive gesture before he leaned in and pressed a kiss to my cheek. "Believe me, she's worth it." He grinned at Charity.

Heat filled my face, and I glanced at the ground, unable to form a clear thought with the burn of his lips still branding my cheek. But I was cognizant enough to refrain from brushing the spot he kissed me with my hand.

Charity glanced at the bar. "I am short bartenders and waitstaff."

"Neither of us have any experience, in either position, but you know I learn fast, and Karen is a quick learner, too."

I put my hands on my hips. "I've mixed cocktails before." It was just on a different realm with different ingredients, but I was sure this wouldn't be a problem. "If you have a mixology book for your drinks, I should be able to memorize them all within a week."

Charity's eyes widened. "Oooo, she has spunk, Ray."

Her teasing tone brought a grin to my face, but Reyfyre just rolled his eyes.

"So, bartenders?" he asked.

"Sure. Are you at the same address here?" Charity asked as she led us to the office in the back and indicated for us to sit.

"No. We, um, don't have a place right now." Reyfyre shifted in the seat. "We're going to check out one of the local shelters until we can get enough to put down a security deposit."

Charity stared at him as she slowly sat in the chair behind the desk. "Nonsense."

Reyfyre's head snapped up.

"My place has been empty for the better part of a year, since I moved into my parents' condo. I just haven't gotten around to cleaning it out, or selling or leasing it. If you can help me clean it out and move the remaining things to my parents' place, you can rent from me."

"No. I couldn't." Reyfyre shook his head, but his tone wasn't completely dismissive.

"Furnished and all." Charity raised an eyebrow. "And I can take rent from your paycheck."

"Paychecks. I don't want Ray to pay my keep," I interjected. A furnished apartment sounded fantastic, especially given his warning that we'd most likely be living on a cot in a room full of other people. I glanced at Reyfyre, wishing I could kick his shin.

He glanced between us and sighed, relaxing in the chair in a way that signaled surrender. "Fine."

Charity beamed and reached into the desk to pull out a set of keys. She tossed them to Reyfyre and then pushed two applications across the desk for us to fill out. "Can I have your licenses?" she asked.

I reached into my pocket and handed mine over. Reyfyre did the same.

"Leave the address blank and I'll fill it in after I make copies." Charity waved the licenses at us and left the office.

Reyfyre leaned forward and started to fill out both forms. Which was a good thing, because I didn't know what half the items were or what to put in the fields. He tapped the signature line. "Karen Johnson," he whispered. "Sign it."

He finished his form as I signed where he had indicated and handed him my pen. He signed his application just as Charity returned with our licenses in one hand and a book in the other.

"You can head up to the apartment and start cleaning up. I should be there in about an hour, and I'll show you the things I need help with getting to my parents' place on the West Side." She handed us our licenses and handed me the book. "Those are the specialty drinks we offer, along with the usual drinks. I'll expect you to know them inside and out before the weekend. I'm putting you two on the Saturday night shift to see how you do."

I smiled, but Reyfyre's grin didn't reflect in his eyes. "Where is your apartment?" He jingled the keys.

"Two blocks down, hang a left and you'll see the apartment building on the right. Apartment 351." She collected the applications and scribbled the address on both and then smiled up at us. "You start Saturday."

Reyfyre nodded. "I don't know how to thank you..."

"Just bring in the crowds. We need some new energy to do that, and I have a gut feeling the two of you will bring some magic to this place."

I nearly snorted a laugh, but pretended to cough to save face. Laughing at the boss-slash-landlord probably wasn't a good thing. But whatever I had sounded like did not seem to offend my new friend Charity. However, Reyfyre sent me a glare as soon as we were on the street, headed toward our new apartment.

"I did not want Charity involved," he muttered at me out of the side of his mouth.

"You have to admit, it's a better offer than the shelter." I cocked a challenging eyebrow at him.

"Yes. It is."

His grumbled admission brought a smirk to my lips, and I dipped my head so my hair would cover it.

"I just hope it doesn't bite us in the ass."

CHAPTER 19

THE ONE-BEDROOM EFFICIENCY was smaller than my bathroom on Asgard, but it was the perfect hiding place for us. I stood in the entrance, appraising the small space, which included a bed, a dresser, and a tiny round kitchen table with two chairs. Boxes dotted the floor with things stacked in them carelessly, some not in any order at all, and there was a layer of dust on everything.

I sneezed as I stepped inside. It seemed our landlord was not a very organized individual. I hoped she ran her business better than she kept her home.

"She hasn't been here in months." Reyfyre stepped next to me and sighed at the state of our new living quarters. "I'll see if I can find some rags in this mess and then we can start by at least cleaning the dust off everything."

"Did you happen to grab my blanket?" I asked as I took in the dust-laden comforter on the only bed in the apartment.

"Yes. But that's not going to keep us both warm."

I pressed my lips against the salty smile that wanted to form. "You can have the comforter wherever you're sleeping."

He snorted at me. "It's as big as the bed on the boat. Besides, if anyone is sleeping on the floor, it's you." He crossed and stripped the comforter and then headed onto the small balcony to shake it out. The dust cloud that came from the fabric resembled a snowstorm and by the time he was done shaking it, nothing seemed to be left clinging to the cotton. Still, he hung it over the railing and leaned the chair against it so it wouldn't blow away in the wind.

A television hung on the wall across from the bed and the remote sat on the nightstand, so I clicked it on to have background noise while we rid this place of dust and dirt and neatly packed the boxes and things gathered on the table.

Reyfyre found a vacuum in the closet and just before he plugged it in, he stalled, his gaze glued to the screen. I turned away from wiping the thick layer of dust from the table and froze in the same way Reyfyre did.

A furious burn lit my blood at the sight of Thor and Odin on the screen. The door opened, and Charity burst in with an envelope with a broken seal in her hand and eyes as wild as a cornered deer. She halted a few feet away from me and pointed at the television with the envelope.

"They expect me to be at their ludicrous ball Saturday night," Charity gasped. "I cannot be in the same room with the bastard who killed my parents."

Her panicky statement held true to the announcement of a ball and those invited were required to attend. If they did not show up, they would be publicly executed.

I glanced at the invitation in her hand and then at her frantic eyes. "They'll kill you if you don't go."

Her glare could have peeled my skin off if she had any magical talent hidden in her blood. She nearly snarled. "Who's to say I'll even walk out of the ball alive? Thor chooses a handful of women at each one of these events and…” She swallowed hard and put the back of her hand to her mouth as if she was about to be sick. “It’s aired.”

“What is aired?” Reyfyre asked.

“Where the hell have you been for the last month?” Charity snapped.

“At sea, bringing a boat up from the Caribbean. Why?”

“Those assholes have been looking for their lost Valkyrie. And he test-drives the ones he pulls aside.”

“Test-drives?” My gaze bounced between Reyfyre and Charity.

“He fucks them on live television?” Reyfyre’s voice cracked.

“Yes. And if they’re human, they die when he…you know.” She rolled her hand without expanding further.

My jaw slowly dropped with the horror reflected in Reyfyre’s eyes. “They die?”

She ran a hand down her face. “He made the first one give him a blow job and when he came, it blew a hole the size of a melon in the back of her head. I guess the same happens inside—we just can't see the damage. And no one has willingly blown the asshole since."

My stomach did the same slow roll it had on the boat, and I ran to the sink, dry heaving a few times before my stomach retreated to a state of less turmoil. But I was still sick at the thought.

"And if they aren't human?" Reyfyre asked, still staring at the television with a glare that could blow the circuits.

"There hasn't been any non-humans pulled aside. I don't know if any exist. And now they are systematically going through New York City looking for someone who likely isn't even here. And dozens of women will die just to satisfy his twisted libido." Her entire form shook. "And now I have to go to a fucking ball." She sat on the side of the bed and buried her face in her hands.

"I can see if any of my clients need their boats moved. And we can take you with us," Reyfyre offered.

Charity stared at him. "No one can leave the city. Once you're within city limits, you are stuck until you've been cleared by attending a ball."

We exchanged a glance over Charity's head. We were just as trapped as she was.

"How many are they planning on doing?"

Charity shrugged. "The target areas are only a couple blocks wide. And there is no rhyme or reason to what section they will choose next. The last one was downtown, so I figured I had more time to get used to the idea of facing them."

"Okay. Well, just try not to bring attention to yourself." Reyfyre sat next to her, draping his arm around her shoulders. "Don't wear anything flashy. And follow whatever the rules they state without question."

"They make the guests drink a truth serum," she whispered. "And I'm likely to tell them to fuck off for killing my parents even before I drink their heinous drugs." Her pleading eyes met mine.

"They can't fault you for being angry that they killed your parents. I would think that should save you from being one of their victims." I didn't know whether that was true or not. I'd seen Odin smite someone for less, but I didn't want to say as much to our newest benefactor.

"If something happens to me, my brother said he'd take over the bar, but he's not stepping foot in the city." She sniffled. "Which is why I haven't been able to get all this stuff packed and across town." She wiped her face and stuffed the invitation in her back pocket. "I think I'll just pack the boxes neatly and store them in the closet here until after the ball."

Charity glanced at the bed and then pointed at the dresser. "There are sheets in the bottom drawer and towels in the linen closet in the bathroom."

"We can't take your things," Reyfyre said.

Charity pulled away. "You only have a suitcase between the two of you. You need this stuff more than I do. I have an entire two-bedroom apartment full of stuff, so I only need to pack my essentials and personal things. Okay?"

Reyfyre nodded, and I followed his lead.

"I'll have the lease papers ready for you to sign on Saturday before your shift starts. I'd like you in at three and then I can show you the ropes." Her chin trembled as she moved to the boxes and started to straighten her pictures and knickknacks up within the container.

Reyfyre helped her in silence while I went back to eradicating every inch of dust that had accumulated in the apartment. But my heart felt sick, like another terrible event was just on the horizon.

CHAPTER 20

REYFYRE AND I DID not speak any further about the pending ball. Instead, we unpacked our meager stacks of clothing while Charity filled three boxes and set them in the closet, so they teetered next to our empty suitcase.

"Anything that remains is a part of the apartment," Charity announced as she wiped her hands on her jeans and stepped toward the door. "I'll see you at three o'clock on Saturday." She didn't wait for a response and left with a small wave over her shoulder.

Reyfyre went out onto the balcony and shook the comforter one last time before he bundled it up in his arms and came back inside with a sour expression. "We are not ready."

"No kidding." I ran my hand through my hair. "Are we in the same block as Charity?"

"No. Her parents lived on the Upper West Side. They owned more than just the bar, so I can see why she chose to abandon this little closet. It's smaller than my boat."

I snorted. "Your boat is actually almost twice as big as this place."

He just nodded and glanced at the news still streaming on the television screen, and his jaw tightened, along with his fists. "If we go after them now, we'll both end up like those women."

The screen had transitioned to a dozen horrific deaths played out for the viewing public. I couldn't tear my eyes from the victim's faces. One moment, they seemed to be in ecstasy and the next, they transitioned into agony as they screamed their pain.

I could not imagine the shame and horror of the moment. Nor could I imagine willfully walking into a situation that could lead to that specific death. All because someone held a certain resemblance to me or just happened to catch Thor's fancy. It disgusted me, and airing this over and over instilled a debilitating fear in the viewing public.

The screen transitioned to a square where several people were on their knees with their wrists and ankles bound together. The caption indicated these were people who had tried to flee the moment they received their invitation. A table with an array of glistening blades stood before Thor. His fingers trailed over each knife until he selected one and approached the first offender, who happened to be a woman. He used the tip of the knife to tilt her head up enough for her to see his face. Her defiant brown eyes glared up at him.

"Your deaths will be as painful as humanly possible."

His sick smile twisted my gut again, and I swallowed the bile. I reached for the remote to turn the television off, but Reyfyre covered my hand.

"Let it play."

His deadly tone made me pull my hand back, and I wrapped my arms around myself, trying to look anywhere but at the television.

"There is a small chair on the balcony." He pointed without moving his gaze from the horror movie playing out on screen.

What Thor did to those poor people made the brutality he rained on Hippocrates seem like a snuggly hug. I noted just how good Thor had become with a simple fish knife before a violent shiver racked my form.

I retreated to the balcony and sat with my hands pressed to my ears and the mixology book open on my lap. I could still hear the screams despite cupping my ears and I just wanted it to end.

Reyfyre finally switched the television off. There were still six more people left to either dismember slowly, or disembowel, or skin them alive and then start carving off visible chunks of muscle until Thor hit an artery or plunged the knife into the victim's heart to stop the noise.

Silence descended like a fresh coat of snow and eventually Reyfyre stepped onto the small terrace.

"I'm not sure what to do," he whispered, pulling my attention to him.

"There's nothing you can do. When it's our time to go, we'll have to go. And then we'll see whether we have some serious award-winning acting skills or not." My mouth ran dry as the words tumbled from my lips. "In the meantime, we train every last second that we aren't bartending or sleeping."

He huffed a laugh. "Who said there was going to be any sleeping?"

My gaze darted to Reyfyre's tight profile. The meaning I thought was imbued in those words was definitely not the same thing that flitted through my brain.

"Um, if I'm going to be at the top of my game, I need at least eight hours of sleep." I could get by with six, but I worked better when well rested. And I had not been well rested since the day Reyfyre sauntered into that cave to free me.

"Then you better get it tonight because tomorrow, we start training in earnest. No more lollygagging."

"Lollygagging?"

"Yes. No more of that. Now the real work begins."

I moaned, but I followed through and climbed into bed after a few minutes of tense silence.

CHAPTER 21

I WISH I COULD have said Reyfyre had been kidding, but he left me very little room to study the mixology book that Charity had given me. Reyfyre had me at the local gym before the crack of dawn each day and he ran me like a pack mule.

The men at the gym tried to stay out of our way, but inevitably Reyfyre would point to one of them and then point to me and command them to beat the shit out of me. I did much better against the non-magical beings than I did against Reyfyre. But a punch was a punch, and I usually left sporting more black and blue than I cared to.

Saturday came fast and by the time we got to the bar for work, I was physically wrecked.

Charity brought us back to the office, handed us smocks with name tags and then pushed a piece of paper across the desk.

Reyfyre scanned the document. "Charity, this rent is insane. It isn't even half that of the slums up in Harlem."

She crossed her arms and jutted her chin out. "And?"

"And we have jobs." He waved toward the bar outside her office door. "We don't need a handout."

"Look. You're the closest thing to family that I have in the city and I'm not willing to rake you over the coals with a high rent. I don't need the money. You do. Let me help you get settled. We can re-evaluate the lease next year." Her eyebrows rose in such a way that I knew there was no arguing with this woman.

"Thank you," I said before Reyfyre could launch into another argument. "And next year, we can look at a figure that is more in line with other apartments in the building."

Reyfyre sliced me an annoyed glance, but then he nodded and signed the lease.

Charity smirked at me for a moment and then ripped off one of the copies and handed it to Reyfyre before stowing the paper in her file cabinet. The moment she left the office, her easy-going attitude tensed.

Charity set us up behind the bar and watched for a few minutes before she disappeared. When she returned, she wore a simple cocktail dress and she clicked the large screen over the bar to the news instead of a local basketball game. Several patrons moaned in response.

Her face paled as she stared at some of the early arrivals and then down at her outfit and then she slammed the remote down on the bar.

"I'm not going into debt for this stupid thing," she muttered and gave Reyfyre a half hug. "Make sure you're more entertaining than that tonight and you'll keep the patrons happy."

"Stay safe," Reyfyre said and glanced at me over her head.

I gave him a nod. "We've got this. You just keep your head low and do everything they demand, and you'll be back before the end of the night." I smiled at her, but my gut did that terrible twist that I remember back on Asgard just before the wraiths attacked. But just like last time, I could not pin down what disaster was waiting at my door.

Charity left and we focused on the patrons, whipping up their orders and chatting it up like we were old pros. By five, the place was packed, and every television was broadcasting the ball.

Festive music filled the bar as Reyfyre and I worked together to mix drinks. I had to reference the book near the register for a couple of the cocktails, but we were slinging bottles back and forth between us like circus jugglers and we had the crowd enthralled with our antics.

I sent a bottle of vodka his way, and Reyfyre's gaze caught on one of the television monitors. The bottle sailed past him and shattered on the floor. But even that didn't capture his attention away from the screen. An eerie silence settled on the bar as everyone stared at what was unfolding at the ball.

I finished the drink I was mixing, delivered it, and then stepped close to Reyfyre. Every muscle in his body was tight, and I threaded my fingers through his as red hair on the screen caught my attention.

Two guards held Charity's arms as she faced Thor. Her glare was murderous, and her mouth moved. I was certain by the expression on Thor's face that what was falling out of Charity's mouth was meant to scathe.

Thor backhanded her, and her head rocked to the side as blood and teeth spewed from her mouth.

"Damn it." Reyfyre's growl swept through me, and he tried to pull his hand from mine.

I tightened my grip, unwilling to let him be the hero. Not when it meant our demise.

"Let go," he growled at me.

"No. If you go running in to try to save the day, you will die. We both know that. We are not ready, Ray." I kept my voice low enough so only he could hear me and met his gaze.

"You expect me to just stand here and let this happen?" He waved at the television.

"No one can stop them. You know that just as well as I do." I stared him down, keeping hold of his hand as if my life depended on it. My heart thundered in my chest. "I cannot lose you."

He blinked at me as if my words hit a defuse button and then focused on the screen as the guards hauled Charity onto a table. Her thrashing and screaming carried over the music, and Thor's twisted smile as he stepped between her kicking legs made me see red.

It was Reyfyre's turn to clamp down on my hand.

"If I can't intervene, neither can you."

The crowd growled their unhappiness. The few who cheered were slapped into submission by the patrons as we all helplessly watched Thor ravage our friend. The vileness of the situation hit me harder than a sword to the gut.

The bar staff came to stand with us as our boss died a horrible death on national television. She wasn't the only one who met their maker tonight, and when I went to turn the television off, Andrew, the manager who had been left in charge, took the remote.

"It's against the law to turn it off." His voice trembled.

"Seriously?"

He pulled a laminated sheet from under the register and handed it to me. It was Odin's decree that all residents of New York must watch the ball in its entirety. Turning off the broadcast would lead to punishment.

I clenched my teeth against the stomach roll. I let my anger take a front seat as I glared at the television and the line of women waiting for death to claim them.

"We need to train more," Reyfyre whispered in my ear while his hard eyes never left the screen.

"GET UP!"

Reyfyre's growl lit my entire body on fire. Fury swept through me as I laid on the mat in the empty gym. We had broken into this building every night since Charity died, and Reyfyre was relentlessly hard.

Harder than he had ever been on me.

"Fuck you, Rey," I snarled from my vantage point on my back. "If you keep going at this pace, you'll break something and then I'll be useless to you."

He wiped his face and stepped back. "You have yet to take me down, Karen." He used my fake name like a weapon.

"But I have landed hits." I rolled and forced my tired body to my feet.

"I'm not a god. Landing hits is not good enough to take one down."

Of course, he was right. We had witnessed five more balls and dozens of women killed on camera since Charity died. Andrew took over the day-to-day operations of the bar for Charity's brother, and we packed in more and more patrons every day with our bartending act. We were in sync on the bar floor but on the mat in the dead of night, we acted like sworn enemies.

And the few scant hours of sleep each night didn't replenish my reserves at all.

"I'm tired," I admitted as I climbed to my feet.

"We'll sleep when we're dead."

His snapping comeback did nothing to quell the growing inferno inside me. I needed to change tactics if I was ever going to lay him out on the mat.

So, instead of charging at him like I had for hours on end, I used my feminine wiles and sashayed forward with my head held low. I slowly licked my lips as I stepped within striking distance. I placed my palms on the tight black shirt covering his chest and glanced up at him as I parted my lips enough to hopefully look sexy.

I didn't wait for any response from him; I yanked him toward me and tossed him over my hip. He landed on his back with a thud.

I swiped my palms together as if wiping dirt off, and Reyfyre's eyes narrowed at me.

"So, I guess honey does work better than brute force."

His leg swept mine out from under me, and I landed on my ass. Reyfyre slammed on top of me, pinning my wrists to the floor above my head. "That is a dangerous game, Kara."

His low voice caressed me in ways that brought forth a different kind of fire that I had thought long since died.

"Time is ticking, love. We don't have time for anything but brute force. If you approach Thor like that, you will be noticed and you will be on his fucking list by the end of the night. I do not want you anywhere near that bastard. Understand?" By the time he finished speaking, his voice had gone feral. "Not until we have a solid plan to bring him down."

He stayed on top of me longer than necessary as we had a stare down. His chest rose and fell as heavily as mine.

I huffed up at him. "We will never have a plan at this rate."

Reyfyre shifted so his knees pinned my sides between them, and he sat up. Running his hand through his hair, he took a deep breath. "Every time I try to put together a plan in my head, it's not good enough."

"Why not?"

He sighed. "Too many damn holes." He climbed to his feet, offering me his hand.

I let him help me up.

"Maybe a good night's sleep will help. We have not slept more than a few hours since we arrived. Sleep deprivation isn't great for making plans. And excuses of whether we are strong enough at this point is just plain procrastination." I didn't add the fact more people would die if we didn't do something soon. The number of deaths already weighed on both of us.

"I wish I had never thought of New York." His gaze slashed to mine.

"I get it. But sooner or later, we would have seen the news and would have come here anyway. The plan of hitting them in the capital is about as ludicrous as hitting them at the ball that Charity died at, and you know it."

"It still doesn't erase the guilt."

I knew enough about that deadly emotion. "Guilt won't change the past."

His lips tilted into a semblance of a smile.

"Let's go get some sleep and then maybe in the morning, we can figure out a viable plan together." I stepped toward the ropes blocking us into the ring.

Reyfyre grumbled under his breath but followed without a fight this time.

We passed another wanted poster with a drawing of my former self plastered on it with a hefty reward, and I scoffed at it. Too bad I didn't resemble the majestic Valkyrie pictured.

Reyfyre glanced at it and a sneaky smile found his lips. "I could be richer than Odin if I handed you in."

I slapped him in the chest with the back of my hand. There was no power in it, and he snickered in response.

Maybe our dreams would give us some answers; otherwise, we would be just as screwed as we were right now.

CHAPTER 22

REYFYRE THREW AN INVITITATION on the table in front of me. "It seems they've finally come to our section of Manhattan."

I stared at the summons and then glanced up at Reyfyre as dread formed in my belly. We both knew it was only a matter of time before this would happen, but we hadn't been able to figure out a viable plan to take out Odin and Thor because every ball had been at a different location with not enough time between the announcement and the actual ball, and this time we were on the invitation list.

"We could leave."

The glare he leveled at me made me shift. All routes out of the city were closed down for specifically that scenario. Even the marina was under scrutiny. They expected me to run if I was indeed hiding in New York City.

"Fine. But you know they are just grasping at this point. Their reward fell flat, too." But I wondered if it was because no one knew who I really was. Not even the few we called friends. If they had, I was sure the lure of easy money would have loosened their tongues. "Besides, you said the world is a big place. They don't know for sure that we are in New York."

He dipped his chin in a disgruntled nod and then turned to the window, scanning the street below. "This is the only city they've systematically been throwing these ludicrous events." He shifted his weight on the balls of his feet. Reyfyre did not like standing still for any period of time, much less when he was agitated. "It's a logical move because it was the first instinct I had, too—get lost in one of the largest cities."

He wiped his face and glanced around our tiny efficiency apartment. "How stupid could I be," he muttered under his breath and ran a hand through his dark hair. His aquamarine eyes found mine.

I stood and crossed to the spot in front of him and put my palm on his chest to try to soothe his self-loathing. "You didn't know."

The invitation on the table was a gaudy mixture of glitter and gold. Certainly, no woman on this planet would have chosen the color palette mixed with chunky block letters. I wrinkled my nose at the words announcing black-tie attire. We didn't have a lot of money and wasting it on fancy clothes was irrational. No one in this area of the city had that kind of money to throw away. "Can you glamour us with clothes?"

"Not unless you want us to both get caught." He glanced at his watch with a sigh. "That kind of magic will be recognizable. We should head to the thrift shops before work to see if they have anything fancy before everyone else picks them over."

We had to be at the bar in a couple of hours, and that job was necessary to keep up our nearly destitute personas. I did not know whether that would be enough time, but the ball was two days away, so if we were late, the bar would just have to deal with it. The idea of mobs trying to get their hands on cheap dresses that wouldn't fit right and the fistfights that were likely sent an itchy rash over my skin.

"Well, let's go. We don't want to be late for work." I grabbed my purse and his hand, pulling him toward the door.

Reyfyre followed as if he were going in front of a firing squad. There was zero enthusiasm in his mopey gait. As much as dress shopping subdued my attitude, the idea of being able to dance like the rest of the citizens appealed to me. I always had been on the outskirts as security staff while we were on Asgard, so I missed that thrilling part of the night.

And for some reason, being dressed to the nines and in Reyfyre's arms warmed my insides, despite the fact Thor would also be in the same ballroom.

We stepped onto the street and headed toward the thrift shop. "Have you ever been to a ball?"

"Can't say as I have." He dug his hands into his pockets and bent his head against the wind. "Why do you look so excited?" He nearly growled the words as he tossed me a side-eye.

"Because we get to eat, drink, and dance." I twirled around in my tennis shoes.

"For the love of... You are not Cinderella, sweetheart."

His curmudgeon surfaced again, and I rolled my eyes at him. He hadn't been this short or impatient with me since his daily beatdowns at the cabin.

"They could recognize you." A current of breath carried his words to me.

The spring in my step faltered. "I am not what I once was. Besides, my hair alone is a deterrent. No one from my past would be caught dead with rainbow hair." I chose my words carefully. There were too many people packing the streets right now, and greed had a way of putting a target on your back if you weren't careful.

"Which is why you will be suspected."

"Stop worrying. There are plenty of people who dye their hair." I slowed my gait as we approached the thrift store. A line wrapped around the building already. At this pace, we'd be lucky to find anything suitable left in the building.

"We're going to have to go into a bit of debt." His frown deepened as he turned me down another street, navigating us toward the more upscale shops on Fifth Avenue. "I just hope I have enough credit on the cards in my wallet to dress us appropriately."

"I will pay you back." It might take months, but I would make good on my debts to him. I expected him to shake his head or something, but his mind was working overtime enough, so I don't think he heard me. "Rey?"

He shook his thoughts away and focused on me. "What?"

"I will pay you back."

"Fine." He went back to brooding with a deep scowl on his face. "We just have to get through this and stay under the radar."

"We go as a couple, right?"

He nodded. "They still think a witch set you loose, so us as a couple will make us a little more invisible to them, especially since the fae were stomped out years ago." His voice was a shred of a whisper among the swish of fabric of those walking along the street around us.

The crowds thickened as we approached Fifth Avenue. He led me to one of the shops with formal gowns in the window and thankfully, the crowds hadn't descended on this shop yet.

"What about you?" I asked as I scanned the dresses. There wasn't any men's attire in this shop.

"I'll go next door to the men's shop and get a tuxedo after we find something suitable and unassuming for you."

Unassuming? *Nope.* That wouldn't do. I wanted to stick out. I wanted something sparkly and shapely that would get noticed. They wouldn't expect that. They'd expect someone on the run to want to blend in.

"You go. I'm sure I'll have found something by the time you get back." I crossed to a dress on display that was exactly the kind of statement I was going for. It shimmered in different colors with the changes in light. "This." I pointed at it.

His brittle laugh had me peering over my shoulder at him.

"Not a chance." Reyfyre scowled at me, but he reached for the price tag anyway. His eyebrows shot up.

"Too expensive?" I leaned over to catch a glimpse of the price.

"It's actually reasonable." He showed me the tag announcing it was well under three hundred dollars. "It's not understated, though."

"Let me at least try it on."

"Can I help you?" A salesperson with the name tag of Kitty approached us.

"I'd like to try this one on, please." I pointed at the dress despite Reyfyre's look of disdain.

Reyfyre moved to a rack of more frumpy gowns. "What about this?" He pulled out an awful dress in green that looked like it was made for an elderly woman. It would cover every asset

I had, and I'm sure make me appear frumpy as hell.

"No." I crossed to where other dresses sparkled and pulled out a blue number that caught my eye. It was sleeveless but had a single shoulder strap that connected the front and back together. It sparkled. "This one as well."

"Dear God." Reyfyre rolled his eyes as I went through and picked a handful of stunning dresses before following Kitty to the dressing room.

"Your boyfriend seems a bit uncomfortable with these," Kitty whispered as she handed me the dresses in my size.

I smiled and glanced out where he sat waiting for me to model each outfit. "Yeah, well, he is a bit insecure." I lifted a shoulder in a half-assed attempt at a shrug. "Do you have silver sandals, too?" I asked, taking in the array of dresses. Silver would go with all of them.

"What size?"

"Eight," I said.

Kitty wandered off as I stripped and pulled on the last dress I chose. I stood, inspecting the bright-red fabric on me.

Ugh. The color made me even more pale, especially with my hair resembling the Bifrost. This dress was a definite no.

I traded it for a black one just as Kitty returned and handed off a pair of slinky sandals.

I put them on and stared in the mirror. The slits reminded me of the outfit they sent me off to Earth to reap Hippocrates in. I tore it off with a shiver.

Which left both the blue and the iridescent dresses to try on. I put on the blue one and was satisfied enough at what I saw in the mirror to venture out to where Reyfyre sat.

He straightened, and his gaze ran down the length of the gown. His lips opened in surprise and then his gaze found mine. He slowly shook his head.

"Why not?" I looked down at myself and then back at him.

"Because." His voice went husky as he spoke the word.

"Fine." I turned and stomped back to the dressing room and stripped off the dress. But I put it on a separate hook. It was a contender. If I could make Reyfyre react like that, it meant I had hit my mark.

I pulled on the iridescent dress. The first one I had chosen. If Reyfyre hadn't given me shit for my choice, it probably would have been the only dress I tried on. And I studied my reflection critically, searching for flaws. But there were none.

The more I turned to view the different angles of the dress, the more I was sure this was the one I was walking out of this store with. I pulled the elastic from my hair and slid it on my wrist so I wouldn't lose it, finger combing my hair to get it in a semblance of order before I took one last glance in the dressing room mirror. This fit as if it had been made for me and it complemented my hair the way an eternity band complemented a solitaire engagement ring.

Reyfyre wasn't going to like this at all, but it was the cheapest out of the ones I pulled off the rack.

I stepped out of the dressing room.

"That's the one," Kitty said with a wide grin.

I smiled back at her and took a deep breath, stepping out into the dress shop.

Reyfyre's eyes widened, and the magazine he held slipped through his fingers. He blinked and wiped his face before meeting my gaze. "That will get you noticed."

I ran my fingers over the fabric, which was silky as opposed sequined like the blue dress. "I want this one."

Reyfyre stood and approached me. He spun me around to the mirror and stood behind me. "You will be noticed."

His tight voice in my ear sent tingles up my spine.

"Yes." I met his gaze in the mirror. "But you have nothing to worry about." I spun in his grip and stared up at him. "I am yours." I winked at him. "Besides, it's either this or the blue dress."

His lips tilted into a grin for a moment and then he seemed to recover.

"This is the least expensive of the lot," I said softly. "And this will look better with a tux than the blue dress."

"Fine." He surrendered to me and stepped back and waved at the silver sandals on my feet. "But if we're going with iridescent, then you should get matching shoes."

I glanced over at Kitty. "Do you have these type sandals that would match the dress?"

The saleswoman beamed and scurried away, only to come back a minute later with shoes that shimmered in the same manner. I tried them on and Reyfyre stepped back with a nod.

"We'll take these," he said, waving at me.

I hurried back to the dressing room and changed into my street clothes. By the time I stepped out, Kitty had the purchase rung up. She took the dress and put it in a garment bag and slipped the shoes into the box and dropped that into a separate bag with a smile.

"You are going to have so much fun at the ball." She winked at me. "Ours was so extravagant and elegant. This will fit in just fine." She handed me the bag.

"Thank you." Fun wasn't what I would call it, but at least I would look more stunning than I ever had. And Reyfyre would have to be very attentive all night. A secret smile slid onto my lips as I thought of his arms around me.

"If you're looking for bargain tuxedos, I suggest going across the street." She pointed at a clothing store that I wouldn't have guessed was a men's store. "Their rental fees are pretty reasonable."

"I'm buying mine, not renting." Reyfyre sent a glare at the saleswoman.

I smacked his arm. "Don't be such an ass. She was just trying to be kind and helpful."

Kitty met my gaze with a forced smile. "Yes. Well, in that case, Saks should have what you are looking for." She bowed her head and left us to help the others in the shop.

"Why do you insist on being nasty," I muttered as we left.

"I'm not wearing a tuxedo that others have worn." He shivered and turned us down the street. "But I'm also not paying Saks' prices either. That would kill my credit." He ushered me a few doors down to a Men's Warehouse store that had a fair number of customers already milling about. Reyfyre crossed to a free salesman. "I'd like to buy a black tuxedo with a white dress shirt and a black bow tie."

"Buy?" He turned toward us.

Reyfyre nodded.

"Right this way, sir." He escorted Reyfyre and me into a larger dressing room. He grabbed a tape measure and began to take Reyfyre's measurements, scribbling them down on a piece of paper. "I'll be right back, sir." He rushed out.

Reyfyre took off his shirt as he waited for whatever the salesman brought back. The wife-beater undershirt hid some of his build, but it gave me enough of an eyeful to wish I had some ice water.

The salesman returned with a rolling rack with an array of shirts and tuxedos in Reyfyre's size.

Without even glancing my way, Reyfyre slipped his jeans off, giving me a full view of his ass clad in the tight fabric of his underwear.

I had been with Reyfyre for close to a year, and I'd never seen him this undressed. He usually changed into his night clothes in the bathroom, sparing me this exceptional view. I did not expect the heat that rose in me as my gaze traveled over his ripped form.

I wanted his body to be against mine.

Right now.

I sucked air in through my nose and blinked, forcing the thought away. The last time I had this overwhelming emotional charge was the first time I saw Hippocrates.

My gaze bounced everywhere around this room except where he was, as I mentally berated myself for even entertaining the idea. Reyfyre was my trainer. My partner in bringing down Thor and Odin. This was not an appropriate response to have. Not when the lives and freedoms of this realm sat on our shoulders.

I slapped down the hunger inside me and glanced back at him as he pulled on a pair of black pants that he had taken from the rack himself.

And those pants looked phenomenal on him. He pulled on one of the tailored shirts and tucked it in before buttoning it and turning toward me as the salesman helped him with the jacket. Reyfyre dressed up in a tuxedo was just as stunning as I had been in the dress.

"You don't need a bow tie." I stood, crossing to him. I unbuttoned the top two buttons of the shirt and stepped back, assessing him. "But you do need a belt of some sort." I glanced at the salesman.

"Oh," he said and then scuttled out of the room.

"Bossy, aren't we," Reyfyre teased me. A smile toyed on his lips. "But black tie means black tie." He raised an eyebrow and went to button up.

I grabbed his hands and shook my head. "This. Just as you are. Well, with shoes, if you have to wear them." I eyed his bare feet.

"If I didn't know better..." He trailed off as the salesman pushed the doors open again.

Our trusty salesman carried both a belt and matching black leather shoes and a pair of black silk socks. "I thought you might need shoes, too?"

The hopeful lilt in his voice made me smirk and step away.

"Yes. And I'm going to pass on the bow tie. My girlfriend likes this look better." He grinned at me, playing up the couple angle. Reyfyre slipped on the belt, then sat next to me and pulled on the socks and slid his feet into the shiny black loafers before stepping before the mirror again. His gaze scanned his reflection and then he nodded. "I'll take it."

"But sir, you haven't tried on the other suits," the salesman said.

Reyfyre turned to me and spread his arms. "Do I need to try on the others?"

I shook my head. "That fits you perfectly."

"This one will do, along with the belt, shoes, and socks." Reyfyre sat beside me and took off the shoes, shoved the socks inside them and handed them to the salesman. He undressed and handed over the outfit as well.

"I'll be at the counter when you're finished in here." The salesman turned away and walked out of the room, but there was no excitement in him like when he came in here with the rack.

Reyfyre pulled on his clothes and glanced at me with a smirk. "I checked the tags before I chose that one to try on. I don't think our salesman saw me do that either. The one I chose is close to what we paid for your dress. The rest on that rack are thousand-dollar tuxes," he whispered as he led me out of the room.

No wonder the salesman was disappointed. I glanced at the rack and couldn't tell the difference between the ones hanging there and the one Reyfyre bought.

As soon as we were outside with the garment bags slung over Reyfyre's shoulder and the shoe bags in my hand, his light mood changed. "That was far more than we could afford right now," he grumbled. "I may have to insist on payment for taking the boat south."

I cocked my head and then nodded. "It would be nice to get paid for that." I smirked at him. "Especially since it took me a bit to get my sea legs."

Reyfyre suppressed a smile. "I'll see what I can do." He didn't say anything more and once our clothing was stowed away in our closet, we headed off to the bar for another noisy night of serving drinks and hot wings to the younger crowd.

A new, more acute tension built between Reyfyre and me, one that could explode, and I wasn't sure either of us could survive the fallout.

CHAPTER 23

THE DAY OF THE ball arrived, and both Reyfyre and I sat in salon chairs. My hair had been washed and trimmed, and the stylist was curling it in small ringlets. Reyfyre sat across from me, and his long locks had been chopped to a length near mine. His stylist was drying it so the sides feathered back. The gentle flow of his hair made his handsome features stand out even more.

I couldn't help staring. Ever since we went to get clothing for this ball, things had been strained. An underlying current weaved between us, threatening to ignite. Even sparring with him in the gym had been more brutal than before, as if our demons were finally surfacing.

He glanced in the mirror and our eyes met. He held my gaze longer than normal and then his eyes roamed over the curls framing my face. A soft smile of appreciation formed; then his line of sight drifted away, punctuating that strangeness that had invaded our relationship.

When we finished, my hair was pinned up with a few curls framing my face in shimmering colors that would match the dress perfectly.

Reyfyre paid for both of our cuts and escorted me back to our apartment a few blocks away. Thankfully, the route he took wasn't one of the wind tunnels that would ruin our hair. We changed in silence and then turned to each other from across the apartment.

"You look..." Reyfyre inhaled and smiled. "Stunning, Kara." He used my real name as opposed to Karen, which had been what he called me here since the first day we arrived.

It's what my fake ID stated and it was close enough to my given name not to totally screw up.

"You don't look so bad yourself."

He crossed and offered me his elbow. "Are you ready for this?"

My belly jumbled with nerves. I was sure I wouldn't be able to eat a damn thing. And I prayed I was able to keep a straight face when confronted with Odin and Thor, especially considering I wanted to see their heads rolling on the floor.

Reyfyre hesitated by the table as he swiped up the invitation. "We both have to act as if this is an honor, and a fun evening to drink and dance, but we can't get drunk. That's a surefire way to screw up. And I rather like your head attached to your neck." His eyes flared with concern. "Can you do this?"

I glared at him. "Can you?"

"I've been acting my whole life. It comes easy to me. But I am worried about you. I know how much you hate them, and I can see it in your eyes right now. If I can, they will, too. So, squash it down and pretend this is our first date or fiftieth date, or whatever you need to do to fake it properly. Got it?" His hard gaze bore into mine.

"A date?" I cocked an eyebrow at him, pulling the only thing I could out of the conversation that would help me, especially considering things had been weird between us.

"You know what I mean." He huffed as he dragged me out the door and locked up behind him.

Instead of walking, like we normally would, Reyfyre hailed a cab and read off the address when we got into the back.

"You and everyone else in Midtown," the cab driver muttered and took off.

It took another fifteen minutes driving instead of what would have taken five walking. And as soon as we pulled up to a red-carpet entry, Reyfyre threw a twenty at the cab driver and slid out of the car on the street side. He came around as I opened the door and offered me his hand.

Nerves bit at my skin and I fidgeted as I stood next to him. He laced his fingers through mine and squeezed.

"Date, remember?" he whispered in my ear and then dropped my hand, planting his firmly on my lower back. Flashes blinded me as cameras clicked off. We weren't the only ones being photographed. I nearly broke away from Reyfyre to smash the camera that captured my image, but Reyfyre tightened his grip on me. "Smile, Karen," he whispered through his own sparkling grin.

I glanced up at him and smiled, but only because he looked so damn handsome that I forgot myself. His gaze dropped to mine and his forced smile softened. That electrical buzz passed between us again.

"Remember, you are mine," he said softly.

I cocked an eyebrow at him.

He responded with an eye roll. "You know what I mean."

Actually, I did not know what he meant. His declaration that I was his made my insides go all gooey. I faced forward, probably reading more into his words than there really was, and I plastered a strained smile on my face. It was as fake as a three-dollar bill.

Reyfyre handed the guard at the door our invitation.

"Names," the guard snapped.

"Karen Johnson and Ray Davis," Reyfyre said.

"Identification." The guard put his hand out.

I was glad Reyfyre had me bring my pocketbook. Both our IDs were inside. The only things in Reyfyre's pocket were the keys to our apartment and his money clip, which only had a few bills on it now that the cab fare was paid. I handed the licenses to the guard.

He studied them and then handed them back with a nod. I stowed them away as we entered the building. Reyfyre guided me and the only indication that I had that we were now in the presence of our enemies was the tightening of his hand on my back. I snapped my purse closed, schooled my features into one of pleasant curiosity, and tilted my head up.

We were in a damn receiving line. My heart hammered in my chest and Reyfyre's thumb started to caress my lower back. The contact didn't help the nerves in my core. It did something entirely different, and heat flushed my cheeks as we stepped closer to introductions to the men I wanted to kill.

Each party who stepped away from Odin and Thor brought us closer, and Reyfyre's thumb kept caressing me on a specific erogenous zone that had my attention on him and not the two assholes in front of us. It was as if he were intentionally distracting me.

And then we were in front of Odin.

Reyfyre bowed in respect but didn't touch his knee to the floor. I curtseyed like he showed me earlier in the day before we went to get our hair done.

"Your Majesty," Reyfyre said in reverence. "I am Ray Davis and this is my girlfriend, Karen Johnson. We are pleased to attend tonight."

Odin's stare fixed on me, and he subtly recoiled enough for me to catch it. "What interesting hair," he said after he recovered from his sneer.

"Oh, thank you, Your Majesty." I let my hand flit near my hair. "I had it done up just for the ball."

"I think he's talking about your color, not your curls," Reyfyre said loud enough to draw a smirk from Thor.

"Oh." I smiled. "I've had it this way for the past couple of years. It's certainly better than my mousy brown hair used to be."

"Ah, well, enjoy the ball." Odin focused on the next guest, dismissing me without so much as another word.

Then we were in front of Thor, and all I could see in my mind was him slicing Hippocrates. I blinked and smiled as I fidgeted. Reyfyre was already bowing, and I rushed through my curtsey. His gaze lingered on me, but Reyfyre pulled me away before I could say anything. It was more abrupt than Odin's dismissal.

Once we got to the line for the bar, Reyfyre's glare caught me off guard.

"What is wrong with you?" I asked in a hushed voice.

"He was looking at you with interest," he hissed in my ear.

I glanced over my shoulder. True enough, Thor's gaze was still on me, and he smiled his signature grin at me, like I was fair game in a sea of women fawning over him. But most of those women were doing it for show. When it came right down to it, they would pass on what he had to offer. At least, if they believed the rumors and the live shots from prior balls.

But Thor was arrogant to a fault, just like on Asgard. He'd take their lives just for his sadistic pleasure.

"I knew I shouldn't have said yes to that outfit," Reyfyre mumbled as we closed in on the bar. "What do you want?" he asked.

"Long Island iced tea," I answered, knowing it would piss him off even more.

"I'm not carrying you home again." He turned to the bartender after reminding me of my last escapade with Long Island iced tea. He indeed had carried me the couple of blocks from the bar because the alcohol in those cocktails rendered me stupid drunk. "Two mimosas please."

"That's for wussies," I muttered. But he was right: if I got drunk, I would blow our cover. Although we couldn't strike them down tonight and live to tell the tale, it still was a rampant desire in my blood.

Music started up, and people either lingered at the buffet table, picking at the food, or made a beeline to the dance floor.

With our drinks in hand, Reyfyre led me to the buffet. He loaded a plate for the both of us and then steered me to a table. I didn't want to waste the night away picking at food and glowering at those dancing.

I'd rather be glowered at. "Dance with me," I said before he could settle into his chair.

He peered up at me with raised eyebrows and nodded toward the plate, as if we could really stomach the food right now. My belly was far too jumpy to eat.

I drained my glass, placed the empty next to the overloaded plate on the table, and parked my pocketbook next to it in plain sight. I didn't care whether someone lifted it. It only had our licenses and some gum.

Then I removed the glass from his hand and pulled him toward the dance floor, where dozens of couples were already swaying to the music.

"Karen," he warned, but he didn't dig his feet in to stop me.

I spun on my toes and faced him.

Reyfyre took in his surroundings and then wrapped his arms around my waist, pulling me close as he stared down at me. "I haven't done a waltz since I was little and standing on my mother's shoes." Then he began to move me around the dance floor like an expert.

My heart soared and my stomach dropped at the same time. "You are such a liar."

Dimples appeared in his cheeks, and he smiled in a way I had never seen. It made his eyes glitter like a thousand suns. Then a hand landed on his shoulder and that gleam disappeared, replaced by irritation so thick, I almost choked on it.

"May I cut in?"

Fuck.

Reyfyre sent a strained smile over his shoulder at Thor and relinquished his hold on me. "Yes, you may, Your Majesty." But his words sounded clipped and the expression of worry on his face made me pause.

Reyfyre backed away and found a spot at the side of the crowd to keep an eye on us. Thor had already started to move me around the floor, and I unglued my gaze from Reyfyre and smiled up at Thor as heat filled my cheeks. I wanted to throw him over my hip and rip his head clean off, but neither of us would get out of here alive if I did that. My gaze kept wandering back to Reyfyre.

"I could make you cry out to the heavens," Thor whispered in my ear.

I had to stomp on the growl that crawled up my throat as I forced my gaze back to his. I slowly blinked up at him. "Excuse me?" I attempted to speak as politely as I could without sounding offended.

"I could make you forget your boyfriend." His Cheshire-cat grin appeared.

It was the one I had always wanted to smash off his face.

Today was no different, but I couldn't react with my usual snark.

My cheeks heated with my building fury, and the flush moved to what was exposed of my chest. I was sure Thor thought he was turning me on, but this wasn't sexual. It was fueled by an anger so raw, all I could do was let it burn through my skin instead of lashing out.

His arrogance fanned the flames, and I pretended to be flustered and humbled by the great god Thor paying extra attention to me. Thankfully, I only had to endure another twirl around the floor before the song ended.

"While I appreciate the attention," I pulled away from Thor, "Ray has my heart." I batted my eyes and turned, sauntering away, swinging my hips a little more than normal as I shot to Reyfyre across the dance floor.

As I approached, he kept his poison-tipped glare to the spot behind me where Thor was. Reyfyre's tight jaw and fisted hands were enough to shoot straight to my heart. It was a look of insecurity and self-doubt, all rolled up in indignation.

I stopped close to him and when he didn't glance down at me, I palmed his cheek. At my touch, his gaze dropped to mine. I rose on my tiptoes and gently pressed my lips to his, staking a public claim in front of Thor, so he'd back off and forget about me.

This was supposed to only drive home my point to Thor, but Reyfyre deepened the kiss, pulling me closer to his hard body. When his tongue ran a slow trail over my lips, I opened my mouth, giving him access. Our tongues rolled together, looping slowly and seductively enough for my knees to weaken. It was tender, yet possessive, and I think my foot lifted off the ground like some smitten schoolgirl.

His hand cupped my cheek; his fingers threaded into my hair and a low groan came from his chest. For a moment, in Reyfyre's arms, the world around us disappeared and there was only this feral connection pulsing through my muscles.

Then Reyfyre gasped and pulled his mouth away from me. He pressed his forehead against mine with his eyes still closed and growled through pants nearly as needy as mine.

"We need to go," he whispered, and his eyes flashed open, meeting mine. Fire burned in his irises like I had never seen. This wasn't anger either. It was something wild in nature, waiting to ravage me. Without pausing for me to speak, he took my hand, grabbed my purse off the table, and started toward the door, weaving through the crowd as if the world were ablaze.

The doorway came into view and then Thor was there, blocking our exit. His eyes sparkled with a challenge.

Damn it all to hell.

We both pulled up short, and Reyfyre tucked me into his side in a protective reflex.

"Where do you think you two are going?" He crossed his arms.

Reyfyre's lips twitched into a ghost of a smile. "To scratch an itch, if you know what I mean." He winked at Thor.

"No one leaves until they've had a drink from the truth fountain." He pointed to a fountain of flowing chocolate. "So, march your asses over there and grab a cup and then we'll have a chat before you go. Or, if you can't wait, you can fuck her in the coat closet over there." He pointed to his right, and both our gazes moved in that direction. "And maybe I can watch."

I recoiled.

Thor tilted his head. "Would you rather I join you?"

"Um. No," Reyfyre said. "We don't need an audience. And I certainly have her needs covered, so while the offer to join us is...interesting...I think not."

Thor's gaze narrowed.

Reyfyre pivoted and led me toward the coat closet. Once inside, he closed the door and slammed me against it. He pressed his body against mine and nipped at the side of my throat. "Can you really withstand the truth serum?" he whispered and licked a line up my throat to my ear.

We had discussed this multiple times over the last couple of days. We had our stories straight, and I was certain I could pull it off.

"Yes." I breathed the word out as he nibbled my lobe, sending shocks through my body.

He pulled back and searched my eyes. "Was that an answer to my question, or me nibbling your ear?" He started to unbuckle his belt.

"Oh." My gaze shot to his hands and then back to his face. His eyes were dark and definitely not what I was used to.

"That's not an answer, Karen," he snarled and pulled at my dress, lifting it up high enough to press his hips against my core.

Reyfyre was harder than stone as he pressed against me.

My mind stalled, and I pushed my palm against his chest. His heartbeat slammed against my hand. My gaze jumped from him to where we were, and I shook my head as he rocked his hips against mine, causing a friction that heated me from head to toe.

He grinned down at me. "So, I'm a two-minute wonder, huh?"

I stared at him a moment and then I snorted a laugh. "I doubt that very much." This was him acting the part.

He leaned close and whispered, "Can you withstand the serum?"

"Yes." This time I shouted the word and banged my palm against the door. At least I thought I could. Especially with the feel of Reyfyre hard against me. That might be all my mind could focus on anyway.

He groaned in a way that added to the heat between us. And then he panted as he pulled away with a smile.

"I'm going to need to find a ladies' room," I said.

"No. I want my cum sliding down your legs. I want every man here to know you're mine." His voice rang out loud enough to make me blush.

He nodded to the door as he buckled his pants. He shook his head, making his hair a little more disheveled than it had been, and he pulled a few locks out of my hair, making me look less put together. And then he stared at my lips.

He stepped in and slammed his mouth to mine. This kiss was wild and untamed and, frankly, exactly what I expected from Reyfyre. And holy shit did my body react. His hands caressed my breasts through the dress until I thought I'd scream.

He abruptly stepped away and scanned me again. This time, he nodded. "Try to straighten out your dress. We wouldn't want anyone to catch sight of your drenched panties." A dimple appeared, and he reached beyond me to open the door. He straightened out his belt as he stepped into the hallway.

I followed, straightening my dress out.

Thor stood near the entrance, acting as a buffer to anyone trying to escape the event. He glanced our way and then nodded at the fountain.

Reyfyre didn't hesitate and he didn't so much as send a glance my way. He grabbed a cup, filled it, and then downed the liquid, smacking his lips together as if it were a tasty treat. He crossed to Thor without looking at me.

Doubts as to what happened in the closet filled me, raging through me like wildfire. I crossed and took a cup, but I took a small amount as Reyfyre and Thor chatted. I drank the sickly-sweet liquid, thinking it would gag me at any moment. Chocolate sweetness slid down my throat, numbing me. My limbs felt heavy, as if I'd drunk too much, but my brain was clear enough to understand this was a truth serum.

I glanced at Reyfyre, but he ignored me, chatting it up with Thor as if I didn't exist. As I approached, he glanced at me.

"You can go," Thor said to him and turned his attention to me.

Reyfyre walked out the door as if ditching me.

A punch in the gut would have been easier to take.

Thor pulled out a picture from inside his vest. It was a pretty Valkyrie with grand black wings. "Have you seen this person around the city?"

I glanced at the picture. My picture. I hadn't seen that person in over three thousand years. And the last time was in the mirror on Asgard. My gaze moved out the door. "No."

"On any of your travels on Earth?" He raised an eyebrow.

"No. I haven't seen her around here." I moved my gaze from him to the door and back. "Why did he leave?" I waved at the door with a whine as Reyfyre's actions hit home. "I mean…" I waved at the coatroom and then dropped my purse as nerves and an underlying devastation crawled into my muscles. I bent over to pick it up, but Thor was faster. He handed it to me.

"Men can be dicks. The offer is still on the table, though." He smiled.

Yeah, offer the poor excuse for a human girl a death sentence. No, thank you.

I shook my head. "He still has my heart. But thank you for the generous offer. I'm sure there's someone here who would be more than willing to take you up on that. But I need to find Ray." I stepped toward the door.

"Kara?"

Thor's question rang in my head.

I turned. "My name's Karen." After all, that was what my license in my pocketbook said. It was the name I had my job under. So, in a way, it was a form of truth. My skin tingled and then settled, as if it wasn't quite a big enough lie to trigger the serum. "It was…interesting meeting you after seeing you on television so many times.”

Thor pursed his lips. “Go on. Your boyfriend is probably waiting for you outside.” He turned away with a bit of a growl.

I didn’t want to stab a gift horse in the mouth, and I scurried outside. Reyfyre stood on the sidewalk, looking in the direction of our apartment. He held out his hand, and I took it.

He had a truth serum in him. So did I, but I wasn’t as concerned with what might drop out of my mouth. But I had to know what had happened to him back in the coat closet.

“How much of the situation in the coat closet was real?”

Reyfyre glanced at me, and his eyes flashed. “You shouldn’t have kissed me the way you did.”

“You did not answer my question.”

His grip on my hand tightened, but he kept silent, gritting his teeth.

The walk home took a little longer than five minutes, but with the busy streets, a cab home would have been longer. Reyfyre’s silent treatment burrowed under my skin, flaring my temper.

The apartment building was empty and eerily silent as the rest of the residents were at the party. Reyfyre held the door for me and as soon as I walked in, I threw my pocketbook across the room and spun on him.

"Answer me!"

The door shut behind him with a bang, and he grabbed me by the arms, slamming me into the closed entry. Before I could balk at him, his lips were on mine, kissing and nipping as his tongue pillaged my mouth. His hands were in my hair one moment and then caressing my body in a way that broke down all my barriers.

When he came up for air, he hissed, "You really shouldn't have done that, Kara."

My fingers fumbled on the buttons of his shirt as he again lifted my dress, but this time, he didn't stop when he got to my waist. He pulled the fabric up and over my head before he tossed it over his shoulder. He clamped my wrists and held them above my head.

Black smoke wisped around him, each tendril caressing me as if they were as solid as his hands. His eyes were the color of cobalt now as he leaned in to kiss the tops of my breasts. "Do you have any idea what you've done," he growled and scratched his teeth across my bra. His free hand slid between my legs, rubbing me in such slow strokes that I moaned.

"What have I done?" I gasped, and my eyes
rolled back as he removed the rest of my
clothing.

"You have awakened the beast in me." His
mouth covered one breast and then the other,
teasing me until my nipples were hard peaks.
His finger dipped inside me, and I groaned in
response.

"Yes," I whispered as every cell in my body
quivered. I wanted the beast right now, not the
calm, controlled man I had lived with for nearly
a year now.

"How much of the closet was real?" He took
my hand and ran it along the front of his pants.
"You tell me?" He released my hands and
stripped his coat as I pushed him toward the
bed. "But if I had fucked you in the coat closet,
every single Asgardian in that place would have
known a wraith was present."

I tore at his shirt, wanting him as naked and
exposed as I was. I couldn't get his clothing off
fast enough, and he chuckled.

One glance at the black smoke traveling from
the corners of his eyes sent ice slithering over
my spine, cooling some of the heat he had
produced.

This was Asgard's worst enemy.

"Truth. Do you really want what you see before you?" His tone mocked me, as if seeing his wraith side would somehow knock this frantic lust right out of me.

My eyes cataloged every inch of him from the crown of his head, down his chiseled chest to his hard manhood standing at attention, and beyond at his powerful legs. When my gaze locked back on his, some of the smoke tendrils had faded, as if my slow inspection of him had softened his need.

His black irises stared down at me, waiting for an answer, but underneath, I could still see Reyfyre. My Reyfyre.

I closed the distance between us. "Yes, Rey. I want what I see before me. Do you want what you see?"

He growled in what I believed was a yes, but he didn't even spare me a glance. His smoke tendrils shot out, yanking me into his arms. His mouth hovered over mine. "Last chance," he whispered.

"Shut up and fuck me." I pulled his lips to mine, and the kiss seared through me like a raging fire eating away at my inhibitions. All these months with him, and I'd only seen the fae side.

His wraith side was wild and even more demanding than the fae.

And my, oh my, he was definitely *not* a two-minute wonder.

CHAPTER 24

WE LAY IN BED, side by side, staring at the ceiling as we caught our breath. Reyfyre covered his face and then ran his hands up into his hair. The wraith had given up control after his last orgasm. The smoke slipped back inside him, leaving only his tired blue eyes.

Eyes that I had grown to adore.

He finally turned his head toward me. "I didn't hurt you, did I?"

"Ha." I couldn't help the outburst. I was Valkyrie. A little rough sex wasn't going to harm me in the least. "You didn't." I met his gaze. "And I didn't break you either."

A genuine smile appeared, one that made his eyes sparkle and dimples appear in his cheeks. It was the kind of smile that I could stare at for an eternity.

"I've had a girlfriend or two in the past, but it never worked out. They left at the first sign of the wraith. And then I had to skip town before word spread." His smile slipped, and he moved his gaze back to the ceiling. "You told Thor that I had your heart while you were under the truth serum."

When his gaze landed back on me, I dipped my head once.

"Since when?"

That's a good question. And one I'd been asking myself since the dress shop.

"I don't know." I chewed on my lower lip, trying to pinpoint just when my heart had gotten involved without my permission. "Things changed after the spiders. You relaxed a little and while you still pushed me to continue on our journey, it wasn't the same as the driving asshole who punished me daily with his sword." I allowed my eyes to close for a brief moment as I inspected my memories. "You let your walls down."

"So, shelving the asshole did this." He waved between us.

A crack of laughter exploded from my mouth, and a new thought possessed my mind. "You did all that shit after the coat closet on purpose, didn't you?"

Reyfyre bunched his mouth into an amused pucker and his shoulders twitched in a shrug. "If you were hurt and confused, you'd be more likely to get away with lying because the other emotions would temper your natural reactions."

"That was genius. But Thor propositioned me again, and he called me Kara as I was walking out. I corrected him by telling him my name is Karen. But the fact I turned may have planted a seed of doubt."

"He let you go." He rolled on his side, facing me. "We've both seen what he does to those he suspects. Or those who try to bypass the truth serum. If he suspected, he would have detained you."

His gaze raked over my naked form. "Besides, you look drastically different than that drawing. Granted, you're still as beautiful, but I am partial to the package before me, including the hair." He lifted a piece of my hair and twirled it between his fingers before he dropped it and put his hand over mine.

"I'm getting used to it." I reached out and ran my hand through his dark hair. The silky strands tickled my fingers. "Is this your natural color?"

"Yes. The only glamour I have is focused on my ears and it's obviously not enough for either Thor or Odin to detect."

I traced the curve of his ear, feeling what I couldn't plainly see. His eyes slowly closed, as if I were lulling him into some hypnotic state. His lips parted and a long sigh dropped.

"Can we not talk about them anymore?" I just wanted to enjoy this after-sex bliss for a little while longer. It would end soon enough.

"We don't have to talk at all." His eyes crawled open and desire burned in them. He waggled his eyebrows suggestively.

"I need sleep and I don't think my body could survive another—" I glanced at the clock and calculated how long we had been going at it. "Three hours of screwing around, anyway." I yawned and rolled closer, curling into the crook of his arm.

Reyfyre's eyebrows arched, and he recoiled. "What are you doing?"

I couldn't tell whether the edge in his voice was from fear or annoyance. "Going to sleep, why?"

He pushed me away. "I don't cuddle."

"Oh, but you spoon." I lifted my head to send visual daggers at him.

He huffed. "That was out of necessity."

His argument was valid, but it still didn't help my wounded pride. "So, you'd screw around again but you won't cuddle?" I clarified, just to be sure.

"Exactly. I need space when I sleep. I don't like to feel restricted."

I snorted at him. "We shared the same sleeping bag all the way across the continent."

"You just made my point. I hated being cramped."

I rolled my eyes at him. "And yet you snored like a bear. You are bizarre." I rolled away from him, intent on trying to catch some sleep but the flare of irritation might not allow that to happen.

The television turned on, and I sent a stern look in his direction. But the way his face blanched had me sitting up and focusing on the screen.

Reyfyre turned up the volume and ran a hand through his hair. My picture, along with two other women, one of whom resembled my former self, filled the screen, along with a demand for information. The screen split, showing each of us at the fountain and the amount of truth serum in the cups we drank. The announcer notified the public that the amount was not acceptable to the rulers and that all three women needed to turn themselves in for further scrutiny by order of Odin.

"Fat fucking chance," Reyfyre muttered.

A camera shot of the auditorium where the ball had been showed at least a dozen people on their knees with their hands bound behind their backs. Thor stepped into the picture with a sword and a smile that chilled me to the core.

"Just to be clear, if the three women we are looking for do not show up, every single guest who remains"—the camera panned to show a larger group beyond the twelve people behind Thor—"will end up like this." He turned and the sword whistled through the air.

At first nothing happened, and then the head of the man directly behind Thor wobbled off, sending a geyser of blood onto the floor.

"You have an hour before another innocent dies."

Thor's stare in the camera sent a rash of chills through me as the crowd screamed their shock in the background.

The camera cut to our pictures again in the background of a very shaken newscaster.

Reyfyre shut off the television.

"I have to go. I can't let those people die." I moved to get out of bed. I could not stay in the safety of this apartment. Not when innocent lives were hanging in the balance.

Reyfyre's hand clasped my wrist in an uncompromising hold and his jaw tightened. "That is what they are betting on. That is what they've done for every ball across the city. You know the outcome."

"No. Tonight, I kill that bastard before he can kill the other women." I twisted my arm out of his grip and headed toward the door, where my discarded dress still lay in a bunch.

By the time I pulled the fabric over my head, Reyfyre in all his glory stood between me and the door. He spread his fingers out toward me, trying to stop me from leaving.

"Kara, do not fall for their tricks." Unease wrinkled the corners of his eyes. "I do not wish to see your execution on television."

I stared into his frantic eyes. I had never seen Reyfyre unhinged before. Anxious or annoyed, yes, but not like this. The edges of his eyes bled black smoke, as if his emotional turmoil was unleashing his wraith again.

I smoothed my dress and straightened my back. "I will not be the only one who returns. I will protect myself, even under the influence of a truth serum. And then figure out how to get one of the guard's swords and end this."

His hands fell to his sides. "You know what happens. You've seen it at least a dozen times. The truth serum does not matter. Thor has decided that the three of you will be his personal entertainment for the night." He ran his hand down his face. "If he chooses you first, he will know. You won't die like the others, Kara." His eyes pleaded with me. "Stay until we can have a better plan in place."

I bit my lower lip as conflicting emotions battered my insides. A large part of me wanted to fall back in that bed and forget this realm. But my values at the core of my soul would not allow me to sit this one out. "I am a protector of the people, Rey. It's what got me into trouble to begin with, but I cannot ignore this. Innocents will die." I pointed to the television. "I cannot live with being the reason for that type of carnage."

His lids dropped closed, draping his cheek with dark lashes. He banged the back of his head against the door a few times before his eyes cracked open. "And if I force you to stay?" Tendrils of black smoke reached for me.

"I will never forgive you." The words slipped out before I could catch them, but I knew as much as it hurt him, it was the truth.

He squeezed his eyes tight and fisted his hands. The smoke stopped traveling toward me, but it encompassed him completely. To the point he became all wraith—a still black form blocking my exit.

"If you go, I will not be here to see if you get back or not." Pain laced the words dropping all around me, as if he filled the room with his essence. "I cannot see another person who I love be torn apart by those monsters." He moved by me so fast that the breeze he created nearly knocked me into the wall.

I turned and scanned the apartment. If he was there, he had cloaked himself well enough for me not to pick him up. My heart thundered in a way that made my chest hurt. "Where can I find you?"

No answer. "Reyfyre?" Silence. "You wouldn't let those people die," I whispered and turned away. I stepped out of the apartment on bare feet without so much as my pocketbook. If Thor and Odin did catch me, they'd have nothing to lead them back to Reyfyre.

My throat tightened and tears threatened, and I picked up the pace until I was in an all-out run with my dress billowing behind me. My vision blurred and my chest hitched. I didn't stop, because if I did, I would turn back. Back to Reyfyre and a future of self-loathing that would eventually tear us apart.

I barreled into the conference center ballroom with the grace and stealth of a bull in a china shop. Heat painted my cheeks, sliding down to my jaw as I skidded to a stop. Reyfyre's words kept looping in my head, crushing my heart. I slowed as my hitching breath made everyone turn my way.

I wasn't the only one who came back, but I was the last one.

Thor was poised with his blade against another innocent's throat, ready to decapitate him.

A guard grabbed my arm and forced a full glass of the chocolate truth serum down my throat, making sure I swallowed every drop. Then he threw me forward. I stumbled, landing on my hands and knees. Tears still streaked my face, and they wouldn't stop running like faucets.

Thor handed the sword off to a guard and strode across the floor. As he closed the distance, his gait slowed.

My reaction was definitely appropriate based on the other televised balls. However, this one felt different. They hadn't killed the attendees. Only those they deemed suspect. My mind raced over the little I had witnessed via the television screen. I stayed where I was and covered my face, trying to get control.

Thor's soft touch on the crown of my head almost blasted the fury through this devastation. "You took your sweet time, Karen." There was nothing friendly in his voice.

"Ray and I argued. He is threatened by you. He's seen the footage of the other balls." My voice hitched with each syllable. I wiped my face and glanced to my side.

Thor crouched down close to me. "I told you I could make you forget him." He tucked a hair behind my ear. "Is your name really Karen?"

I met his gaze, trying not to glare. "Yes." It was on my license. It was the name my paychecks came in with; it was on the lease to the apartment. At the thought of the apartment, the tears threatened again.

"Why are you crying?"

"Because Ray doesn't want me to die tonight." It was the truth without any hidden innuendo to it. "And neither do I. But you're Thor." I waved my hand at him. "And we've both seen the televised balls." I covered my face again. None of the words burned. I didn't even wince once. I sniffled. "No matter how hot you are and whatever pleasure you may give, it still means my death. But I couldn't watch another person die instead." I realized I was prattling on. "I'm sorry for babbling, Your Highness."

He ran his hand down my back, as if checking for wings. "Are you the traitorous Valkyrie?"

My throat tightened at the familiarity of his hand, and I stared at him over my fingertips. "No." It came out with a whine, as if I couldn't believe he would ask me that. Besides, I was not a traitor. I protected the innocent. That was why I was here and not on the run again.

He smirked and helped me to my feet. "Let me rephrase that. Are you a Valkyrie?"

Without the word traitorous, I wasn't sure I could pull off the lie. "Why are you asking me that? I already told you I wasn't." I nearly gagged out the last sentence. I sniffled and grabbed a napkin off the nearest table to blow my nose.

Thor's smug smirk fell into confusion as I cleared the snot from my nose in the discarded rag. It was very unladylike, and quite gross if you asked me, but it sidetracked the questioning enough to save my ass. I put the cloth napkin back on the table and turned back to him.

"May I please go back home now? I have to try to salvage my relationship." I pointed toward the door, knowing it was a long shot. None of the other women had ever asked to leave. They all cried as they kneeled, waiting for their turn at being pleasured before dying. It was quite pitiful.

He shook his head. "No one is leaving until I can make a determination on who is being truthful and who isn't."

Same operating procedure as the last dozen balls that had been aired. It was his twisted game, and I openly glared at him. The other two women were on their knees, staring at the floor as if too stunned to speak.

He grabbed my upper arm and led me to a spot near them and pointed to the ground.

Although every muscle argued with me not to fall to my knees, I did without hesitation. I would have never knelt for Thor back on Asgard. I had knelt for Odin, though, and that little sign of respect still burned.

Thor pulled out a chair with no arms and set it down in front of us. He straddled it and unbuckled his pants before settling down on the seat. "Who wants to go first?" He glanced at the three of us as he pulled his cock free of the fabric.

Not one of us moved. The hush that fell over the room sent a shiver down my spine. I had seen this time and time again. It was his sick idea of driving out the non-humans in hiding. But in all the cases I'd witnessed, the women were only mere humans, and they died a slow, painful death when his jizz tore through their bodies like steel bullets.

"Do you not want me?" he asked the first woman.

She stuttered and stumbled over her words. "Are the rumors true?" she finally asked while her entire form trembled.

I guessed she must live under a rock. Anyone who watched the balls knew the rumors were true.

He grinned. "That my orgasms kill humans?"

She gulped and nodded. "D-d-do they?"

He leaned forward with that arrogant smile of his. "Yes. This is how we test for other if the truth serum doesn't work." He stared at her. "Are you human?"

"Y-y-yes," she stuttered.

"I do not believe you." He nodded to the guards, and they rolled a table with chains next to where Thor sat. "If you're not willing to ride me, you'll be chained, and I'll take you however I deem fit."

The first woman climbed to her feet and inched toward the door as everyone focused on the spectacle of the table. Her face pinched into a mask of horror and panic. The same emotions reflected in the second woman on her knees.

Anger blew through my body, tinting my vision red. "You are going to kill all of us just because..." I couldn't finish the statement, but it was enough to pull Thor's attention to me.

He grinned in a sick way that made me recoil. "I'll get to release this pent-up sexual energy, and if that means a few die for my pleasure...so be it." He snapped his fingers, and the guards caught the first woman before she could flee. "And if they survive, then they will carry my heir."

I slowly climbed to my feet and turned toward the makeshift dais where Odin sat, as if bored of this. "And you allow this to happen?" I waved at the spectacle.

"It is a valid way to flush out enemies of the state."

"What of your people? Don't they have a suitable surrogate for him?" I waved toward Thor again.

"We are all that is left of my people," Odin snarled. "So no, this is how we find a surrogate." He pointed to the woman being restrained on the table.

"No." I turned toward Thor. "Just. No." I raised my hands in a boxing stance. "If you can beat me in a fair fight..." I gulped and shook myself. "Then maybe I will let you have your way with me. But only if you let everyone go."

Thor's mouth popped open into a small O, and his eyelids fluttered with disbelief. "Are you challenging me?"

I licked my lips and nodded even as Reyfyre's face flashed before my eyes. "I, um. Yes." I stumbled. "I am a black belt," I added and flipped my hair behind my shoulder before straightening my back. Reyfyre had taught me a lot of earthly defense arts, to the point he said I was better than most of the black belts who had taught him. "In exchange for their safety." I twirled my finger at the rest of the people in the room.

I was willing to take a beating to make sure these people were safe from harm.

"Why?"

"Because they are *my* people. And they do not deserve to be played with in this manner." I remained in my ready stance. "Someone needs to take a stand against this tyranny."

His eyes narrowed and he stood, tucking himself back into his pants. "I don't think you understand, little girl. I am a god." Thunder rolled through the ballroom. "I take whatever the hell I please."

"Then do so without your guards and without the threat of death." I lifted my chin. "Start acting like a goddamned god and let these prisoners go," I demanded. "Using them is beneath you." I spit the words out, letting some of my venom bleed into my voice. Playing on Thor's vanities had always been an easy mark. And this time, he bristled and glanced at his father.

Odin stared at me with a crease between his eyes. Finally, he gave a sharp nod. "But not the television crew." He pointed at the man holding the live camera. "Or the other two women. Their fates were sealed along with yours the minute you disobeyed and did not initially drink the serum."

Fuck.

If glares could kill, Odin would be dead ten times over.

"We drank it, just not the entire cup. Sometimes chocolate disagrees with me, and I didn't want to spend the evening in the bathroom," I snapped. "And for having gastric issues, you're sentencing me to death?" I tightened my jaw and closed my mouth before I told him to fuck off.

The guards escorted the crowd out the ballroom door. When the last one left, the doors closed behind them.

I inhaled through my nose and when they returned, I added, "The guards cannot intervene."

I knew that was pushing my luck, but if they were here, I might be subdued before I could get the other two out of the building. "And no magic. That's cheating." I pointed at Thor. "This will be a fair fight, understand?"

He laughed, so sure of himself. "For every punch you land, I will let someone go free."

"Thor." Odin's reprimand came through in his voice, but the deal was already out there and televised live to the masses.

Arrogant asshole. But I nodded. "That works."

"And for every punch I land, you'll suck my cock dry," he said with a smile. "Before I fuck you over that table." He pointed at the table still holding one of the women.

"I sure hope you'll unlock her first." I batted my eyes.

He snorted a laugh as he stepped closer. He did not wait for me to engage. He swung his fist. I bent back, using gravity to pull my hands to the ground behind me. I flipped over, catching him under the chin with my foot and snapping his head back before I bounced to my feet. Thankfully, my dress hardly moved.

"I'm also a little bit of a gymnast." It was my turn to smirk.

Thor rubbed his chin as he stared at me.

"I believe that is one point for Karen." I held up my finger, digging the cockiness in my voice.

Thor shook off the hit. "It doesn't count. That wasn't a punch."

I growled my disdain.

He moved and jabbed to the side at the same time as I tried to spin away. His fist caught my cheek, sending flares of light across my eyes. I flew to the ground as a buzz filled my head.

"I am going to so enjoy those pouty lips around my cock."

I shook the stars from my brain and stood, a little warier than before. But this time I didn't wait for him to make a move: I charged and at the last minute, bent back out of the trajectory of his punch and dropped to my knees, sliding under his wide-set thighs. I punched straight up with a tribal cry.

I think I lifted him off the ground with the power of my junk punch. I slid beyond his reach and spun to my feet.

His wheezing breath filled the room, and I landed a kidney punch, driving him all the way to his knees.

He spun, leading with his elbow, catching me in the ribs. The crack of bone echoed in my head and my chest tightened as if a rope had been banded across it. I hit a table on my landing, banging my head enough to warble my vision.

Thor towered over me and held up three fingers.

I raised two. "The elbow doesn't count, just like my foot doesn't." I kicked out, aiming for his dick, but he punched my ankle aside, pulling a cry from my lips as fire engulfed it.

"Three." He reached for his belt.

"None of it counts unless you honor my deal." I rolled off the table and hopped away from his immediate grasp. My ankle was raw and sang a wailing scream every time I put my full weight on it.

"Let the girls go," he said.

I moved farther away until my heels hit wood. Out of the corner of my eye, I saw the girls who had been pictured next to me on the television escorted out of the building.

The only possible innocent in the room was now the cameraman. He aired this crap willingly, almost salaciously, so I wasn't concerned they'd decapitate him.

Thor advanced, and I went to slide toward the door, but a hand gripped the back of my neck, holding me in place in a punishing grip. Something solid hit the back of my knees and I fell to the floor. I reached to grab the hand still clasping the back of my neck, but metal clasped around my wrist.

Terror washed through me as the binding locked both my hands behind my back. I was helpless without my hands.

"You promised no guards would intervene," I challenged Thor.

"It is not a guard," Odin's voice whispered in my ear.

Damn it. I should have clarified *no one* was to intervene. Semantics just screwed me. But Thor approaching wasn't the worst situation I could be in. I'd have to do what I swore I never would. His hands unthreaded his belt as he stepped closer. With the leather folded in half, he struck out, slapping my cheek with it.

Hot agony blared through the cheek his fist hadn't connected with, and if Odin wasn't still holding the back of my neck, I would have sprawled on the floor from the force of it.

He snapped his fingers and the doors to the ballroom opened. A battalion of guards corralled the guests along with the other two women back into the ballroom.

"You fucking liar," I snarled at Thor, even though speaking hurt my bruised face. I struggled against the bonds.

"This is what happens when you challenge your rulers," Odin announced loud enough for the entire room to hear and then he crouched down next to me. "These manacles are charmed, just like the ones in the cave." Odin's whisper sent goose flesh all over me. "You remember the cave, right, Kara?"

I gulped. "I don't have any idea what you are talking about." My voice shook as the lie made my mouth sour.

Thor's eyes narrowed as he stalked forward. "Don't you?"

He looked more like a predator cornering his prey than I cared to see, and my heart thundered in my chest.

"After I lost the only woman I ever cared for due to this curse, I went to the cave to retrieve the only being left on this godforsaken planet who wouldn't die from having sexual relations with me. Imagine my surprise to find the cave empty."

"Aww. My heart breaks for you," I sneered, without an ounce of compassion. "And now you just kill whomever you please to satisfy your fucking libido? That's just pathetic." If I could only manifest daggers with a look... But all my snarling did was make the bastard more cocky.

Thor grinned and unzipped his pants. "I've got three blow jobs coming."

Fury raged through me, burning away the terror like pouring a fire accelerant on an already out-of-control forest blaze. "You reneged on your end of the deal, so if you put that thing in my mouth, I will bite it off." I glared up at him, and the entire room gasped.

Thor snapped his fingers, and a guard dragged a man to Thor's side, keeping a sharp sword at his throat. "Then I will start killing these people until you comply." He waved toward the huddled and terrified crowd and then glanced at the guard before bringing his glare back to me.

"It's time to pay up." He stepped close enough to rub the tip of his hard length on my lips. He took a handful of my hair and yanked back. "And if your teeth so much as scrape my shaft, I will make sure they pay dearly. Now open your fucking mouth and suck, you traitorous bitch."

"Do not touch her."

The words echoed around us, and my heart squeezed. Reyfyre's growling command froze Thor in place, and I turned my gaze to the entry. Reyfyre was equipped to the hilt—blades on his belt and swords in his hands.

His rage pounded through the room like a tribal beat just before a wave of magic plowed over us all.

My restraints blew off my wrists, freeing me from Odin's hold. Although, Thor still held a handful of my hair. I junk punched him again because there was no way I wasn't fighting now that Reyfyre was here. Thor dropped to his knees, wheezing from the hit. His grip on my hair faltered, and I spun away.

Odin raised his staff, meaning to cut down Reyfyre. I kicked, hitting the rod dead center. It snapped in two, and Odin screamed as if I had chopped him in two instead. He collapsed over the staff, blubbering like a demented fool.

Then I bolted toward Reyfyre, but a hand caught my foot, tripping me.

"Hold her!" Thor's growl raged. "I want her to see me beat the living shit out of another lover of hers before I kill him."

My chest squeezed enough that my shattered rib felt like a hundred knives digging into my soul. I couldn't watch another who I cared about cut down. I would not survive it.

Hands gripped my arms and yanked me into a kneeling position. Thor stepped near me and placed the sharp edge of his sword on my throat before swiveling his gaze to Reyfyre.

"Drop your weapons," Thor ordered. "Or I'll run my blade through her throat."

"You're going to do that anyway," Reyfyre snarled.

"No. But I am going to chain her back up, but this time in my bedroom so I can fuck her any time I please."

Reyfyre measured his reaction, but the flick of his eyes in my direction was enough. "So, you're bluffing?" He raised a condescending eyebrow.

Thor moved the blade and slashed my cheek. "She doesn't have to look like much. She just has to spread her legs and bear my children."

Reyfyre's eyes widened.

I gagged on the fiery pain, but shook my head. If Reyfyre put his weapons down, Thor would kill him. I could not allow that, even if it meant Thor permanently disfigured me.

Movement behind Reyfyre pulled my gaze away from his.

Reyfyre reacted, spinning with swords slashing. The guards who had almost been upon him died swiftly. Reyfyre twirled back in our direction with blood splattered on his cheek and the white shirt.

"Now I'm pissed. You've ruined my new tuxedo shirt." His sharp gaze locked on Thor's. "Stop your guards from attacking and swear on your mother's grave that this will be hand-to-hand combat only between the two of us, and I will gladly put away my weapons and school your self-righteous ass. But if you draw another drop of blood from Kara, I will castrate you and then force you to choke on your own dick."

Gasps echoed around the room.

"Don't." I couldn't help the warning, but Reyfyre didn't even glance my way. His gaze was locked in challenge with Thor.

Thor's sword dropped to the ground, and he moved toward Reyfyre. Thunder rumbled overhead. "I swear on my mother's grave." He fisted his hands.

"What do you swear on your mother's grave?" Reyfyre was fae. He knew how to manipulate oaths or how to omit critical pieces to leave a loophole.

"That my guards will not intervene and that this will be hand-to-hand combat between the two of us." The words hissed through his clenched teeth. "But no magic."

"You can't invoke magic either." Reyfyre pointed a sword at Thor.

"I will not invoke magic."

Reyfyre pushed the swords and knives attached to his body to the ether, but before he navigated the few steps to the ballroom floor, he waved in my direction. The guards holding me dropped to the floor, stone dead. "Anyone but me touches her, and they die." He grinned at Thor and set his feet. "That includes you." He cocked his finger at Thor.

I climbed to my feet, shaking my head. "Please, Rey," I whispered just as desperately as he had before I left the apartment. I couldn't watch another man I loved get beat to shit and then get slaughtered. It would break me.

Reyfyre's grin widened. "And that spell that I just cast does not die with me."

"You son of a bitch!" Thor bellowed his anger and charged.

He used brute strength to intimidate, and I waited for the impact. But Reyfyre casually evaded him and swept Thor's feet from under him.

Thor sprawled out on the floor, crashing into tables as he slid.

Reyfyre caught my gaze and winked.

Thor charged at his back, but Reyfyre spun and parried, knocking Thor's punch to the side before he stepped in and used his inertia to land a blow to Thor's chest, knocking him into a group of people who couldn't scramble away fast enough.

Thor shook his head as if dazed and then he growled and launched directly at Reyfyre. At the last minute, Reyfyre sidestepped, but Thor corrected himself and tackled Reyfyre.

"Rey!" I yelled as his head banged the hard floor.

Thor's hands wrapped around his throat, squeezing as he pounded Reyfyre's head on the floor. Protective black tendrils shot out of Reyfyre, launching Thor across the room. He turned onto his hands and knees, coughing.

I rushed to his side but when he looked beyond me, his eyes widened, and he knocked me to the ground. Air grazed my hair, and I turned, hopping to my feet.

Reyfyre climbed to his feet next to me.

Thor swung his hammer, making it whistle in the air. "A wraith, Kara?"

Reyfyre dropped all glamour, revealing his true form, and he glowed with power. His pointed ears poked through his hair. "And fae," he said with a raspy voice. Thor had done damage to his voice box with that choke hold.

Thor released the hammer and Reyfyre dove to the ground, trying to take me with him, but I spun out of his grip and shot my hand out with my fingers splayed. Thor's hammer hit my palm square. Pain radiated up my arm from the impact, but Mjölnir recognized my righteous nature, and did not shatter my bones the way I'd seen it do to countless enemies over the centuries.

Reyfyre stared up at me from the floor with an open mouth, mimicking both Thor and his father.

I had no idea how Thor still wielded this weapon. But I guessed even the magical elements could be duped when there wasn't anyone else to stand in to protect the people.

"Give me my hammer," Thor commanded with his hand out, trying to call it back.

I flipped Mjölnir, catching the handle before I caressed the metal. Its sigils glowed, and I looked beyond the hammer at Thor. "I don't think she belongs to you anymore. You are no longer worthy of her."

I jumped in the air, closing my eyes as I felt her power fill me, and then I aimed the hammer at the floor, willing it not to harm the innocent and to strip those unworthy of their immortality. Lightning splintered across the room and when Mjölnir hit the marble floor, it snaked out, lifting Thor and Odin into the air.

The crowd gasped and then the lightning zapped out of existence, leaving a faint ozone smell. Both Odin and Thor crashed to the ground with as much of a bang as the hammer hitting the floor.

Thor rolled and groaned as he glared at me.

Reyfyre hopped to his feet and gave me a curious side-eye that encompassed more of me than just my face and body. I waved the hammer away like I had seen Thor do hundreds of times and was startled when it actually disappeared. I guess she was mine now, and I would only wield her to protect the people. I also did not want Thor to get hold of her again, even though I was reasonably sure the hammer wouldn't allow him to hold it. Not with his blackened heart. But I didn't want to tempt fate.

"Don't just stand there like a bunch of idiots. Kill them," Thor yelled.

Reyfyre pulled his weapons from wherever he stowed them and handed me my sword as we moved back-to-back.

"Be mindful of the innocents." His whisper caressed my ear. "And you might want to pull your wings in, so they don't get chopped."

His words made me glance over my shoulder. Iridescent wings fluttered and I heeded his warning, snapping them back inside. Although the excitement of having them back buzzed through my muscles, energizing me.

The legion of guards surrounded us, their knives and swords at the ready. I centered my mind like Reyfyre taught me, and when they lunged as one unit, we parried and slashed and twirled away from their blades. My movement flowed as if all my injuries had healed.

I caught sight of Reyfyre, and his fluidity was beautiful. He had grace and power all rolled up into this vicious form that I adored.

Watching him take down guard after guard reminded me of fighting the wraiths on Asgard. I refocused on the renewed effort of the guards surrounding me. I relied on the balls of my feet, almost like a ballerina, twirling and striking until none of our enemies were left breathing.

Blood painted the floor and us. My beautiful dress was officially ruined. I pointed my dripping sword at Thor and crossed the room. My bare feet squished in puddles of warm blood, turning my stomach.

I swallowed bile and took a breath. The stench of iron in the air did nothing to help my roiling abdomen, but I couldn't lose it here. I needed to project as much power and grace as possible to win over every viewer watching us.

"You have ruled long enough. Now it's time for the people to rule once again." I snapped my wings out to punctuate my statement as I stopped next to the woman he had strapped to the table earlier.

"They are mortal now," I said to her and offered her the sword. "Justice is in your hands."

The sword wavered in her grip, and her wide eyes stared at it and then at Thor. The one who would have killed her had I not intervened. The blade steadied and anger finally overrode the fear pulsing from her.

"Do with them as you wish," I said to the crowd and waved at Thor and Odin.

A few of the guests dropped to a knee, muttering, "Goddess," with such reverie that I bristled.

"I am not a goddess. Please do not bow to me. I am Valkyrie. I am the one who will rain righteousness on those who wish to harm the people of this realm. My people." I scanned every face in the room. "So, make sure you put someone in power who is just and honest. Otherwise, I will come back and wreak havoc on

you." My gaze moved to the rolling camera, and I
gave the audience a curt nod before I turned and
marched to where Reyfyre stood.

Reyfyre kept his eyes on me, and I reached
for his hand, lacing my fingers through his, and
led him out of the destruction around us. In the
lobby, I caught my reflection in the elevator
doors and halted. My wings were as magnificent
as my hair. Both matched the colors of the
Bifrost and I smiled, despite the blood streaks
on my dress.

I flexed my back and they stretched, and then
I snapped them away.

"Oh, I want to play with those," Reyfyre said,
pulling me out of the building just as the night
sky opened up, drenching us.

CHAPTER 25

"I THINK YOU ACTUALLY may be a goddess now," Reyfyre said as he surveyed the apartment littered with broken furniture and our discarded clothing from his vantage point on the edge of the tilted bed.

I breathed a chuckle out. We had destroyed the place in our wild lovemaking. I guess death and destruction bred one hell of a sexual appetite in both of us.

"Thankfully you didn't bring me to the boat. Otherwise, we would have sunk the damn thing."

A laugh ripped from Reyfyre, and he threw his head back with it. It rippled his abdomen and bounced off the walls with a musical quality. When he calmed down, he splayed his arms wide on the bed.

His euphoric smile faded away. "I'm not sure what to do with myself now that we've succeeded. I honestly thought I would never see this day."

"What do you think they did with them?" I couldn't help but ask now that all my itches, and then some, had been satiated by this wonderous man next to me.

The tilted television clicked on with a twitch of Reyfyre's hand. Of course, the scene at the ball with me wielding the hammer was the news of the day, along with our battle with the guards. Once that looped through, a new scene had both of us sitting up.

Thor and Odin were bound and beaten and on display in Times Square. I couldn't tell whether Odin was breathing or not. But Thor was still alive as people continued to beat him. It was as brutal as anything they had done, and a sense of wrongness overwhelmed me.

I climbed out of bed and rummaged through my smashed bureau for clean clothes. I still had blood streaked on my skin, so I opted for a quick shower.

Reyfyre stepped in the shower with me, and his hands began to wander.

I knocked them away. "Not now."

"What's wrong?"

"I thought that's what I wanted." I waved absently toward the bedroom and the television still droning on. "But it doesn't sit right."

"He's getting what he deserves."

"No, Rey. Justice should be swift and severe and merciful." I stared up into his blue eyes as I soaped up my hair. I rinsed and slid by him, giving him the shower while I toweled off in the bathroom and dressed.

By the time I combed out my knotted hair, he was standing next to me, doing the same.

"You're going there, aren't you?" He put down the comb and folded both our wet towels over the bar before he pulled on a blue T-shirt the same color as his eyes and tucked it into his jeans. The points of his ears peeked out of his wet hair. Without the glamour, he was even more stunning. A fae glow kissed his skin, distracting me.

"Yes. I need to make this right. Brutality for brutality's sake is no better than Odin and Thor's tyranny. *We* need to be better."

His sigh followed me out of the bathroom.

I searched the mess and found Reyfyre's boots. I tossed them to him and righted the table and chairs, looking for mine. He attempted to straighten out things as well.

"Found them." He pulled out my boots from under the crushed side of the bed and tossed them to me.

I slipped them on near the door as we surveyed the damage.

"I don't think much is salvageable."

"Well, when you're done doling out justice, we can come get our clothing and go back to living on the boat," Reyfyre said. "Until we can build a marble home we can't destroy in a fucking frenzy." His grin surfaced like a fresh beam of sunshine.

We turned away from the mess and stepped into the hallway.

People in the building stopped and bowed as we passed, making my mood just a little fouler. The same with on the street. They scattered, letting us through as if we were royalty.

When we got to Times Square, the murmurs preceding us swept through the crowd and they parted like the Red Sea had for Moses.

Odin's body was still. Multiple stab wounds dribbled thick, dark blood and he just swung in a slow circle from his wrists with his legs bent and his toes anchoring him to the ground. It was a gruesome sight.

Thor wheezed with each breath and one eye stared out of a slit. The other was completely closed. Blood dripped from his lips, and his legs couldn't hold his weight.

"Come to gloat," he mumbled through broken teeth and swollen lips.

"No."

He lifted his head with a wince. "He certainly is."

"Rey has a right to his feelings. You slaughtered his parents."

His lips tilted in a bloody smile. "I slaughtered many." His smile fell as someone passed by behind him and slammed a punch into his kidney.

"Enough!" I yelled, and my wings ripped through my shirt.

The crowd backed up with wide eyes.

"You could have ruled by my side," Thor whispered as his gaze traveled over my wings.

"No, Thor. You were always too arrogant and self-centered. You have no clue what justice and mercy are. I hated everything you stood for, even back on Asgard. Freya was the one who taught me what mercy truly means."

"And yet you killed her."

He was much more talkative than anyone else in his situation would be.

"Yes. In a kill or be killed situation, I will survive, but it wasn't without scars. You don't seem to have any remorse for what you have done."

"I am a god. I do not need to justify my actions to you."

I put my palm up, and Reyfyre handed me a dagger. It was as if he read my intentions. "I am a warrior. The protector of this realm. And you are no longer a god." I slammed the blade home in his chest to the hilt. With a vicious twist, I pulled it out of Thor's heart. "It is not as quick a death as beheading you, but your death will be mercifully quicker than your father's."

"I will be waiting for you in Valhalla," he gasped.

"No. I think you're heading to Hel, my friend."

He coughed blood, and I stepped back so it wouldn't splatter on me.

I spun to the crowd. "What you did was not justice. It was cruel and brutal, just like they were. Do better. Find mercy in your punishments. Protect your humanity, for God's sake!"

I walked away from the dead bodies with the dripping blade still in my hand, and my wings fluttered in aggravation. Reyfyre matched me step for step as I mourned an entire conglomerate of realms. My home. Reyfyre's home. And countless others decimated out of greed for power.

Thor could have been magnificent, but he fell into the same trap his father had slipped into.

I studied Reyfyre with a side-eye. Both of us were the last of our kinds. And I wondered whether there were other survivors from different realms here, hiding in the dark like we had for the better part of a year. Hell, Reyfyre hid in the shadows all his life.

Someday, maybe we'd seek them out, but for now, the sea was calling.

Bonus Epilogue

Reyfyre

I STOOD AT THE controls of my boat while Kara whipped up something in the kitchen below deck. From the scents drifting on the air, it was a combination of scrambled eggs and cheese and some tangy fruit. I scanned the aqua waters of the Caribbean and leaned back in the seat, waiting for her to deliver on the bet she lost last night.

A rare smile curved my lips. She wagered I couldn't go again without sinking the ship. On retrospect, perhaps she didn't really lose after all. A snort of laughter escaped.

Before I rescued her from the cave, I had built up the lost goddess in my mind so much that when she told me she was Valkyrie, I nearly lost control and let my darker side extinguish her life. Valkyrie had let all this happen. They, along with Odin and Thor, had been the reason the realms fell.

But Kara's eyes still held a stubborn fire even after an eternity in chains.

That made me pause and stirred something inside me.

And, of course, she had agreed to help me destroy Odin and Thor. If she had refused to help, I would have taken her life.

I had to reset my expectations all over again at the sight of her. But at least I had planned on her being an invalid, especially with how long she had been chained in a cave in Alaska. Truthfully, I thought she'd be frozen solid. It was fucking cold up there at twenty thousand feet. If I hadn't been so good at planning for the worst, I wouldn't have gotten both of us down that mountain without a shitload of magic. And that would have raised red flags all over the world. That would have been our demise.

Once Kara got a little meat on her bones and I changed her hair with dye and magic, I didn't anticipate the attraction that bloomed. It took everything to keep my wraith side caged during our sparring sessions. And I knew if I let myself go down that path, I'd probably lose her when the wraith came out. And if not, I'd never be willing to put her in harm's way. I'd give up trying to set this world right, for her, and end up condemning us both to certain death.

I let my pent-up frustrations out on her. But she kept swinging the sword and fighting back like a true warrior. I can't really pinpoint when my heart jumped into the mix, but the more my attraction grew, the more demanding my training became with her. It was the only way I could deal with the storm of feelings brewing inside me and win this damned war against the gods.

I lost my fucking mind when she kissed me at the ball. My wraith almost slipped out and that would have been a big mistake. Same thing came close in the closet. Having her against me with her heart fluttering in her chest and her tongue in my mouth, I almost forgot where we were. Almost.

Thankfully, I didn't lose my shit until we got to the apartment. Having anyone beyond my parents accept me, all of me, was a new experience and even now I can't quite believe it. Especially since Kara had transformed into a stunning goddess when she wielded Thor's hammer.

I mean, she was immortal before, but now she had those magnificent wings, which she let me play with at length.

Her footsteps pulled me from the memory, and I turned to see her step into the cabin with a tray piled with different culinary delights.

"I should blindfold you while I feed you," she grumbled and set the tray down on the counter next to me.

"Don't be a sore loser." I grinned and opened my mouth expectantly.

Her eye roll stretched my smile further. She just griped some more as she fed me the meal she had made.

After the last bite, I dropped anchor and shut off the engine. Then I turned my chair and hoisted her into my lap before she could wander away with the dishes. Her warmth wrapped around me.

"You are far more playful now than you've ever been," she glowered.

I laughed and then nipped at her neck. "That's because all the reasons to remain stoic and distant have been eradicated." I followed the line of her throat and then nibbled her ear. "Now you need to take me for a quick flight. And maybe we can try something more daring this time." I reached for the waistband of her shorts, tugging at them to get my point across.

She pushed at my chest, and her wide eyes met mine. "You want to screw around while we're..." She pointed to the ceiling.

"That is precisely what I want to try." I thought it would be a cool experiment.

Her mouth opened and closed, but no sound came out. Although, her eyes sparkled, and a slow smile emerged. Finally, she asked, "What if I lose concentration?"

"Then we take a swim." I could protect us from going splat on the ocean if she lost control. I did not have to keep my magic under wraps anymore. And this was an experience that would be worth it.

Her melodic laughter turned me on beyond reason, and I smashed my lips to hers, taking liberties with her tongue before I stripped her of her shorts. Mine followed and I hiked her around my waist, plunging inside her as I walked out onto the deck.

Coupled with her, I pulled away from her lips. Her wings sprouted, tearing through yet another shirt. Her giggle filled my world.

"When we dock at the next island, let's get married." I did not phrase it as a question. I knew she was it for me back when we were at the cottage in the middle of the Canadian Rockies. I didn't know whether we would succeed in our mission, but we did, and now there was nothing left on this earth that could tear me away from this woman.

Her wings fluttered and her legs tightened around my hips, sheathing me completely inside her. She adjusted her arms under mine, instead of around my neck to keep me against her, and lifted us into the air.

Her lips crushed mine as she flew straight up.

"Did you hear me?" I asked against her kiss.

"Yes, and yes, I will marry you, Reyfyre. Just as soon as we are done with this crazy experiment."

Her answer along with the slow twirl of her hips brought a growl to my lips and a thrilling jolt of joy traveled through my form, giving way to the reality that we were traveling up into the blue sky. My heart stuttered, and I pulled away from her kiss. One glance down at the speck on the ocean that was my boat caught my breath in my throat.

"I think that's far enough." My voice actually cracked.

Her grin widened, and she slowed us to a hover. "Do I detect a little fear in the mighty fae-wraith?"

I did not want to admit that to her, but unease wrapped around me as tight as her arms and legs. I let out a small chuckle and focused on trying out what I intended for this ride. The gentle rocking of our hips took all my energy and concentration. The color in her cheeks heightened with each slow thrust.

"Bring us down so I can make love to you right and proper," I said, meeting her gaze.

That twinkle that always worried me sparkled in her eyes, and she tilted us, so her wings were underneath her, fluttering to keep us stable in the air. "Better?"

Her teasing tone zinged through me like a bolt of lightning. She wasn't going to let me out of this precarious position.

Left with no choice based on the dare dancing in her eyes, I employed a little of my wraith magic, wrapping it around us in a secure blanket, and then I did my very best to satisfy my crazy-ass Valkyrie wife-to-be.

THE END

If you enjoyed the FALLEN VALKYRIE DUET please consider leaving a review.

About J.E. Taylor

J.E. Taylor is a USA Today bestselling author, a publisher, an editor, a manuscript formatter, a mother, a wife, a business analyst, and a Supernatural fangirl, not necessarily in that order. She first sat down to seriously write in February of 2007 after her daughter asked:

"Mom, if you could do anything, what would you do?"

From that moment on, she hasn't looked back.

In addition to being co-owner of Novel Concept Publishing, Ms. Taylor also moonlights as a Senior Editor of Allegory E-zine, an online venue for Science Fiction, Fantasy and Horror, and co-host of the popular YouTube talk show Spilling Ink.

She lives in New Hampshire with her husband and during the summer months enjoys her weekends on the shore in southern Maine.

Visit her at www.jetaylor75.com to check out her other titles.

If you enjoyed the FALLEN VALKYRIE DUET, check out more of her dark fantasy titles:

SHADES OF NIGHT

The Monster Defense Agency demands loyalty, and once you become an agent, the only way out is in a body bag.

When Sarah Stone and Robby Young train together at the agency's academy, sparks fly. And when they are paired as partners, they must muzzle their attraction, or they will face a firing squad.

All their pent-up frustration sharpens them into finely tuned monster hunters. Their ability to neutralize entire nests of vampires becomes the stuff of legends.

But hunting vampires has its own risks. Especially when Sarah and Robby uncover duplicity and corruption at the highest echelon within the Monster Defense Agency.

With a bull's-eye on their backs from both the agency and the vampires they hunt, Sarah and Robby's only hope is to take down the Monster Defense Agency.

But two against an ancient organization that trains monster-killers and knows all their tricks is even harder than it sounds. It's going to take all their skill and intelligence to kill this beast.

And being caught is not an option.

Shades of Night delivers forbidden mates, cool magic, and a kick-ass heroine in this fast-paced urban fantasy series.

Books included in this special edition hardcover:

Young Blood – A Shades of Night Prequel

Wicked Heart – Shades of Night Book 1

Crooked Soul – Shades of Night Book 2

Tainted Mind – Shades of Night Book 3

Find these and other title on her website:
www.JETaylor75.com